Empyrean's Fall

By

Nicole L. Bates

To: Meghan

Reach for the Stars!

Nicole L. Bates

To my Mom and Dad for always

saying *when* instead of *if*

COPYRIGHT

ALSO BY NICOLE L. BATES

Novels

<u>The Leron Series</u>

Empyrean (The Leron Series Book One)

Empyrean's Fall (The Leron Series Book Two)

Empyrean's Future—
Coming Soon!

Short Stories

"Fairy Tale Redux: A Short Story"

"The Mortal Years"—Published in *TV Gods Anthology* released by
Fortress Publishing, Inc.

Contents

DEDICATION 3

COPYRIGHT 4

ALSO BY NICOLE L. BATES 5

CHAPTER 1 9

CHAPTER 2 21

CHAPTER 3 27

CHAPTER 4 39

CHAPTER 5 47

CHAPTER 6 53

CHAPTER 7 61

CHAPTER 8 67

CHAPTER 9 83

CHAPTER 10 91

CHAPTER 11 99

CHAPTER 12 111

CHAPTER 13 121

CHAPTER 14 131

CHAPTER 15 141

CHAPTER 16 147

CHAPTER 17 159

CHAPTER 18 171

CHAPTER 19 179

Chapter 20 193

Chapter 21 201

Chapter 22 213

Chapter 23 219

Chapter 24 229

Chapter 25 237

Chapter 26 253

Chapter 27 261

Chapter 28 267

Chapter 29 281

Chapter 30 297

Chapter 31 311

Chapter 32 323

Chapter 33 335

Chapter 34 345

Chapter 35 355

Chapter 36 371

Chapter 37 381

Chapter 38 389

Chapter 39 399

Chapter 40 411

Dictionary of Leroni Words 420

Acknowledgements.. 424

About The author.. 425

CHAPTER 1

Orange and blue flames leaped toward the stars in the center of the clearing where two distinctly different groups gathered for a celebration feast. The bonfire formed a barrier between the blue-white glow of the Leroni and the wide-eyed stares of the humans. Firelight danced across shadowed faces. The divided groups watched and waited, wondering what to say, or what their new neighbors would do.

"Well, this is awkward," Magnar whispered.

"Give it some time," Jahira replied. "It's going to take more than a few hours for everyone to get used to each other."

Magnar scratched at his hairline.

"Everything alright?" Jahira asked.

"This second-skin stuff itches."

"Well, don't scratch it or it will come off," Jahira whispered.

Medic had given Magnar a small supply of second-skin, a substance that could be painted over a wound to keep it clean while allowing it to breathe. The second-skin also changed color to match the pigment of the user's skin. They thought it would be the best option to hide his scarred forehead from the Leroni. The scars, which Grollon had given him to purge him of the silver liquid he'd drunk, were a sign of the enemy to these people.

A few more tense minutes passed before heads began to turn toward the long covered tables set out under a large tent at one end of the clearing.

"Oh, thank goodness, the food is here," Magnar said.

Several humans bearing trays appeared out of the darkness beyond the tent and began to fill the tables with fruit, garden-fresh vegetables, roasted fish, and dried meat. The savory smells drifted from the tent, beckoning the waiting crowd.

General Thayer motioned for Ellall to begin. The Akaruvel of the Leroni nodded in acknowledgement. Measured graceful steps carried her toward the waiting bounty. The bioluminescent glow of her fur waxed and waned as she moved away from the light of the fire into the surrounding dark, and then back into the glow of the solar lamps hanging from the supporting beams in the tent.

The elders followed, and then a line began to form. Like a carefully choreographed dance, the Leroni moved into position without ever bumping, brushing, or jostling. There were a few whispered questions from the children in the group, but most of the Leroni were silent. Only the subtle tilt of a head or slight change in facial expression let Jahira know they were communicating mind-to-mind.

Krnar and Allnall stood at either end of the table. They appeared to be translating as needed while the Leroni filled their plates, though Jahira was too far away to hear what was being said. The fruit, fish, and dried meat dwindled rapidly. The Leroni seemed wary of the trays of unfamiliar vegetables.

Jahira's gaze kept returning to Krnar. He talked and smiled, occasionally even laughed...showing more emotion than she'd seen from him since she'd met him. Her heart filled and ached at the same time. It made her happy to see him happy, and it made her miss her own family, whom she'd never see again. She wished Krnar could meet them.

The Leroni automatically separated in to small groups, sitting on the ground and eating in small circles with their closest friends and family members.

The humans filled their plates next and then found places to sit among the Leroni, trying to find the right balance between appearing welcoming yet not getting so close that it became creepy. Jahira had warned them about not touching anyone, even by accident.

Ellall waved General Thayer over to join her and the group of elders. Allnall rose from where she'd been sitting and joined the group.

Probably to serve as an interpreter, Jahira guessed. She wondered if it had been her choice or if Ellall had asked. Jahira couldn't read Allnall very well yet.

Krnar waited for Jahira and Magnar to get through the food line, and then escorted them to a small group of Leroni. Jahira recognized Krnar's brother, Arkan, and his sister-in-law, Ulletta. There were four others she did not recognize.

Jahira bowed. While maneuvering into her seat, she tried so hard not to accidentally brush against Krnar that she nearly tipped her plate.

Ulletta caught her eye and smiled. Jahira smiled back, grateful that Ulletta seemed to like her, and that the feeling was mutual.

"Jahira, this is Erget, Klleallan, Erknok, and Tllakall." Krnar gestured to each of the Leroni she had not previously known. Nodding to each in turn, she searched for distinguishing features that would help her remember who was who. When she locked eyes with the one she thought was Erknok, a shiver ran down her spine. His eyes were narrowed, and though his face showed little expression by human standards, it didn't seem friendly.

Krnar introduced her and Magnar, distracting her from trying to figure out Erknok. Everyone nodded politely and then turned their attention toward the food.

Jahira inhaled the steam rising toward her nose. Her mouth watered and her body screamed for the fresh steamed vegetables she'd piled across one half of her plate. The fresh fish looked appetizing as well. A week of fruit and dried meat while she'd waited aboard the ship on the third continent had left her body in need of some variety...and nutrients.

The first bite of green bean fueled her hunger. Jahira happily tucked into her meal. Soft growls and low trills punctuated the conversations taking place around her but she didn't even try to follow. Magnar seemed equally taken with his meal, barely taking time to swallow between bites.

Loud and unfamiliar laughter drew Jahira's attention away from her food. She grinned once she'd identified the source of the merriment.

Ryan sat with a large group of Leroni.

Most likely without an invitation, Jahira thought.

His cheeks were flushed, his eyes bright, and he spoke at great volume without pausing. Elaborate gestures accompanied his words.

Jahira knew he'd been working hard to learn Krnar's language. Unfortunately he did not have a gift for tongues.

The Leroni around Ryan were holding their sides and barely kept themselves from tumbling into each other as laughter overtook them.

"I wonder what he's saying," Magnar asked.

"I wonder what he *thinks* he's saying," Jahira replied. "I'm pretty sure they're not the same thing."

"It's not deterring him in the least."

"That's Ryan. You've got to love his enthusiasm."

"Clearly the Leroni do."

Whether he intended it or not, Ryan making the Leroni laugh helped ease the tension in the surrounding humans. The fur-covered faces and foreign gestures made The People hard for humans to read. Jahira remembered how intimidated she'd felt when she'd seen Krnar back in that mountain cave for the first time.

Watching him now, she realized how much had changed. She could see in the relaxed set of his shoulders and the way he leaned toward his brother that he was comfortable, happy.

Drumbeats began to thump an enticing rhythm.

Heads lifted and turned toward the sound.

The humans, with the help of Krnar and Allnall, had prepared a musical surprise for the Leroni.

Having revealed The People's love of dance, Krnar and
Allnall worked with the musically inclined in the settlement on a
playlist for the evening. Some of the selections were traditional
Leroni chants, like the one starting now; others were a blend of
human and Leroni rhythms that were sure to get bodies on the
dance floor.

Several couples jumped up and made their way to the
hard-packed ground in front of the band. Children tumbled out of
the shadows and twirled between the adults.

Jahira smiled but her body tensed. Part of her wanted to
dance, wished Krnar would invite her to dance with him perhaps.
Another part of her drew a deep line in the sand at the very
thought of being the center of attention in a situation like this.
What if she did something wrong? She felt a strong need to make
a good impression on Krnar's people. Making a fool of herself the
first night was definitely not part of the plan.

She tried not to let her body language give her away, and
hoped that Krnar had his mind blocked.

He caught her eye and smiled.

Damn telepathic alien, she thought.

15

Glowing Leroni bodies moved between the dark silhouettes formed by the humans. Jahira became mesmerized by the contrast, engrossed with following the intricate steps that fell somewhere between a waltz and a sparring match.

A tingling sensation along Jahira's scalp alerted her to someone else's presence in her mind. She glanced at Krnar, assuming it would be him, but he'd engaged in conversation with Erget and didn't notice her.

She looked at Ulletta and Arkan to see if it might perhaps be one of them. Arkan told a story to Erknok and Ulletta flagged down Mrkon, who had not yet touched the food on his plate.

Jahira's brow wrinkled. She scanned the crowd for some clue as to who might be trying to read her thoughts.

Eventually, she caught the eyes of a Leroni female watching her. When they made eye contact, the woman immediately looked away, and the crawling sensation disappeared.

That's strange, Jahira thought. *Most likely someone being curious*, she guessed, but it was disconcerting to say the least. The thought of someone rifling through her mind without her being able to do anything about it bothered her more than she'd realized. She'd have to start taking Krnar's lessons more seriously.

What would the other humans think? she wondered.

They knew that Krnar could communicate by sending pictures to their minds, but not having much experience with telepathy, no one had thought much about the possible downside.

Except Lusela, Jahira realized.

When Lusela had refused to vote in favor of Jahira taking Magnar to the southern continent, she'd mentioned Jahira being under the control of Krnar.

What if they could control human minds? Would they?

Krnar had explained that he almost always had to keep his mind blocked around humans; too much *noise*, he'd said. But that didn't mean he had to. What would stop one of the Leroni from trying?

Because they're good people, she told herself. *It's the same as us having weapons that could kill them; it doesn't mean we would go around shooting people whenever we feel like it. It's a matter of human decency.*

But the Leroni aren't human...

No, she had to trust what she knew of Krnar, and even Allnall. They wouldn't do something like that.

What about the others?

Then, of course, there was still the question of Grollon. He chose to remain in hiding for today, not wanting to incite panic among The People, but he'd caused a war once. Would the temptation to repeat his actions prove too strong? Would the humans be caught in the middle?

"Hey, this is supposed to be a party. You look more like you're at a funeral."

Jahira jumped at the sound of Magnar's voice. She turned toward him and tried to relax the lines from her brow. "Sorry," she said. "Just thinking."

"Yeah, well, as much as I'm enjoying trying to hide in plain sight, I think I've had enough. I'm gonna catch up on my beauty sleep." Magnar winked.

"Good luck with that," Jahira replied with a grin. She kept the smile on her face as Magnar waved goodbye and retreated, but she worried about him, too.

He'd been doing better on the ship, but it would be hard for him to be back here near the pools. She could tell he felt anxious around the Leroni, afraid he'd slip up and let his scar show.

Jahira sighed and took a sip of her fruit juice. The tart flavor slid over her tongue and soothed her dry throat. The mild effervescent effect invited her to take another sip.

The conversation around her came to a halt. Jahira looked up to find a Leroni woman standing behind Krnar's shoulder. Jahira thought it looked like the woman who'd met her gaze earlier, maybe the one who'd been trying to get into her head.

"Jahira, I'd like you to meet Tllomell," Krnar said.

Jahira started to reach out to shake the woman's hand, then stopped and pulled back. She tried to hide her foible with a bow of her head. "Nice to meet you, Tllomell," she said.

Tllomell tipped her head slightly then addressed Krnar.

He looked up at the woman and responded.

Tllomell cut her eyes toward Jahira before bowing and then walking away.

"What did she say?" Jahira asked. She watched Krnar's reaction. Did he look...embarrassed? Jahira glanced around the circle and noticed that no one met her eye.

I really wish I could read minds, she thought.

"She asked me to dance," Krnar said.

"Oh." Jahira wasn't sure what else to say. Obviously Krnar had said no, at least for now. Jahira felt oddly relieved, but wasn't sure why. Did it matter if he danced with someone else? More important, who was Tllomell and why had she asked Krnar to dance in the first place?

All of these questions and speculations helped to distract her from her biggest worry, the one that had been gnawing at her ever since they'd landed.

That was probably the last flight of my life. What am I going to do now?

Nicole L. Bates

CHAPTER 2

Tllomell didn't have to read Krnar's mind to know why he'd re-fused her. He'd looked to the human female before answering. Watching them sit at the same hearth and share a meal with Krnar's friends and family stabbed her in the heart.

Her brisk walk carried her to the edge of the dance floor where she stopped and watched but did not join.

Something bumped her from behind and then brushed along the fur of her arm.

Tllomell hissed and turned toward the offender. A human smiled and stumbled past her onto the dance floor. Her heart thumped against her ribs and her entire arm tingled. Chills ran up her spine.

It was just an accident, she told herself. Krnar had warned them that the humans did not share the same laws about touch, but she hadn't comprehended quite how extreme the difference would be. Watching them was like watching untrained children with adult libidos. They held hands, hugged everyone, couples pressed their bodies and lips together right out in front of every-one! They had no control over their bodies or their minds. She had been alternately appalled and jealous all night long.

How does Ellall expect us to live alongside them? she wondered.

"Tllomell, would you like to dance?"

Tllomell turned her head to the right and saw Frmar, head bowed, hand extended. She hesitated. Frmar was a friend, respected among The People, and he'd been a comfort to her these last moons. He was also apprentice to the Akaruvel. He would one day become the leader of The People. Therefore things could never go beyond friendship.

Perhaps that was exactly the kind of person she needed.

"Yes," she agreed. "I would."

Frmar straightened and smiled. He gestured for her to lead the way.

For a blissful and untimed duration, Tllomell allowed herself to get lost in the music. She twisted and flipped, ever aware of those around her but also able to let go of the restraints normally required of her. She reached for Frmar and felt the jolt of energy move from her fingertips to her spine.

Touching was allowed on the dance floor, and the Leroni took advantage of this one loophole in their everyday formality. Not quite to the extent that the humans went, perhaps, but the occasional brush against an arm or a leg, fingertips trailing down her back; the sensation intoxicated.

Accustomed to dancing on the rock and ice of the frozen third continent, her body soon overheated. Sweat rolled through her fur and her mouth felt coated with the unfamiliar dust kicked up by stamping feet.

I need to get a drink. Tllomell projected into Frmar's mind rather than attempt to shout over the music.

Frmar nodded and pointed to the food tables where containers of water and fruit juice waited.

They wove through the bystanders and came to a stop beneath the vast hide the humans had propped up over the food. Tllomell stared at the tiny containers of light, wondering how they worked. Were they alive, like glow-worms stuffed inside a clear shell?

"Here you go. I hope water is alright."

Tllomell tore her eyes away from the lights and accepted the glass that Frmar held out to her, careful now not to brush his fingers. "Water is perfect. I'm not sure I approve of the humans turning the alara fruit into a drink. It seems wasteful, exorbitant, especially with the abundance of fresh water nearby."

"I agree with you." Frmar paused and sipped his own drink. "It's strange to be here, in person. I've remembered this place so many times with Ellall that I feel as if I might be dreaming, except that the sounds and smells are so much more vivid."

23

Tllomell nodded, and then tipped her head when a thought occurred to her. "Did any of the memories ever show the humans here?"

Frmar frowned. "No, actually. There are the memories of the silver mountains, of course, and those are similar to what we remember, but none of the humans that I'm aware of. Perhaps that piece was lost over the generations because we did not know who or what they were. Or perhaps Ellall had not yet shared that with me. It's hard to say since the memories are no longer passed directly from Aruvel."

"How close are you to completing the training?" Tllomell felt suddenly very curious about the secrets Ellall and Frmar held locked away in their minds. She'd always taken for granted that the Akaruvel shared what was needed, that no more was necessary, but she began to doubt.

"Very close," Frmar replied. He glanced to the left and the right, and then leaned a bit closer to Tllomell. "Ellall did not expect to survive the next Season of Ice."

Tllomell's eyes widened. "She told you this?"

"Not in so many words, but I could tell by the ways in which she'd changed her approach to my training."

"And now?"

"Now? Who knows? There is enough food and water for everyone. The weather is mild. There is plenty of fuel to burn. We might all live a handful of seasons longer than before."

"Everything's going to be different, isn't it?"

Frmar paused, took a sip of his water, and then answered slowly. "A lot of things will be different, yes, but it doesn't have to change who we are."

Tllomell considered this before responding. "I suppose you're right. It's been our goal since our ancestors left this place to return to the warm land. This *used* to be our life. Perhaps it can be again."

Frmar nodded and Tllomell took a long drink of water.

"Would you like to dance some more?" Frmar asked.

"Hmm, I'm getting pretty tired. I think I'll..." Tllomell's voice trailed off when she realized she had no hearth, no place to call her own, no place to go.

"Give it some time, Tllomell. Things will get better."

She glanced back to where Krnar leaned in to say something to the human female.

A bitter seed took root in her soul and began to grow.

Nicole L. Bates

CHAPTER 3

A long curl peeled away from the main body of the stick and fell to the ground to join the pile of shavings at Krnar's feet. He'd gathered some fallen branches from the dancing forest before leaving to rescue his people. The cache waited for him. He'd been itching for an opportunity to shape the new material. This morning proved perfect.

In spite of the late night celebrating, he'd risen early and seemed to be the only one awake. Even the birds had barely begun to herald Allorkan's return.

The quiet washed over him, soothing, like the waves lapping the shore. His mind could wander without interruption while his hands worked.

The sharp blade of the knife Jahira had given him bit into the soft surface of the branch. The material yielded in a way that bone never did.

Another dark curl joined the pile and Krnar began to see the image hidden beneath the surface. A soft trill of satisfaction vibrated through him. This was his favorite part of carving, the moment when the chosen medium revealed its form to him.

Fingers worked tirelessly while he held the picture in his mind of the final outcome.

A gentle push against his mind broke his concentration. Krnar paused and scanned the area around him.

Not seeing anyone, he opened his mind and felt Grollon's commanding presence.

Krnar, I need you to arrange a meeting with your Akaruvel.

Surprised by the request, he didn't know quite how to respond. *A meeting? With Ellall? You want me to arrange this?*

Isn't that what I just said? Grollon's impatience made Krnar's hands twitch.

Uh, I will speak to her and see what she says.

Good.

The link snapped, leaving behind a brief hollow feeling in Krnar's skull.

Doubting that Ellall would be awake yet, he tried to return to his carving. It was no use. The peaceful, creative zone he'd been in had evaporated with Grollon's interruption.

After carefully placing his materials and tools into his pack, Krnar walked deep into the grove until he reached on of the many springs bubbling from the ground and feeding the stream that wove through the silver trees.

Cold water coated his mouth and cascaded down his throat. His esophagus worked to keep up with the flow from his joined hands until his thirst had been satisfied. He rose and pulled a golden fruit from the nearest tree. These fruits were less sweet than those that had been growing in the grove upon his arrival. They seemed to have more substance, lasted longer in his gut. He found it difficult to describe the taste, having never tasted anything like it before.

Though the shade of the canopy blocked much of the light, Krnar knew that Allorkan had made its appearance. Tiny feet scurried through the underbrush, feathered wings flapped and fluttered in the branches overhead. The frtikdi screeched a constant warning to any who might wander into their territory.

When he stepped out from beneath the bright red leaves, he smiled. It hadn't been a conscious decision to visit Jahira, but he wasn't surprised that his feet had carried him to her hearth.

A few of his belongings were neatly arranged by the fire pit, right where he'd left them before they had embarked on their rescue mission. Seeing them there, waiting for his return, he felt torn. Until he had formally declared a union with Jahira, he should not continue to stay here, not with his people watching.

It had all been different before. The humans barely took notice of where he spent his nights, but the Leroni would, he knew.

How could he explain this to Jahira without hurting her?

He'd noticed the tension in her face during the celebration when the dancing had started, the uneasy expression when Tllomell had asked him to dance. With his people here, he felt like he was treading water between two shores, unsure of which way to go.

In an effort to distract his mind, he set to work starting a fire and heating water for tea so that it would be ready when Jahira woke.

Water bubbled in Jahira's cookpot when he heard the tell-tale sounds of Jahira waking and preparing to step out of her tent.

A dark hand pushed aside the door flap and then Jahira emerged, rubbing the sleep from her eyes.

When she locked her gaze with Krnar's, her green eyes glowed in the morning light.

"Good morning," she said, her voice still rough from disuse.

"Allorkan a tal," he replied. "Tea?"

"Yes, please." Jahira sat on the stump next to him, hugging her body and rubbing her hands along her upper arms.

"Cold?"

"Just a little," Jahira replied. "The sun will warm me up soon...and the tea."

Eyes lighting in anticipation, she accepted the cup he offered. Long dark fingers wrapped around the warm mug and she inhaled the scent with her eyes closed before taking a cautious sip. "Mmmm, perfect. Thank you."

Krnar nodded and relaxed back on his seat with his own cup. He forgot sometimes how easily the temperature affected these furless humans. He wondered, not for the first time, what it would be like for them when the snows came.

"It's getting colder at night," Jahira said, as if reading his thoughts. "A few more months...moons...until it's supposed to snow. It might be time to cut some holes in my new sleeping bag."

Krnar smiled at the inside joke. Her words brought back memories of their time in the cave after he'd rescued her and Magnar. "You have new srlen hides," Krnar said. "I can help you make some warm covers."

"I would appreciate that. I've never had to do much sewing before." Jahira took another sip and then nodded toward his belt. "How's the new knife working?"

"Excellent," Krnar replied, pulling the tool from its sheath to admire the fine workmanship and sharp edge. "Thank you."

Jahira nodded. "So, what's on the agenda today? It's the Leroni's first official day in the alara grove. Are there more ceremonies?"

"Grollon has asked me to arrange a meeting with Ellall."

Jahira's eyebrows crept up her forehead. "Already? Does Ellall know about him?"

"Yes, Allnall and I told Ellall about The Marked. I did not think he would ask to meet her so soon, but I suppose there is no reason to wait."

"When are they going to meet? And where?"

"I have not yet spoken with Ellall. I came here first. Would you like to come with me?"

Jahira's eyes widened slightly, as if surprised by the request, but her response came quickly. "Yes, of course!"

"I think a human should be present in case it does not go well. I do not yet fully trust Grollon. Perhaps Magnar should come also? He and Grollon have grown close."

"Okay, that's probably a good idea. I can about guarantee that Magnar is working on his boat, or sleeping next to it. We can go get him, and then go ask Ellall."

Krnar nodded.

Jahira downed the last swallow of her tea and then excused herself to take care of other pressing matters. Krnar put out the fire while he waited for her to return from behind the stand of nearby trees.

When she returned, she poured a bit of the hot water he'd set aside over her hands, scrubbed some powder on them until it bubbled, then rinsed with the remaining water. She claimed this ritual got rid of *germs*, which could pass from person to person and cause illness.

Considering her people had built ships that could fly from one world to another, he decided not to completely discount their theories, no matter how strange they sounded.

After Jahira retrieved two sticks of dried meat from her pack that hung from the branch of the nearest tree, they were on their way.

They walked in companionable silence, Jahira chewing her dried meat, Krnar thinking about how to approach Ellall. The sounds of the human world waking echoed across the field. The clinks of their hard utensils against equally hard bowls and cups, the rise and fall of clipped high-pitched voices—these sounds had become familiar to him but now, after his time away from them and back among his own people, their foreignness again intrigued him.

The four ships rose against the skyline, just like the mountains his people had thought them to be. Only one stood whole and untouched, the one that had been fixed in order to rescue his people. This was not the one they entered.

Inside the cargo hold of the ship on the far left, Magnar stared at a hovering image of his watercraft. A hot metallic smell filled the air.

He and Jahira waited on the edge of the entrance ramp for several heartbeats before Jahira cleared her throat.

Magnar shifted his eyes, focused on them, and smiled. "Good morning! I didn't expect anyone else to be up this early. How're you two doing?" He tapped the glowing disc on the table in front of him and the hovering image disappeared. Magnar stood and gave them his full attention.

"We're doing well," Jahira replied. "We were wondering if you'd like to join us for a meeting."

Magnar's eyebrows rose.

"Grollon wants to meet with Ellall and Krnar..." Jahira paused and glanced at him.

"Wants witnesses?" Magnar guessed.

Jahira nodded. "Something like that, yes."

Magnar glanced back at his pile of materials, looked at Jahira, and finally shrugged.

"Sure, should be interesting." He grabbed his head covering off the table and pulled it low over his forehead, hiding his scars. "After you."

They walked three abreast along the outskirts of the human settlement. Once they reached the silver-trunked trees capped in brilliant red, Krnar took the lead. They wove through the evenly spaced trees accompanied by the calls of the grove's avian residents and the whir of insect wings.

Once inside the ring of trees, Jahira and Magnar waited at the edge of the field. Krnar picked his way carefully across the field that looked like white rocks had been randomly dropped into the tall grass sometime during the night. Between the exhausting journey across the Great Ice and the late night of celebration, not even the rising of Allorkan had the power to wake his people...most of them, anyway.

A lone figure sat atop the highest hill in the center of the field, silhouetted against the pale grey sky.

That has to be Ellall, thought Krnar.

Thankful for the soft ground that absorbed the sounds of his footfalls, Krnar made his way to the edge of the largest of the five silver pools.

The Akaruvel sat with legs crossed, eyes closed, and one hand resting on each knee. Her chin lifted toward the rising sun and slow, deep breaths expanded her ribcage and then let it fall in a steady rhythm.

This is the first time she will witness the rising of Allorkan, the sun of the warm land, he realized.

Not wanting to interrupt or ruin the moment for her, he sat a body length away, closed his eyes, and waited with long-practiced patience.

Heat soaked into his fur, warming his skin and forcing tense muscles to relax. The blades of grass that had fought their way out from under his weight and sprung toward the light tickled the sensitive hairs on his feet and legs, interfering with the calm state of mind he attempted to achieve.

With his eyes closed, his hunter's senses tuned in to the world around him. A warm breeze carried the heady scent of alara fruit to his flared nostrils. The fur covering his ears picked up the faint rustlings drifting up the slope of the hills, letting him know the Leroni were beginning to wake and greet the day. Krnar opened his mind to the buzz of energy, feeling the collective excitement of his people as they realized where they were and noticed the light spreading over the tops of the red-crowned trees.

Fully immersed in the experiences of those around him, he lost track of time.

A push against his mind reminded him why he had come.

Before opening his eyes, he blinked the protective tinted lens in place and turned to face Ellall.

"You came to see me, Krnar."

He bowed his head and projected, acutely aware of the need to keep Grollon's presence a secret for the time being.

Yes. Grollon wishes to meet with you.

Ellall's body stiffened, but her inner voice remained calm. *When?* she replied. *And where?*

The exact first questions Jahira had asked.

He did not say, only asked me to arrange a meeting with you.

Is there somewhere unseen that we can speak? I do not wish to invite him among The People. Not yet.

Krnar nodded in understanding but did not respond immediately. It had to be somewhere neutral, yet also a place that would not be disturbed by accidental wanderers. *There is a place in the dancing forest, not too far from the grove, but far enough that no one should see the two of you. You could be well hidden by the roots of the dancing trees, if you choose.*

Ellall nodded. *That should work well.*

I have also invited two humans, Jahira and Magnar. They helped to fly us here and have become friends. I felt they should be aware of what was happening, in case there are any...issues.

37

You do not trust The Marked.

He has not shown any signs of wanting to cause harm, but a lifetime of belief that he is not trustworthy is difficult to set aside.

Yes, I agree. Ellall paused and then added, *Is Allnall aware of this?*

Allnall? I hadn't thought to ask. I will invite her also, if that is your wish.

Ellall nodded.

I will tell Allnall and Grollon. We can meet at mid-sun?

Yes, thank you, Krnar.

Krnar bowed his head and then rose in one fluid movement. *I will return to escort you to the meeting location when Allorkan is here*, he said, pointing to the sky.

Ellall nodded and then closed her eyes.

He was dismissed.

Interesting that Ellall wishes for Allnall to be present as well, he thought as he made his way down the series of hills. It made sense, he supposed. He, Allnall, and the Akaruvel were the only Leroni aware of Grollon's existence. Perhaps Ellall wanted more people there who were on her side.

Soon they would find out just how far The Marked could be trusted.

CHAPTER 4

Tllomell made the mistake of opening her eyes without the tinted lenses in place. Tears leaked from the corners of her eyes when she squeezed them shut again. Two bright yellow spots hung behind her eyelids. The spots remained, though faintly, even after she blinked the protective lenses in place and opened them again.

Dark soil clung to her fur and her overheated skin seemed to crawl as if a thousand eroki had burrowed into her and began to melt. After a vigorous brushing, most of the dirt returned to the ground where it belonged, but she still felt unclean.

Water, she thought. *I need water.*

Like a fish to bait, Tllomell felt pulled toward the stream she knew flowed through the grove. Unfamiliar chirps and squawks accompanied her through the maze of silver trunks that soared above her head and exploded in a brilliant display of color. The grass was shorter here. It didn't tickle her legs like that of the inner field. The smell of sun-warmed fruit filled her nostrils.

Finally, the soft bubbling of water over rocks could be heard over the din of animal life.

Once she reached the spring, she dropped and her knees pressed into the soft cool dirt along the shore. Deliciously cold water coated her fingers when she cupped her hands together below the surface.

Glistening beads dripped from the backs of her hands when she pulled her cupped palms out of the stream and brought them to her lips. She drank in long gulps, tasting the soil and rock and grass, which infused the water with a flavor so unlike the brackish, stale, or frozen liquid of her former home.

Her mind drifted to memories of the underground caves, the dark, the stale air, and the moons of starvation, which were barely worse than eating raw krska or moons-old dried fish. If Krnar and Allnall had failed, if the humans hadn't come, that's where she would be right now, and likely, where she would have died.

Tllomell's ears perked at the sound of approaching voices. Her body stilled and she strained to hear enough to distinguish the speakers.

When they drew closer, she could make out the familiar lilt of one of The People, but the other voice spoke the human language in a high-pitched tone, with an occasional lightly-accented Leroni word thrown in the mix.

A human and Leroni together, she thought. There were on-ly two people she knew of who might be conversing together in mixed tongues. *Krnar and the human female.*

Without consciously deciding to do so, Tllomell crept through the trees toward the voices. A mix of curiosity and trepidation swirled inside her chest. She felt unable to resist.

When she drew close enough to identify the source of the voices, surprise rooted her feet to the ground. Krnar and the human female were walking together, as she'd suspected, but Allnall and another human, a male, accompanied them. Tllomell vaguely recognized the human male from the feast; he'd sat with Krnar and the female.

From her position behind one of the smooth silver trunks, she listened with her mind blocked.

Krnar did most of the talking, using a hybrid of the two languages that made it difficult for her to follow the thread of conversation.

He said something about Ellall and the dancing trees. Then Krnar spoke a name that froze her to the core: Grollon.

Why did he say that name? she wondered. *Did he mean Grollondi? Were The Marked living here still? Surely not. They would have told us, warned us.*

Or would they?

Would everyone have come if they knew their ancient enemy waited?

Did Ellall know?

Don't get ahead of yourself, Tllomell thought. *You don't even know what he's saying. They wouldn't have brought us here if it was not safe.*

Krnar's head lifted. Tllomell straightened and shifted fully behind the trunk just as Krnar cast a glance over his shoulder. Did he sense her presence? Was he afraid of being followed?

What do you have to hide? she wondered. Tllomell needed to know.

She trailed the group from a distance, far enough that even if spotted, it would not necessarily look as if she had followed them.

The group left the grove but did not head toward the human settlement. They walked toward the forest of towering dark trunks and deep purple-red leaves...the dancing trees.

A sense of awe filled Tllomell as she approached the forest. She had, of course, heard of the dancing trees, but she'd never seen anything like them. Great curving roots radiated out from massive trunks. Some of the root walls grew to a height over her head. Following the line of the massive trunk upward, her eyes tried to focus but kept darting about, watching the leaves that never ceased their tilting, trembling movement. From here the leaves appeared tiny, yet those scattered about the forest floor were larger than her head.

New noises assaulted her here; more intermittent, more distant than those in the alara grove, and somehow more ominous.

Unease crept along her spine as she made her way deeper into the shadowed forest. In this place, she had the feeling she would be easy prey.

Fortunately, the roots provided excellent cover.

What else they might be providing cover *for*, she tried not to dwell on.

Keeping track of her quarry here proved far more challenging than in the grove. She lost sight of them several times. Luckily, when she drew close enough, the humans' heavy foot-coverings stomping and crunching through the dried leaves got her back on track.

"This is the place," Krnar said.

Tllomell stopped and pressed her body close to the nearest root-wall to listen.

He continued in the human language, and then switched again to address Allnall.

"Allnall, would you please bring Ellall to this place? Magnar will bring Grollon. Jahira and I will wait here for you both to return."

A trill followed by soft footfalls let her know that Allnall was on her way.

The human male spoke. *Magnar*, Krnar had called him. Then the crunch and scrape of heavy steps rebounded off the trees in the opposite direction.

Krnar and Jahira were alone.

Part of her wanted to find a vantage point that would allow her to see them. Another part of her wished to be anywhere but here, with them, alone.

Soft voices drifted to her, but she could make out few of the words. Eventually she gave up trying to understand and simply waited.

In her haste to follow, Tllomell had forgotten to bring any provisions. Her stomach ached, punishing her for her lack of a morning meal. Fortunately, she knew well how to turn her mind away from food and push her body through hunger.

While she slowed her breathing and heart rate, Allorkan reached its midpoint in the sky.

At least I don't have to worry about freezing to death while I wait, she thought, recalling her time spent in the crevasse of the Great Ice after she'd fallen during the trials—the place where Krnar had found her, and had rescued her. On the contrary, even in the shade her skin felt uncomfortably hot.

A twinge in her calf let her know she needed to shift from her half-sitting, ready-to-spring-at-any-moment position before she lost all feeling from the knee down. Careful not to make a sound, she shifted her weight and sighed in relief.

She'd just started to make out shapes in the whorls of the tree bark when she heard footsteps approach.

Tucking her body deeper into the junction of root and trunk, Tllomell waited until she heard Krnar greet Ellall before moving out to the edge of the root wall.

Before she'd even worked up the nerve to peek out from behind her hiding place, heavy footsteps sounded from the opposite direction. Again she retreated.

Tllomell caught glimpses of the human male and another figure moving through the open spaces between the roots. When they drew close enough that she could make out some detail, her heart stopped and a cold sweat broke out along her spine.

It was an old man, an old man with wings.

She sucked in a gasp of air, restarting her heart, which began to pound like she'd just swum a race. *He has true wings.*

Krnar had even said his name was Grollon. He must be a descendant of the original. *The* Grollon couldn't possibly still be alive...could he?

Over the generations, those who fled to the third continent evolved into what they were now: fur-covered against the cold, dark-adapted vision, incredible lung capacity, and the triangles of fur-covered tissue that had once been true wings but were now much smaller and assisted only in maneuvering through water. The People could no longer fly. But the Grollondi, if they still existed, wouldn't have had reason to evolve physically. They had remained in the warm land, surrounded by food, water, and a sun-warmed sky.

This must be the leader if Ellall agreed to meet with him.

How many more are there?

Muscles twitched with the desire to run, not only away from the descendant of The Marked, but to warn her people. She had to tell them that their enemy still existed.

Against all instincts, she remained still. She had no desire to be discovered, and she wanted to learn as much as she could about this new potential threat.

Had Krnar and Allnall known before they led the people here? They must have. But they would not knowingly or willingly put the Leroni in danger, would they?

With long, slow breaths she calmed her racing heart and listened.

CHAPTER 5

A sense of calm spread through Jahira's system like a time-release drug. She loved this forest. She loved the huge trees, the moving canopy, and the quiet. It was nice to get away from the settlement and the constant press and presence of people.

Ellall and Grollon sat a short distance away facing each other. Jahira assumed they were communicating mind-to-mind. Either that or they were staring at each other in silence for an uncomfortably long time.

Krnar and Allnall stood on either side of their Akaruvel like sentries on high alert.

Jahira and Magnar had taken seats on the dry ground, backs against a root wall, legs stretched out before them.

"So how are you doing, now that we're back?" Jahira asked.

"I'm doing okay," Magnar replied. "The trip to the third continent was a lifesaver. I felt almost like myself again. I could think clearly, slept better, I even got a ton of research done for my boat. Now that we're back it's...hard. I'm always distracted by those damn pools."

"How long until you finish the boat and can get some distance between you and the pools?"

"Hard to say. I make a lot of mistakes and have to tear things apart and redo it."

"You? Make mistakes?" Jahira grinned and Magnar snorted. "Maybe you should get some help. Dan would do it, and he'd be amazing. Cholie, Tala, Leiko...I bet I could get them all to pitch in."

Magnar shrugged.

"Well, let me know."

They sat in silence for a while, watching Ellall and Grollon watch each other, and then Magnar spoke, quieter this time. "Grollon came to visit me last night while I was working on the boat," he said.

"Yeah?" This was not a terribly uncommon occurrence, so she wondered where he was going with this.

"He seemed a bit more introspective than usual so I asked him what was up." Magnar paused and grinned. "Well, I didn't use those exact words because, you know, he wouldn't understand what I was saying..."

Jahira smiled. "Yeah, I get that with Krnar. I'm always surprised by how many things I say in a day that really don't make sense to someone who didn't grow up with our language."

"Really? That doesn't surprise me at all."

Jahira raised an eyebrow and said, "Ha. Ha. Ha. Well, what was his response?"

"He said he's been *remembering* things and he is concerned."

Both of Jahira's eyebrows rose this time. "Things? What kinds of things? And why is he concerned?"

"That's exactly what I asked."

"And?"

"He said he wouldn't tell me. The gist of it was that if he told me, it might make it happen. Or, if he told people what would happen and they changed their actions, something worse might happen."

"Huh, sounds confusing."

"Yeah, but he did say to be careful who I trusted."

"What? Really? So he had a vision about you?"

"Seems that way, but I don't know."

"Is that what prompted the meeting with Ellall?"

"I'm guessing that's at least part of it. He might want to share some of his *memories* with her. I think he also wants to try to make amends, you know, to be a part of a community again."

"It must have been hard for him to be on his own for so long."

"Yeah, I can't imagine."

"You can't? Isn't that exactly what you're planning to do, go off on your own for long stretches of time?"

"Well, a few months is different than a few hundred years, and I'm not opposed to company. I just don't know who would want to go floating around for weeks at a time with *me*."

"Hmm, yeah, you're right."

"Ha. Ha. Ha."

"So, do you have visions of the future? Or did you see things when you were drinking the silver?" She had never asked him anything like this before, but he seemed more comfortable talking about it now.

"Not exactly, or not that I remember. I knew I needed to go to the mountains, I felt drawn there, but I think that was just Grollon sending out an SOS."

"Interesting."

"Grollon thinks the 'soul' might react differently in humans or that we can't 'hear Aruvel.'"

"That makes sense."

"Well, I'm really looking forward to moving on. I'll explore the oceans, the southern continent, map the coastlines. I'll go wherever I can go that will keep me away from those pools."

"You'll come back and visit though, right?"

"Of course. I'll have to make repairs and get supplies and all that."

"It will be an adventure, that's for sure."

Before Magnar could respond, a flash of movement drew Jahira's attention.

Ellall stood abruptly and spoke to Grollon in a low growl.

Simultaneously, like synchronized athletes, Krnar and Allnall drew their spears and unsheathed their knives with opposite hands.

Jahira sprang to her feet. Beside her Magnar did the same.

For a full five seconds, no one moved. Grollon remained seated on the ground. Finally, Ellall spun on her heel and marched away.

Allnall hurried after the Akaruvel.

When they were out of sight, Grollon rose in a series of slow, laborious movements. With both feet finally under him, he brushed the dirt from the seat of his borrowed pants—it was a bit strange to see an old guy with wings in the blue PT pants—turned and began to walk in the opposite direction.

Krnar sheathed his weapons.

"I'd better go with him," Magnar said. "Make sure everything's okay."

"Sure, I'll catch up with you later."

Magnar nodded and then jogged over to Grollon's side, falling in step beside The Marked.

Jahira turned her attention to Krnar, who had walked over to join her. "Is everything okay?" she asked.

"I think so," Krnar responded. "Things seemed to be going well, they were exchanging memories, and then Ellall blocked him out, and stormed off."

"I saw. What did she say right before she left?"

"She said, 'I will not listen to lies.'"

"But you don't know what he said, or showed her?"

"No."

"Hmm, I guess that could have gone better. Now what?"

"Now we wait."

CHAPTER 6

Tllomell's thighs screamed and her back throbbed. She'd pressed her body as far into the junction of tree and root as she could go, waiting until she heard only the sounds of the forest, and then waited some more.

She did not hear what was said, only that Ellall's voice rose in anger and then everyone departed. *That can't be good.*

While contorted in the shadows, she'd decided her first stop when she returned to the grove would be to speak to Frmar. If he knew about this meeting, perhaps he would have more information to share. If he didn't know about it, he needed to.

Using her hands pressed against the rough bark, she worked her way to standing and then stretched her aching muscles.

To be cautious, she peered over the root before stepping out from her hiding place. There were no signs of anyone else around.

By this time her stomach felt as though it had started to eat itself and her tongue stuck to the roof of her mouth.

While making her way back to the settlement, she stopped to eat her fill of fruit and drank from the stream until she could feel the slosh of water moving in her gut.

Once she reached the inner field, she saw her people had been busy.

Sticks and rocks neatly outlined each family's hearth. Small fires flickered beneath the stone and bone pots that had survived the journey. Children raced through the long grass between hearths, laughing and squealing. Tllomell smiled to see them crouch down and disappear, only to pop back up with a shout while their friends ran and screamed. They seemed to be at home here already.

She wished she felt the same.

Frmar sat with the elders sipping water from a small bone bowl.

Tllomell approached the circle, bowed, and then addressed Frmar. "Frmar, may I speak with you?"

"Yes, of course." He placed his bowl on the ground, rose, and bowed to the elders before following Tllomell away from the circle.

Tllomell scanned the field for a private place to talk. They could communicate without being heard, of course, but she didn't know how Frmar would react to her news and she didn't want to draw attention.

"Will you walk with me?" she asked.

Frmar gestured for her to lead the way.

Tllomell returned to the cover of the alara grove, continuing until she felt confident they would be hidden from curious eyes.

"Tllomell, what is this about?" Frmar asked once she'd finally stopped.

Tllomell turned to face him and suddenly felt tongue-tied.

Frmar smiled encouragingly.

"I followed Ellall today," she began, thinking that if Frmar knew where Ellall had gone, he would understand what she was talking about.

His brow furrowed.

"She was accompanied by Allnall and Krnar, as well as two humans. They went into the dancing forest."

He still looked confused, but interested.

"In the forest, they met with another, an old man...with true wings."

Frmar's eyes widened. "One of the ancestors?"

"That is my belief, yes, and they called him Grollon."

"Grollon! *The* Grollon?"

"I don't know for sure. I did not get a close look at him; I was trying not to be seen."

"Was he marked?"

"Again, I did not see."

"Were there more?"

"No, not today, only the one. He connected with Ellall's mind."

"What was Ellall's reaction when she saw him? Was she surprised? Angry? Did you hear what was said?"

"She did not seem surprised to see him. I think she knew who and what he was. I did not hear anything that was said, only that before she left, she spoke in anger."

"How is this possible?" Frmar said softly as he paced in front of Tllomell.

"You knew nothing of this?"

"No, I have heard nothing, seen nothing. I did not know our ancestors still lived." Frmar continued to pace, and wrapped the fingers of his right hand around the hilt of his knife. "Allnall and Krnar were there? They knew about this?"

"Yes."

"So they must have known about the ancestor's existence before they came to rescue us."

"That is what I think as well."

"So at some point they told Ellall, but none of them saw fit to share this news with the rest of us."

"It would seem so."

Frmar stopped pacing and met Tllomell's gaze with a look of determination. "I must confront Ellall. I must know what happened, and if there are more of them."

Tllomell nodded.

"Thank you for telling me this, Tllomell."

"Will you tell me what Ellall says? What you find out?"

Frmar nodded slowly. "I will. I think this is something that everyone should know about."

"When will you speak to her?"

Frmar thought for a moment. "I will wait one sleep, to see if she approaches me, or addresses the elders. If she does not volunteer the information, I will confront her."

Tllomell nodded.

When they parted ways, she couldn't help but feel a bit guilty. Maybe she should have spoken to Ellall first, or Krnar, to see what they knew. Maybe they had a good reason for not sharing this information.

She also felt relief and even validation knowing that someone else knew and shared her opinion about the issue.

With a heavy heart, she returned to the space she'd claimed as her own. She thrust one hand into her pack and fished around until she felt the telltale spiny surface and soft tentacles of her last vrmefur. Flipping it over, she cut a slice in the soft underbelly and placed it in the center of a smooth dirt circle. The click of her fire-rocks sounded twice in quick succession. A small spark jumped into the slice she'd made and a small blue and orange flame rose up and tested the night air.

Over the growing flame, she set up a stand and placed a bowl of water to heat. Once it began to bubble, she added bits of dried fish and dried glow weed to simmer together.

Tllomell rocked back on her haunches and waited for her food to cook. Normally, every man, woman, and child would be catching and preserving all the fish, glow weed, and vrmefur they could find in an effort to store enough to survive the Season of Ice.

This day, most of the people relaxed, visited with family and friends. Laughter and conversation drifted on the warm breeze. Juice from the alara fruit stained hands and chins.

Some of the Leroni even napped!

This is good, Tllomell thought. *It's why we came here, to live a life free of the worry of death by starvation, or death by freezing; to live a life in the light of Allorkan and to watch our children grow strong.*

They came for the promise of hope.

But at what cost?

CHAPTER 7

"Krnar, come quickly," Allnall said, once she'd regained her breath.

Krnar set down his bowl of stew, nodded a farewell to Jahira, and followed Allnall into the alara grove. "What is it?" he asked.

"Frmar found out about Grollon. He confronted Ellall."

Alarm quickened Krnar's pace. "How did *he* learn about The Marked? And if Ellall didn't tell him, how does he know that Ellall knows?"

"I have no idea. At first they were speaking mind-to-mind and everyone ignored them, but then Frmar began to get more and more agitated. Finally, he began shouting about Grollondi. Of course everyone nearby stopped to listen and I ran to find you. I think the news is going to spread fast, and I hoped that together we could explain how Grollon was discovered and what we know about him. Also, since you were the one to encounter him first, perhaps your testimony would carry more weight."

Krnar nodded in understanding.

When they broke through the trees and entered the inner field, a crowd had gathered.

Krnar and Allnall projected to those at the back. People began to shift to allow them through. At the center of the throng, Frmar and Ellall faced each other.

Frmar's rigid posture and narrowed eyes told Krnar that it wasn't going well.

Ellall cut her eyes to the side and nodded to acknowledge their arrival.

Frmar followed her gaze and rounded on them.

"You! The Chosen!" he spat the word like a curse. "You knew The Marked lived and even had contact with him before coming to rescue us, but you said nothing!"

"We told our Akaruvel," Krnar replied calmly.

"Yes, and the three of you kept it a secret from everyone!"

"We didn't wish to deal with reactions like this when we had a dangerous journey ahead of us."

Frmar growled, "Dangerous journey indeed. It makes me question your motive in bringing us here."

"*What?*" Krnar roared, indignation unfurled inside his chest, filling him and pushing him up straight.

"Don't be absurd!" Allnall exclaimed at the same time.

"We have all been told since birth what The Marked could do. They'll take over your mind, control your thoughts, even your actions. How do we know this didn't happen to you?"

Krnar growled low in his throat and took a step forward.

"Frmar, enough." Ellall stepped forward, creating an obstacle for Krnar if he wished to reach Frmar. "You of all people can feel that their signal is unchanged. Their mind is their own."

Frmar's eyes narrowed but finally, he nodded.

Krnar didn't believe Frmar was convinced, only that he was standing down for now.

"How many are there?" Frmar asked, his voice softer now. "And why did The Marked wish to meet with Ellall?"

Krnar glanced to Ellall, seeking permission to speak. He didn't know how much she had revealed, but considering the number of people listening, he thought it best to present the truth now and prevent the spread of far more damaging rumors.

Ellall tipped her head slightly and gestured for him to proceed.

"There is only one to my knowledge. He claims to be the last and that all the others killed each other or themselves many seasons ago. He had nothing to do with rescuing our people, and even seemed apprehensive about it, not eager for it. As to why he wished to meet with Ellall, only she can answer that."

Frmar's attention returned to Ellall.

Ellall stood straight, shoulders pulled back, and met Frmar's angry glare with complete composure. "He wished to apologize. He regrets his actions, so long ago, and wants to atone for his wrongdoing."

Krnar was certain this was not the whole truth, but didn't think this would be the time to ask questions about her angry departure from their meeting.

"His actions so long ago...this can't possibly be *the* Grollon," Frmar said.

"Yes," Ellall replied.

Gasps and trills sounded from the gathered crowd.

"And you met with him, knowing he is the reason our ancestors fled. He is the one who murdered an Akaruvel. How is it possible that he still lives?"

People leaned in, fully engaged and hardly daring to breathe lest they miss a single word.

"As difficult as it may be to accept, he is an Akaruvel. He passed through the gateway. This prolongs one's life. He lived in a land of plenty, without threat of starvation. No doubt our children will live much longer than we could ever have dreamed."

Krnar noticed that she failed to mention the consumption of Aruvel's soul, the silver liquid of the oranlodi.

"Yes, he passed through the gateway. He is filled with the memories of past, present, and future. He has the power of a *true* Akaruvel."

Ellall's grip around her spear tightened and her eyes narrowed. The crowd collectively held their breath. "Are you challenging me?" She spoke slowly, her voice controlled, her words measured.

Silence reigned.

Even the birds and insects seemed to be waiting in tense anticipation for Frmar's response.

Some of the air seemed to leave Frmar as the weight of her question hung between them. Krnar thought Frmar looked as though he realized he'd gone one step too far. "No, Akaruvel, I only wish to know the truth."

Ellall nodded, and then raised her voice to address the crowd. "I will keep all of you informed of any new developments." She looked pointedly at those surrounding herself and Frmar.

People bowed their heads and the crowd dispersed, all except the elders and Frmar. Krnar noticed Tllomell lingering a few body lengths away. Frmar met her eye. A few heartbeats later, Tllomell nodded and then returned to her hearth.

What was that about? Krnar wondered.

"Krnar, Allnall, you should join us," Ellall said.

Krnar groaned inwardly. He glanced at Allnall, who raised her eyebrows and gave him a *you first* look.

They'd participated in the trials in part to avoid this duty, the endless meetings, the long circular discussions that never seemed to resolve. In this way they were alike; they understood each other.

But, Krnar told himself, *you succeeded where no one else did*.

With success came a certain measure of responsibility. They'd elevated their status and had become that which they had tried to run away from.

It was going to be a long day.

CHAPTER 8

After Krnar's abrupt departure, Jahira decided to see how Magnar felt about having some help on his boat.

Walking through the heart of the settlement, her jaw dropped to see the progress in the short time she'd been gone. Now that three of the four colony ships were essentially scrap, thanks to Lusela's efforts to sabotage the rescue mission, they were being slowly dismantled for parts to build the settlement.

The frame for the greenhouse stood like a giant rectangular skeleton patiently waiting for its skin and innards. Clear panels, which had previously been the windows of the colony ships, were stowed in racks nearby. Solar panels would be placed on the roof to power the irrigation system and, voilà, garden fresh vegetables all winter. Most important to Jahira, the coffee trees would be protected.

Several more permanent housing structures had sprouted up as well, replacing most of the tents. Those with sod houses were "winterizing," but not rebuilding.

Jahira had opted to keep her tent...for now. She knew she would need something else for winter, but the empty rooms aboard the ship would always be available. Honestly, she couldn't decide what to do. Most of her indecision had to do with Krnar.

Where would he want to stay? What type of shelter would he feel most comfortable in? She hadn't approached this subject with him and didn't think that so soon after his people had returned would be the best time to have that kind of conversation. Maybe he would decide to stay in the grove with the Leroni.

"Jahira! Hey!" She recognized Tala's voice before she saw her friend wave and began to jog toward her. "Where are you headed?"

"I'm going to see if Magnar needs some help with his boat."

"Oh, fantastic! Can I join you?"

"Of course! I actually want to convince him to get a crew together to help. Maybe you can help me persuade him."

"I am very persuasive," Tala responded with a smirk.

Jahira grinned.

"I'm so glad you're back," Tala said. "I've been going crazy. I am not a gardener, not much of a hunter, and I'm tired of holding up beams. It really stinks not to be able to fly."

"I know what you mean," Jahira said. "It's all I ever wanted to do and now…"

"You don't know what to do with yourself?"

"Yeah. I mean, there's a lot to be done, and I want to help, there's just not much that I feel passionate about besides flying. I never imagined that it wouldn't be an option."

"I know." Tala paused. "Well, maybe if the boat thing works out, we could become sailors."

Jahira smiled. "Yeah, maybe."

"Ooooh, how about pirates? We could be pirates, Jahira."

This made her laugh out loud.

Tala raised her eyebrows and asked in her most innocent voice, "Will it depend on what a certain fur-covered alien wants to do?"

Jahira gave Tala a measured look and raised one eyebrow.

Tala raised her palms and shrugged. "Just asking."

The problem was, it *did* have something to do with a certain fur-covered alien, and she didn't know quite how to handle the situation. She'd always been decisive and independent. She made her own decisions and stuck to them. It was probably why none of her previous relationships had lasted very long; she'd never made the effort to compromise with anyone before.

"How are things with you and Leiko?" Jahira asked.

Tala smirked, knowing full well Jahira was deliberately changing the subject, but she went with it. "Great!" Tala said. "Actually, we're thinking of having a baby."

"Really?" The news stopped Jahira in her tracks. "That's so exciting! You two will be great parents. Are you thinking soon?"

They resumed walking as Tala responded, "Well, we figured we wouldn't be doing much this winter, so we made an appointment with Medic to pick the frozen father next month. He said it can take a few tries, so we'll give it a few months and then hopefully, grow a baby on board the ship while it snows."

"On board the ship? Are you going to incubate it in the nursery or will one of you carry it?" Jahira asked.

"Are you kidding? I can't even grow lettuce. You think I can grow a whole human?"

Jahira laughed. "Well, I think your body kind of knows what to do."

"Yeah, well, no need to test that theory."

"Ok, what about Leiko?"

"She might, but I don't want to assume. I guess we'll figure all of that out when we talk to Medic and look at the options."

Jahira nodded. "That's really exciting, Tala."

"Thanks."

At this point, they'd reached the base of the entrance ramp to the *Seyfert*. The hollow clang of boots on raised metal echoed through the hold.

Magnar was, as expected, hard at work on his creation. He turned when he heard their approach and smiled. "Hello, Ladies. To what do I owe this honor?"

"We were bored and decided to bother you," Tala replied with a wink.

"Ah, well, you'd be the one to do it," Magnar said with a grin.

Tala and Magnar loved to give each other a hard time.

"We actually want to see if you need some help. The bored part is pretty accurate, though," Jahira said.

"Okay, well, the first thing you'll need to do is go get your lifesuits," Magnar said.

"Lifesuits? Why?" Jahira asked.

"Because we're going to do a little cold welding."

"What is cold welding, and what does it have to do with lifesuits?" Tala asked.

"We had training in that, remember?" Jahira said. "Our tools were all coated with that spray barrier so that they didn't stick to anything when we did repairs in space."

"Right," Magnar said.

"I don't remember," Tala admitted.

"We are going to shunt all of the air out of the cargo hold and create a vacuum, like in space. Then, when we place the metal panels against the metal frame, all the pieces adhere permanently without using heat. No gaps, no leaks, no maintenance."

"Wow, how does that happen?" Tala asked.

"Without the oxide layer, the air or dirt molecules clinging to the metal, the panels don't know where one begins and the other ends. They *become* one piece of metal."

"Cool!"

"How are you going to shunt the air?" Jahira asked.

"I linked the *Seyfert* to the *K.C.'s* power," Magnar said. "The holds are designed to adapt to the atmospheric pressure of the outside, and contain its own atmosphere separate from the rest of the ship. We just close the door, turn on the pumps, and go to work."

"We'll be right back," Jahira said.

She and Tala left to retrieve their suits. When they returned, Magnar was dressed and ready.

A sense of nostalgia filled Jahira as she pulled on the familiar suit. She'd thought she'd never wear it again. The thin, flexible material wouldn't be too hard to work in, but it still felt a little strange after so long.

When she turned to join her friends, Tala and Magnar's faces glowed from the lights of their hood displays.

"Comm-link check," Jahira said, her voice echoing inside the helmet.

"Check," said Magnar.

"Checkmate," said Tala with a wink.

Jahira grinned. "Okay, boss, what do we do now?"

"First, I get rid of the air," Magnar said. "Everyone's oxygen good?"

"One hundred percent," Tala replied.

"Green and go," Jahira said.

Magnar walked to the wall and flipped the cover off a control pad. He began pressing buttons.

Jahira could feel the half second of expansion in her suit before everything adjusted to space-op levels.

"We have a vacuum, ladies," Magnar said. "Now we need to scrub down the frame and panels. I scrubbed them once, and shaped the panels before we went on our rescue mission, but there can't be any clinging particles. Once they're clean, we put everything together."

Magnar retrieved scouring pads from his worktable and handed one to Tala and then Jahira.

Gripping the scouring pad in her gloved hand, Jahira scrubbed until her shoulders ached.

"Okay, I think that's good," Magnar said. "Let's try a piece."

They gathered around one of the metal panels, each taking a side.

"On three. One, two, and three."

Jahira's thigh muscles flexed, straightening her bent knees while her fingers curled around the bottom edge of the metal sheet.

The panels were easy to lift, thanks to the lack of gravity, but rather awkward to carry in unison and hold perfectly still.

"Now, the pieces can't touch until everything's exactly where it needs to be," Magnar said. "A little left, and up, up another centimeter, left two centimeters...okay, and...connect."

Nothing dramatic happened.

She'd expected some kind of noise or sudden suction. It was a little anticlimactic. It appeared to work, though. She felt a small thrill of satisfaction when they stepped away and the sheet of metal stayed in place.

They all stood back to admire their work.

"Perfect!" Tala said.

"One down, dozens to go!" Magnar said.

Tala rolled her eyes and Jahira snorted.

For the better part of the day they worked steadily, watching the hull of the boat form before their eyes. When the last piece adhered to the frame, Tala and Jahira high-fived.

"Well, I think that's it for today," Magnar said. He stepped back and surveyed the progress they'd made, nodding with satisfaction. "I don't think I'll even have to tear any of that apart."

"Uh, of course not, *we* helped," Tala said waving her hand between herself and Jahira.

Magnar walked over to the panel on the wall and pushed more buttons. Jahira felt her suit compress and adjust this time. Magnar stared at the screen for several seconds before he turned back to them and gave a thumbs-up.

With a sigh of relief, Jahira released the seal on her helmet and removed the claustrophobia-inducing hood. She wiped the sweat off her forehead with the back of one hand and then finished removing her suit.

"You know, Jahira, that work crew idea might not be so bad. We got more done today than I thought I'd get done this whole week. With help, I could definitely get this in the water before the snow hits."

"Great!" Jahira exclaimed. "I'll talk to everyone tomorrow and see who's interested and available. Maybe I can make a work schedule."

Tala and Magnar exchanged a glance.

"What?" Jahira asked, glancing from one to the other.

"A work schedule...for a fun project..." Tala said and shook her head. "Only you, Jahira."

"Hey, it's efficient! You want to get this done, don't you?"

"Yeah, yeah, make a work schedule. Put me on all day, every day," Magnar said. He turned and walked to the long table where various tools were spread and began to organize.

"All right, good night, Magnar, we'll see you tomorrow!" Jahira called over her shoulder.

"G'night! Thanks, Ladies!"

A cool, starlit night pulled them into its embrace, sending chills down Jahira's spine.

A few fires blazed at random intervals, pockets of light dancing against a black backdrop. Most of the settlement was quiet, everyone snug inside their homes and resting up for another day of work.

They returned their suits and then made their way to Tala's door.

"Goodnight, Tala. Say hi to Leiko."

"Will do. 'Night Jahira." The door closed behind Tala and Jahira continued toward her tent.

After a day of company, conversation, and laughter, the knowledge that she would be returning to an empty tent instead of a house filled with her mom's cooking or Zarya's practical jokes made her chest constrict with anguish.

When she rounded the last building and saw a fire crackling in her fire pit and Krnar's blue-white glow, a smile split her face and her heart filled with gratitude. Maybe, together, they could make a home.

She had to admit, she was surprised to see him here so soon after his people's return, not to mention his hasty departure this morning. "Hey," Jahira said, taking her seat by the fire. "It's good to see you."

Krnar nodded. "And you," he replied.

"What happened today with Allnall?" Jahira asked.

"We had trouble with Frmar."

"Frmar, he's the one who's training to be the next Akaruvel, right?"

"Yes."

"What kind of trouble?"

"He found out about Grollon."

"Oh, wow. How did he find out?"

"I don't know, but he knew about the meeting as well. I'm sure Allnall would not have told anyone. Someone must have seen us." He shook his head, clearly having no idea who might have revealed the sensitive information. "Frmar confronted Ellall. Now all the Leroni know."

Jahira made a sympathetic noise. "How are they taking the news?" she asked.

"Hmm, they did not panic, but there is fear, anger. Frmar is most angry, I think, because he was not told. The elders are divided, of course. Some wish to meet with Grollon, others wish to banish him."

"What do you think?"

"I do not fully trust him, but I do not believe he means us any harm...for now."

"What do you think will happen?"

"I think there will be many meetings and very little will be decided."

Jahira couldn't help but smile. "Sounds a lot like how humans handle things."

Krnar nodded. "We are not so different...on the inside." Krnar caught and held her gaze until Jahira felt heat uncurl in her belly and spread through her entire body.

Clouds had moved in to obscure the light from Leron's three moons. Darkness surrounded them, making her feel hidden, and brave. It was the first time they'd been alone in a long time.

"Have you eaten?" Jahira asked, clearing her throat after hearing the odd thickness in her voice. She moved about the fire, gathering bowls, water, and ingredients.

"Some, but I could eat more," Krnar replied. "Let me help."

Krnar took over roasting two day-old fish. Jahira sliced up fresh fruit and vegetables, arranging them artfully on a platter. Once the fish were hot and the skin peeled off the flaky flesh, they enjoyed the meal in comfortable silence.

Krnar picked through the slices of fruit and avoided the vegetables. Jahira smiled, remembering the first time he'd popped a whole radish into his mouth and began to chew. The look on his face had her doubled over with laughter, but he hadn't found it very funny. She could tell he was trying to be polite, but desperately wanted to spit the offending item onto the ground. Ever since then, he'd been hesitant to try "human food."

After a last bite of the mildly sweet and somewhat chewy filet, Jahira began to clear the plates. She reached out to take Krnar's bowl and felt the fur of his fingers brush against her skin.

Her movement halted and she met his intense blue gaze. With a human, she'd have thought nothing of the minimal contact, but with Krnar, she knew it was no accident.

His lips pulled up into a smile, revealing a row of straight, white teeth. He reached up with his opposite hand and trailed a finger through her hair, then behind her ear and along her jaw. Jahira felt goose bumps rise along both of her arms.

When Krnar stepped toward her, she met him halfway. She ran her fingers along the silky fur on his arms and watched his pupils dilate.

When their lips met, Jahira felt a tingling along her scalp, followed by an explosion of sensation that rocketed through her entire body.

She gasped and pulled back.

Immediately, the sensation left her, leaving her wanting.

"You connected with my mind." It was a statement, not a question. "Is that what you feel?"

"Yes," Krnar answered. "Every time you touch me."

"Wow."

"I am sorry. Is that not okay?"

"No! I mean...uh, yes, it's okay. It's more than okay."

She leaned in for another kiss, but Krnar didn't open his mind. She felt her own racing heart, the spike of awareness everywhere that her body touched his, but she wanted to feel that again, to feel what he felt. "Do it again," Jahira whispered against his lips.

She was rewarded with the tingling along her scalp, which traveled down her spine and then then out to her fingers and toes, growing in intensity until she moaned.

Jahira deepened the kiss and brushed her hands down Krnar's back.

Electricity hummed along her skin where Krnar touched her and her blood pounded with the added sensation from his mind.

Jahira pulled Krnar toward the tent without breaking contact.

"Are you tired?" Krnar asked.

"No," Jahira replied. "I want more."

CHAPTER 9

After an eternity of tossing, turning, and cursing under her breath, Tllomell gave up trying to sleep. She sat up by her cold fire circle and stared at the remains of her last vrmefur. Tears pricked the corners of her eyes. She blinked them away, feeling ridiculous, but seeing the burnt crisp of one of her last pieces of home speared her heart.

A gentle push against her mind brought her chin up. Her eyes widened in surprise when she saw Frmar standing outside the ring of rocks she'd used to claim her space.

Though she really didn't feel like entertaining company, she very much needed a distraction from her depressing thoughts.

She bowed her head slightly to Frmar and waved him in.

"Are you alright?" Frmar asked, taking a seat an arm's length from her.

Tllomell nodded. "I'd offer you tea but that is my last vrmefur," she said, pointing her chin toward the pile of ashes in the center of the dirt circle.

"I have branches and leaves from the dancing forest. Let me get them."

He stood and walked to his hearth, gathered an armload of branches, and returned to her side.

"Have you used them yet?" Tllomell asked.

"No."

"Have you seen anyone start a fire with them?"

"No, but the person who brought them to me told me to put the leaves and small pieces down and light them like you would a vrmefur, with the rocks, then slowly add branches until it's the size you want."

Tllomell tipped her head, giving him permission to give it a try.

Frmar made a small pile of dried leaves. "If you would do the honors," he said.

Tllomell picked up her rocks and clicked them together until a spark jumped onto the pile of leaves. Like a voracious animal, the fire began to consume the small pile. Frmar and Tllomell took turns adding leaves and small sticks, feeding the flames until they could safely add larger pieces.

Very soon a cheery blaze warmed her shins and face.

"That was pretty easy," Frmar said, his voice full of awe.

"Yes," Tllomell agreed. "I guess now I can start some tea?"

"Please."

"How did the meeting go?" Tllomell asked as she gathered her cooking implements and dried glow weed.

"Not the way I'd hoped," Frmar replied. "Some of the elders agree with me and want nothing to do with any ancestors of any kind, especially The Marked. But others are curious, and they expressed interest in meeting this Grollon. I believe they are fascinated by the idea of meeting one who has passed through the gateway, perhaps learning from him."

"With no concern about his motives? Or his past actions?"

"They're old. They no longer fear death. They only want to learn as much as they can before they go."

"Hmmm, well, many of the rest of us are still young enough to fear death very much."

Frmar's lips twitched with amusement.

"In fact, I spoke to some friends, discreetly, trying to gauge how they feel about the news."

"And what was the general feeling?"

"Everyone I spoke to, or overheard talking, had fears, concerns, questions of course, but many are waiting to hear what Ellall will say. They trust her to guide them, and believe she withheld information to protect, not to harm."

Frmar nodded slowly. "Any idea what might persuade them to feel otherwise?"

Tllomell cocked her head and regarded Frmar for a moment. "Do we want them to feel otherwise? I personally don't condone meeting with The Marked, but I don't wish to sew distrust of our Akaruvel."

"No, of course not," Frmar responded hastily. "I only meant what might persuade them to support a ban against this Grollon."

"Oh, of course." Tllomell paused and carefully poured two bowls of glow weed tea, passing one bowl to Frmar, who accepted with a nod.

"Well," Tllomell continued, "if there was proof that he meant us harm, or if he threatened Ellall in some way, I'm sure people would agree to keep him away. As I said, I don't know what he said or did to anger her. Did she reveal more in the meeting?"

"No. She carefully avoided specifics on their meeting. She said they exchanged memories of what happened between our departure and return, but that Grollon had little to share. I don't know if I believe her."

Frmar paused and tipped his head. "I think it would be a good idea to watch The Marked. Find out where he goes, what he does, whom he interacts with. Perhaps we can find some evidence that will convince The People to oppose any further contact with him."

Tllomell listened and nodded through his speech, then stopped mid-sip when she found Frmar staring at her.

"What is it?" she asked.

"Could you do this, Tllomell? Follow him, see what he does with his days, try to find something we could use?"

Tllomell finished her sip and swallowed. "I suppose I can try." A nervous flutter spread through her belly at the thought of following The Marked or, more to the point, potentially being *caught* following The Marked.

"Excellent. Start next sunrise. This will be your mission. You will bring information back to me and we will make a plan from there." Frmar tipped his bowl and finished the last of his tea in one swallow.

After carefully placing the bowl on the ground before him, he rose, bowed, and then stepped over the ring of stones that formed her hearth.

Tllomell watched his glowing form retreat to his own hearth. Dread and fear wormed their way into her heart, doing nothing to quell the anxiety that had kept her awake in the first place.

How did I get myself into this? she wondered.

Perhaps, at the very least, it would give her something to occupy her mind, and her time, so that she could stop thinking about Krnar. A glance at Arkan's hearth let her know that Krnar had not returned. He had not set up his own hearth near the oranlodi. Where was he sleeping?

Do I really want to know?

Tllomell lay back down and watched the flames shrink and finally die out as the fire's sustenance turned to ash.

After another fitful attempt at sleep, she woke to the single most unusual sensation she'd ever felt. Fat droplets of water splatted against her fur at random intervals. When she opened her eyes to try to discover the cause, water splashed into her right eye, causing her to trill in surprise and blink rapidly while rolling onto her hands and knees.

The water is falling from the sky!

By the time this realization sank in, the random drops had become a steady fall, soaking her fur and all of her belongings.

She jumped up and scrambled to roll up her sleeping hide. After scanning for any items that might be damaged by the water, she grabbed her pack and followed the rush of people heading for the shelter of the trees.

"What is this?" Tllomell called to Plldoll as they crouched beneath the canopy.

"Ellall called it *tllafar*—water from the sky," Plldoll called back.

Tllafar, Tllomell thought. She'd never heard the word before, and never in her life had she imagined anything but snow falling from the clouds.

Her tongue slid between her lips and tasted the liquid.

Fresh water, like a gift from Aruvel.

The fall was steady, but not as heavy under the cover of the alara leaves. Water trickled through her fur, tickling the skin of her arms and back.

Suddenly, a boom sounded overhead. Tllomell flinched and heard those around her cry out. People hugged their packs or their children close and with wide eyes watched the sky.

It is a storm. Tllomell heard Ellall's voice in her head, calm and reassuring. *This is nothing to fear. The sunlight and water are necessary for the plants, the alara fruits, to grow. This is good. It is good.*

It is good, Tllomell repeated to herself.

Then a bolt of light tore through the clouds, leaving her momentarily blinded.

It is good, she chanted, hugging her pack to her chest and closing her eyes. *It is good.*

There were no caves here, no shelter to retreat to.

Tllomell slid down a smooth silver trunk. Her bottom rested in the ooze of mud and grass while the heart-stopping booms shook her bones. Just when she thought she'd recovered from the last, another assaulted her ears.

Eventually the noise and light faded, the rain slackened to a soft mist that clung to the tips of her lashes.

Tllomell rested her forehead on her pack and tried to sleep.

There was nowhere else to go.

CHAPTER 10

The staccato rhythm of the rain played its soothing music against the tent cover, while inside Krnar and Jahira curled into each other, neither one wanting to end the exploration of the other.

Thunder boomed and Krnar's body jerked.

Jahira laughed softly. "The only thing you're afraid of," she said, tucking her head against his shoulder.

"I am not afraid. It is unexpected. We never had *thunder* where we lived." Krnar trailed a finger along the back of Jahira's arm. He felt the small bumps rise on her flesh in the wake of his touch and marveled at her response to his attention.

"Oh!" Jahira exclaimed, rising up onto her elbows. "What about the others? Do you think they're alright? This is the first storm since your people arrived."

"You are right," Krnar said, surprised that Jahira had thought of this before he had.

He quested out with his mind, but found he was too far away to connect with anyone.

"Allnall will know; she will reassure them. Ellall may remember as well."

"Do you need to go?" Jahira's face hovered above his. Her green eyes glowed in the light given off by his body. A crease formed between her eyebrows and he could feel her warring emotions.

"No, they do not need me there to survive a rain storm." Krnar pulled Jahira down against him again. "Besides, I don't want to leave."

"Oh good, because I don't want you to go."

Krnar smiled, pressed his lips to the top of her head. The gesture still felt somewhat foreign to him, but he could feel Jahira's response to it, which encouraged him to do it more often.

His own body still hummed with energy like he'd never felt before.

For a time, Jahira's focus had been entirely clear. No other thoughts had interfered. Her emotions had been strong, clear, and unquestionable.

He'd been shocked by her intensity, and by the intensity of his own response.

Did every couple feel this way? he wondered, and then realized what he'd thought: *Couple.*

Gazing down the length of Jahira's smooth, dark body pressed against him, absorbing his light, he realized he wanted to be.

But does she? And what would his people think?

Most of the humans already considered them a couple; he read it in their thoughts and in their looks. Most didn't seem to care...most.

But they come from a different world, he thought. *Which is now a part of our world.*

Jahira's leg twitched. Her eyes were closed and her face relaxed. She'd fallen asleep.

He closed his eyes and let his mind drift until he joined her in a peaceful, satisfied slumber.

The next morning, they both slept late. Krnar woke first to find Jahira still pressed against him. Feeling had left his right arm, which had been cushioning Jahira's head all night.

An attempt to gently extricate himself without waking Jahira failed.

Green eyes lifted and met his, sparkling mischievously. She pulled him down and ran her fingers through the fur on his chest.

His body responded instantly. It was also telling him there were more urgent matters to attend to.

A low growl rumbled through him. "I have to get up. I need to go outside."

Jahira groaned. "Me too, but I don't want to get up yet."

Krnar chuckled, pulled on his shorts, and then opened the tent flap.

A rush of cold air filled the tent. Jahira yelped and rolled into the covers. "Shut the door!" she yelled, her voice muffled by the barrier of her sleeping bag.

Krnar obliged before moving off into the trees to take care of business.

By the time he'd returned, Jahira had managed to get dressed and drag herself outside. She gave him a crooked half-smile and then took her turn in the trees.

Together they prepared the morning meal; a familiar routine with an added dimension after last night. They intentionally touched on several occasions, smiling each time they did.

Once they both had a plate of food and bowl of tea, Jahira sat down and sighed. "I don't suppose you can just stay here with me today?"

Krnar trilled. "I wish I could, but after yesterday's unresolved meeting, I'm sure I'll be expected. What will you do today?"

"I'm helping Magnar with his boat," Jahira replied. "I promised I'd gather a crew today. He wants to get it done before the snow comes."

Krnar nodded.

"Speaking of Magnar and meetings, do the Leroni know about Magnar? Do they know he's got the scars like Grollon?"

"No," Krnar said. "Perhaps it would be best to tell them now. I do not want them to think we are withholding more information, and it may help Grollon's cause. After all, he did help Magnar."

"That's true. I think Magnar might be more comfortable too if he didn't have to worry about slipping up and revealing his scars to the wrong person."

Krnar nodded. "I will tell them today." He cut his eyes toward Jahira. "They may request a meeting with him once they learn of him."

Jahira's brow furrowed. "I think he'd be okay with that, as long as he knew he wasn't going to be stoned."

"Stoned?" Krnar asked.

"Oh, uh, it's when people throw rocks at someone until they die because that person did something wrong."

Krnar's eyes widened. "Your people do this to each other?"

"Oh, no! Well, not anymore. It's just kind of a saying now."

Krnar still felt alarmed by this idea. "We do not do this."

"Well, nothing to worry about then." Jahira smiled but Krnar didn't understand what was funny. Her smile fell and she added, "I could join him for support. You could be a witness also. The more truth they hear, the better."

Krnar chewed his last piece of fruit and washed it down with lukewarm tea.

Jahira put out the fire and stacked their plates and bowls in a bucket of sudsy water.

"I will see you tonight?" Krnar asked.

"I hope so," Jahira replied with a smile.

Krnar reached out and drew a circle on her forehead. Jahira rose up on her toes and placed her lips against his and then drew away.

Reluctantly, he turned and walked into the grove. He did not look forward to revealing this new information, but he knew it was the right thing to do.

When he arrived at the base of the five sacred pools, the circle of elders was gathered and appeared to be waiting for him.

Where were you? Allnall asked, her tone teasing. She kept her face neutral but he could feel her amusement.

Krnar didn't bother to answer.

He bowed to Ellall and the elders before he took his seat.

Ellall opened by highlighting the questions and concerns from yesterday.

Krnar half-listened while glancing around the circle. He stopped on Frmar and noticed the apprentice to the Akaruvel wasn't paying attention, either.

Frmar's gaze fixed on some distant point. He tipped his head ever so slightly and one finger twitched. Sure signs he was communicating with someone mind-to-mind...but not anyone in the circle.

As discreetly as possible, Krnar followed Frmar's line of sight. His eyes widened in surprise when he saw Tllomell across the field, watching.

She tipped her chin in a slight nod and then turned to leave the grove.

When Krnar looked at Frmar again, the man stared directly at him.

CHAPTER 11

"Okay, this all looks pretty good. I think you're going to have too much weight here," Dan said, pointing to a section of Magnar's hovering diagram. "And I wouldn't use these rotating panels."

"Why not?" Magnar asked. "It's the best way to maximize the sunlight. The panels will follow the sun."

Jahira approached slowly, not wanting to interrupt. She paused a few feet behind the two men and waited for an opening in the conversation.

"Yeah, great in theory, but you're going to be on the open sea. Small parts that stick up and move around—you're kind of asking for trouble. They're more likely to break, get stuck, corrode, blow away—"

"Alright, alright, what do you suggest?"

"Well, you've got this whole enclosed front end that could be covered with panels and it looks like you're planning to enclose the flying bridge?"

Magnar nodded.

"I'd use the solar glass to encase the whole thing. It'd give you an unobstructed view and get the light from all angles, plus it's just pretty."

Magnar smirked. "Pretty, huh?"

"Yeah, well, very functional also."

Magnar gripped his chin and then nodded slowly. "Okay, I like it. Panels on the surface of the enclosed bow," he tapped and slid things on the screen to adjust his plan. "And solar glass encasing the flying bridge." He stepped back and smiled. "What do you think, Jahira?"

Jahira took a step forward and examined the changes in the rotating 3-D image of the projected finished product. "I like it."

"Me too," Magnar said.

"I'll go scrounge up some solar glass. The strips you were going to put on the upright panels can just be moved to the bow."

Dan left and Magnar turned to give Jahira his full attention.

"I think the hull is ready for that sealant. You want to come check?" Jahira asked.

Magnar closed the data screen and followed Jahira to the center of the cargo hold where the completed bottom of the boat hung suspended from cables and carabiners hooked to the ceiling. Tala and Cholie waited.

"Yeah, looks ready," Magnar said. "So, the sealant's going to go on pretty thick and it has to be even. Like I said, it really shouldn't be necessary, but I'm not willing to take any chances."

"I got it," Cholie said.

Magnar nodded.

"So, what's next?"

"Well, once the sealant is on, we'll have to build the hold and put in the engine, cover it all with the deck, put on the solar strips, and I think the last step will be the flying bridge on top if Dan can get the solar glass."

"Hey, Magnar, come take a look at this!" Dan called from a shadowed corner.

Magnar raised his eyebrows and waved to Jahira before jogging over to see what Dan had discovered.

Jahira walked over to the prep site where Cholie and Tala were getting ready to apply the sealant.

"Can I help?" Jahira asked.

"Yep," Cholie replied. "Grab a brush and spread this on thick and even. Tala will follow with the heat, I'll follow with the curing light."

"Sounds good."

After donning safety glasses, gloves, and a breathing filter, Jahira began, focusing on smooth, even strokes. She made sure to keep the same amount of sealant on the brush with each dip and took extra care around seams, where the metal had welded itself together.

The buzz of the heat rod followed in her wake, smoothing out the brush lines. The faint whine of Cholie's curing light added to the chorus. The blue light hardened the sealant on contact so there would be no waiting time and no chance of smearing and damaging the watertight seal. The glow in the corner of her eye reminded her of Krnar.

The three women worked their way around the hull without pausing.

Once she'd returned to the keel line on the bow of the boat, Jahira stepped back with a sigh and rolled her shoulders. The burn reduced to a simmer. She tipped her chin from side to side and was rewarded with a loud pop in the center of her cervical vertebrae.

When Tala and then Cholie joined her, they stepped back and examined their work.

"Looks great!" Magnar exclaimed, startling Jahira. She hadn't heard him approach. "Now you can do the inside."

Tala groaned.

"Hey, who volunteered to help here?" Magnar said.

"Sir, yes, sir," Tala replied, her voice dripping with sarcasm.

"Do we at least get a lunch break?" Cholie asked.

"Only if you make up for lost time at the end of the day," Magnar replied with a wink.

He stepped closer to the hull and ran a hand along the smooth, even surface.

"Seriously, though, my stomach is yelling at me right now," Cholie said.

"Okay, lunch break, and then we tackle the inside," Jahira said.

"How are we going to do the inside without Cholie and me stepping on the sealant?" Tala asked.

Jahira's brow wrinkled in thought.

"Let's figure it out over lunch, please," Cholie begged.

"Want to eat outside?" Tala asked.

"Definitely," Jahira said. "Without the filter, the smell of that sealant is making me dizzy."

"Hey, better take this," Tala said, grabbing a tarp off the floor. "The ground's pretty wet after that storm last night."

Once they'd each grabbed their pack, Jahira led the way down the ramp.

"Let's get out of the shadow of this beast and into the sunlight," Cholie said.

They picked a warm spot in the field and laid out the tarp.

Jahira sat cross-legged on one corner of the tarp. From her pack, she pulled out three strips of dried meat, four medium-sized purple carrots, a piece of fruit from the alara trees, and her canteen of water.

"Not quite the bounty we had on *The Aquilo*, huh," Tala said, frowning at her collection of vegetables.

"Not yet, but we'll get there," replied Cholie, ever the optimist.

"I want cake, and chocolate, and pudding, and ice cream," Tala said, her voice dreamy and her eyes distant as she chewed on a spinach leaf.

"You know that was all created in a lab, right?" Cholie said. "This is so much better for you!"

"It doesn't *taste* better for me," Tala lamented.

Jahira grinned. "The Leroni might be able to help us find more edible plants, and maybe once Magnar gets underway we'll have a supply of seafood," she added.

"How will the Leroni help if they've never lived here?" Tala asked, not in a confrontational way, but out of genuine curiosity.

"Well, Krnar talks a lot about memories and his people remembering things from this place. I think they've passed down stories and images from generation to generation. And don't forget Grollon, he lived here, and he remembers everything."

"That's really cool," Cholie said.

"What if the things that are safe for them to eat aren't safe for us to eat?" Tala asked.

Jahira shrugged and said, "I suppose that's possible, but so far, so good."

"So, are they happy, the Leroni? I hardly ever see any of them except Krnar, and once in a while Allnall."

"Well, it's only been three days. Give them some time."

"Oh, right. I guess it's a pretty huge adjustment for them."

"How's Krnar handling the new situation?" Tala asked, waggling her eyebrows.

"Fine," Jahira said. She studied her food, trying to think of a way to change the subject.

"So, you two are...still...together?" Cholie asked.

Jahira looked up, her eyebrows pulled together. "Um, yeah. Why do you say it like *that*?"

"Well," two spots of color grew over Cholie's cheeks as she paused and cleared her throat. "Some people, not me, but some people, thought that once *his* people were here you two would, well, he'd be with one of his own people."

"Some people, huh?" Tala said. "Which people?"

"It's okay, Tala," Jahira said. "I'm not worried about what other people think."

"Me either. It's what they say about my friends that I'm worried about," Tala replied.

Jahria turned to Cholie and said, "So, how's the greenhouse coming along?"

Cholie visibly relaxed. Tala smirked and Jahira ignored her. "Great! It's really looking good!"

"That's good to hear. Will everything be ready before the snow comes?"

"Hey, is that Kato and Creed?" Tala asked, squinting and pointing toward the river.

Cholie squealed, dropped the salad she'd been eating, and raced toward the two approaching figures.

The two men waved and then sprinted toward her. Jahira and Tala rose and followed Cholie.

Kato dropped his pack as Cholie leapt and he caught her in mid-air.

By the time Jahira and Tala caught up, Cholie had covered Kato in kisses.

"Hey, where's my hug?" Creed asked.

Cholie let go of Kato long enough to squeeze Creed and stand on her toes to give him a peck on the cheek.

"You're back! You both look great!" Tala exclaimed.

They looked even more alike with their matching deep tans beneath two heads of wavy black hair in serious need of a trim.

"I hope this is the last time you'll have to go away," Cholie said.

"Should be," Kato replied, pressing his lips against the top of her head. "Magnar can take over from here."

"So, how's Lusela and the gang of misfit maintenance workers?" Jahira asked.

"They're doing fine. Still refuse to return to the settlement or return the food they took. In fact, she sent a list of supplies they need for the winter."

Jahira's eyebrows rose. "She's making demands now?"

"Well, not demands, per se," Creed said. "She wants to establish a trade agreement."

"What does she plan to trade?" Tala asked.

"Oh, maybe freeze-dried meat," Jahira said.

Tala snorted.

"Well, they were building rafts to cross the channel. They're definitely headed to the southern continent. The herd animals have already crossed and they're following. I guess they'll be able to hunt through the winter. They might be able to trade fresh meat. Who knows what else they'll find?"

"A few people came back with us this time," Creed added. "Not everyone had planned on this being a permanent move."

"Yeah, they got spooked by the idea of living so far away from the ships and a doctor, one of the women is pregnant, and a few have had some bad rashes on their arms and legs, but don't know what caused it." Kato said.

"Are they really that afraid of the Leroni that they're willing to risk their lives to get away from them?" Jahira asked.

"Honestly, for most of them, I think that was just an easy excuse. A lot of the ones who left are workers who've filed complaints about the leadership…"

"Or who've had complaints filed about them," Kato added.

"Good luck to Lusela then."

"Yeah, we'll see how it goes."

"Kato! Creed!" Dan and Magnar stood at the top of the entrance ramp and waved.

"Come on, come say hi to the guys. I think you'll be surprised by the progress," Jahira said, waving the brothers toward the ship.

Creed fell in step between Jahira and Tala. Kato and Cholie hung back, glued to each other's sides.

The lunch break turned into an hour of exchanging stories and catching up on all the news before Magnar put them back to work, including Kato and Creed.

"No time to lose," said Magnar. "I've got three months to get trade goods to the south, return, and then leave again before I get snowed in!"

The crew set to work with fresh enthusiasm.

CHAPTER 12

After a fruitless day of trying, and failing, to find The Marked, Tllomell returned to her hearth to find Frmar pacing just outside her circle of stones.

Her eyebrows pulled together in a frown. *What is he so upset about?* she wondered.

Once he noticed her, he started to reach out and then withdrew his hand, as if he'd had to restrain himself from grabbing her.

"What is it? What is going on?" Tllomell asked, trying to decide if she should sit or stand since Frmar continued to pace, though now inside her circle of stones.

There's another! he shouted inside her head, causing Tllomell to flinch. *One of the humans, if that's what they really are, is marked!*

"What?" Tllomell exclaimed.

Those at the nearby hearths cut their eyes her way. Tllomell bowed in apology and switched to projecting.

What do you mean? she repeated.

Krnar told us today, Frmar explained. *One of the humans drank from the oranlodi. Grollon saved him with the blood of Aruvel and now this human bears the scars of The Marked.*

Is he the only one?

So they say. My fear is the more we push, the more will be revealed. I'm beginning to doubt the entire story about these humans. I mean, they have proven that at least one of the mountains can fly, but from another world? From a place beyond the stars? Frmar shook his head at the incredible thought. *Then we arrive and learn The Marked still lives. I think it's all a trick to bring us back so they can finish what they started.*

But how did they build these ships? And where are their wings?

Grollon passed through the Gateway. He has been given the knowledge of eternity. What couldn't he do? And as for the wings, perhaps they evolved, as we did.

What about their minds? Their language? They cannot project, or shield their thoughts. They do not understand what we say...

Frmar growled in frustration. *I don't know, but I don't trust any of them!*

What are you going to do? Tllomell asked.

I don't know.

Frmar exhaled and finally sat down. *Did you learn anything today?* he asked.

Tllomell looked down and away. *No, I could not find him, not with my eyes anyway, and I dared not try with my mind.*

Frmar's lips tightened into a thin line. *Well, keep trying.*

Tllomell nodded.

Frmar rose, bowed, and without another word he left.

The following day, Tllomell had more success, if one could call it that.

She rose to the crest of the riverbank and caught a glimpse of Grollon walking away from the river on the opposite side.

Dropping to one knee, she watched his retreat. When the distance was enough that she felt safe, she began to follow. Her heart hammered and her palms grew slick with sweat. With every step, she prepared to drop to the ground and hide in the tall grass, but he did not look back.

Even with her protective lenses in place, Allorkan's light made her eyes water. She squinted each time she scanned the horizon to find Grollon continuing toward the dancing forest. When he reached the edge of the trees, he disappeared from sight.

Tllomell moved parallel to his last position and stepped out of the long grass to see him sitting cross-legged with his back resting against a root far down the tree line.

A quick search revealed a perfect place to watch and, hopefully, not be seen.

Tllomell took up her position and sat...and sat...for the entire sun. Truly, she began to wonder if he knew she was there watching him and meant to torture her with absolute boredom.

No one came to see him. He did not move from his seat on the fallen leaves to go anywhere, not even to eat or relieve himself. He just...sat.

Tllomell dared not move too much and risk drawing attention to herself. In the safety of her own mind, she sang every song she knew. She tried meditating. She even began to pick the surrounding grass and stems and weave them into various random designs.

She'd nearly completed a complicated pattern that would be just long enough to wrap around her wrist when the crunch of dried leaves drew her head up.

"May the light of Allorkan shine upon you." The Marked stood no more than a body's length away, bowing slightly.

"Uh," Tllomell cleared her throat and attempted to compose her expression. "And upon you."

The Marked straightened. He wore a bemused expression. "What are you making?" he asked.

Tllomell stared, taking in the wings, the scars across the wrinkled forehead, the piercing blue eyes that seemed older even than the wizened body. His eyebrows lifted and she realized she hadn't answered. "Oh, uh, a bracelet," she replied, holding up her creation and feeling completely inane.

Grollon, The Marked, was talking to her about pieces of woven grass.

"It's very nice."

"Thank you."

Grollon looked up toward the darkening sky. "It is getting late, and I am hungry. I must be going. Have a pleasant evening."

"Yes, you as well."

The heat of embarrassment began to replace the cold shock she'd been filled with at hearing Grollon speak for the first time.

Then he turned.

Dread stabbed her in the heart and took her breath away. What would he do?

"You know, Tllomell, there are some decisions so big, so life changing that, once made, things can never return to the way they were. Believe me, I know."

The breath she'd been holding left her in a huff of relief when The Marked continued on his way, but her brow furrowed when his words registered in her brain. Why had he told her this? What did it mean?

He knows my name, she realized. *Did I tell him my name?*

She didn't think that she had.

The lack of food, the heat of the day, and the gut-churning fear of Grollon calling her by name made her head spin. She wasn't sure she could make it back to the grove.

An unfamiliar hoot echoed through the trees, followed by an eerie silence.

Tllomell rose to her feet and quick-walked through the grass back toward the river.

The next day she chose not to look for The Marked. She still felt unsettled by their encounter the previous sun and had no desire to repeat the experience.

Instead, she decided to go fishing.

After she'd packed her supplies for the day, she walked to Plldoll's hearth and invited her along. For the first time since arriving at the warm land, she enjoyed herself.

A belly full of fresh fish sustained her through a peaceful night's sleep. She woke refreshed, almost happy, and then she opened her eyes to find Frmar standing outside her hearth.

With a sigh of resignation, she waved him in.

What have you discovered? he asked.

I did find him two suns past; he sat under a dancing tree. He met no one, he went nowhere. I'm not sure how helpful this is going to be.

Well, you can't quit yet. We need something.

Tllomell closed her eyes briefly before she nodded.

This time she would be more prepared. She filled her pack with food, water bags, tools that needed sharpening, and clothing that needed mending along with her needles and gut-line. If she had to sit all day again, she would at least be productive.

The old man sat in the same spot as before, eyes closed, body relaxed. He reminded her of a plant, soaking in the sun and sustaining himself on the light alone.

After choosing a place in the shade a good distance away, she pulled out the contents of her pack and arranged them on the ground in front of her.

It did not come as such a shock this time when The Marked approached her late in the day. "A new project," he remarked.

"Yes, some mending," she replied.

"It's a peaceful place, isn't it? Good for thinking."

"Yes," Tllomell replied. She paused, working up the courage to ask what had been on her mind since their last encounter. "What did you mean before, about 'some decisions being so big they changed everything'?"

Grollon's eyebrows rose. "I trust you know my story." It was more a statement than a question, but Tllomell nodded. "Well, I made choices that changed the course of history. Things can never return to the way they were."

"So you were speaking of *your* choices."

"Anyone's choices."

"Do you regret these choices?"

"Many of them, yes. But, if I had not made them, we would not be here. You might not be here."

Tllomell thought about that in silence for several heartbeats. "What is going to happen now?"

Grollon stared off into the distance. "I am going to go eat, and then sleep."

Tllomell felt her anger start to rise, and then remembered to whom she spoke. Tamping down the anger, she reached for patience. "Yes, but I mean in our future, as a people, what will happen?"

Grollon waved a hand. "Many things."

Tllomell ground her teeth in frustration. "What, specifical-ly?"

"That depends on your choices."

Tllomell began folding the mending she'd had on her lap. She'd had enough of this conversation.

"Perhaps I'll see you here again," Grollon said.

"You should know," Tllomell muttered.

Grollon did not respond. Either he hadn't heard her, or chose to ignore her. "May the light of Allorkan shine upon you," he said, and then walked away.

Tllomell cursed and shoved items into her pack. A sharp sting on her right index finger caused her to yelp and pull her hand from the pack. A sewing needle protruded from her finger-tip.

After removing the needle, she placed the fingertip in her mouth and sucked the blood from the tiny puncture.

Digging through her pack with more care this time, she found a spare strip of hide. With her belt knife, she sliced a thin piece, held one end with her teeth, and wrapped the other arcund her finger. When there were two short ends left, she wound the free end around the taut piece still secured with her teeth and then pulled them into a knot.

This had turned out to be a very bad idea.

CHAPTER 13

"How are the meetings going, Krnar?" Ulletta asked.

Steam rose from the bone bowl that Ulletta filled and passed to him. The smell of salty fish and rich oil filled his nostrils. His stomach grumbled in anticipation.

"Nothing has been decided," he said. "Frmar grows angrier every day. He argues instead of listening. I feel he is determined to oppose whatever I say."

Krnar waited for Ulletta to finish passing out bowls and finally take her own seat before picking up his spoon. Tiny waves rippled across the broth when he blew on the first bite to cool it down. The familiar, savory flavor melted on his tongue and slid down his throat. "This is delicious, Ulletta. Thank you," he said.

Ulletta nodded then said, "Arkan and Mrkon caught the fish today, fresh out of the river."

"Ah, well done. I wish I had been there." Krnar took another bite, swallowed, and then said, "Do you enjoy fishing in the river, Mrkon?"

Mrkon nodded once.

Either Ulletta or Arkan must have mentally admonished the boy because a heartbeat later he looked up, met Krnar's eyes, and replied, "Yes, Uncle."

Krnar nodded and Mrkon's stare returned to his bowl.

Krnar glanced at his brother from beneath his lashes. Mrkon was quiet, unusually so for a boy his age, and so serious. He reminded Krnar a bit of himself as a child.

"When will you get to join us again?" Arkan asked.

Krnar trilled in frustration. "Hopefully soon. I certainly didn't anticipate the number of meetings I'd have to attend once everyone arrived here."

"Some thanks, isn't it?" Arkan grinned.

Krnar chuckled. "How is the baby, Ulletta?" he asked.

Ulletta placed a hand on her swollen belly and frowned. "She seems to be moving less since we got here," Ulletta replied.

Concern drew Krnar's eyebrows together.

"The humans have a very good healer here. I have seen him help some of the human women who are with child. Would you like to see him?" Krnar asked.

Arkan reached out a placed a hand over Ulletta's. "She will be fine," he said. "I told her there's been so much going on she probably hasn't noticed the baby moving."

Arkan smiled at Ulletta. She returned the smile, but Krnar could see the worry around her eyes.

"We heard a rumor," Arkan said, his voice lowering so that it would not carry beyond his hearth. "Is it true that one of the humans has been marked?"

Ulletta paused and watched him. Even Mrkon picked his eyes up from his bowl.

Krnar nodded slowly. "It is true," he replied. In equally hushed tones, he told them the story of Magnar.

"I thought you were hiding something back at the cave. You omitted those details from the story you shared." Arkan raised an eyebrow. Krnar knew his brother wondered why he hadn't shared the news at least with him.

"We told Ellall right away. She felt it would be best to wait to tell anyone about Grollon and Magnar. We didn't want anyone to panic."

"And you think I would have panicked?" Arkan asked.

"No, of course not, but you know as well as anyone, there was no way to keep a secret in that place."

Arkan grunted.

Krnar wasn't sure if it was in agreement or not.

"We noticed you haven't set up a hearth here, near the pools," Ulletta said.

While grateful for the change in subject, Krnar wished it had been a different subject. He filled his mouth with stew to give himself a moment to think.

The corner of Arkan's mouth twitched.

Krnar swallowed and said, "Yes, I had established a hearth during my time here, closer to the human settlement, that I chose to keep."

"Ah, I see, and is it...working out for you there?" Ulletta asked, her voice casual and innocent.

Arkan could no longer suppress his grin. His attempt to bury it in his bowl of stew failed miserably.

"Uh, yes, so far it suits me very well."

"Oh, good. Well, you are always welcome here if your...situation...changes."

"Thank you," Krnar replied. Embarrassment oozed from every pore. He reinforced his mental shields, hoping to prevent further awkwardness.

"You know, I really like Jahira. I haven't seen her since the welcoming feast. You should invite her here to eat with us some-time."

Arkan tipped his bowl up, supposedly to finish the last swallow of stew, but Krnar could see him shaking with silent laughter.

"I will pass on the invitation," Krnar said.

"Wonderful." Ulletta smiled.

Krnar tipped his own bowl, licked the last drop of broth from the rim, and then set it gently by the fire. "Thank you, Ulletta, that really was wonderful. I need to be going."

"Of course. We wouldn't want to keep you," Arkan said, still grinning.

Krnar bowed his way out of his brother's hearth, then turned and walked away, shaking his head.

Allorkan had begun its daily descent on the horizon. A faint lavender tinted with rose splashed across the sky above the grove.

Once he stepped beneath the canopy of the alara trees, it was dark enough that he could blink back his protective lenses. The world sharpened instantly, going from the blurry shadows of waning dusk to crisp lines. His bioluminescent fur glowed with a faint light that would grow more intense when full dark came.

Through the silver trunks, he saw another light move. Krnar altered his path to intercept the approaching Leroni.

"Tllomell," Krnar said, once he'd gotten close enough to identify the figure.

She stopped, eyes wide, and then glanced from side to side. "Krnar," she said.

"Were you out fishing?" he asked, scanning for any evidence of her catch.

"No, uh, just, exploring."

Tllomell continued to look around, as if expecting someone to appear. She shifted her weight from one foot to the other.

"Oh, by yourself?"

"Yes, why not?" Tllomell's eyes focused on him and narrowed. "Don't you think it's safe?"

What is going on? he wondered. Aloud he said, "I have no doubt you can handle yourself, I was only...surprised. Few of The People have left the grove at all, not to mention alone, since we arrived."

"Few except you, of course." Tllomell tilted her head to the side. "Where are you going so late, Krnar?"

"I, uh...my things are on the other side of the grove."

"Hmm, I see."

Tllomell began to walk away.

"Tllomell, wait." She paused and turned to face him. "How are you adjusting? Do you like it here? Are you happy?"

Tllomell's expression fell, almost as if she were about to cry. She quickly looked away and then said, "It's amazing, Krnar. Everything Ellall said it would be."

He could hear the lie in her voice but he didn't understand why she would lie to him.

This time, when she walked away, he didn't try to stop her.

Stars began to appear in the sky, creeping out from their hiding places to decorate the night. The fire in Jahira's hearth had already been smothered and no sound emerged from the closed tent.

Bracing himself for the inevitable noise, Krnar pulled the tent flap open. Jahira lay curled on her side, eyes closed.

Krnar crawled inside, closing the flap behind him, and then lay down with his stomach to Jahira's back.

"Hey," Jahira murmured sleepily.

Krnar reached out and covered her hand. She curled her fingers into his.

"Magnar thinks he'll be ready for a test run soon. He wants to take his boat to the southern continent. He asked if I would join him, and I said yes. Would you want to come?"

"When will he go?"

"I'm not sure. Maybe a week, uh, seven sleeps. Depends on how fast everything comes together."

"Seven sleeps. Perhaps by then the elders will have come to some agreement."

Jahira chuckled. "Do you want to go? If you can."

"I would like to see the first continent." Krnar paused. "This is where the others are? Those who left?"

"Yes."

"I do not think I would be welcome at their hearth."

"Screw Lusela."

"I do not understand."

Jahira yawned. "Oh, uh, I don't care what Lusela thinks."

"Still, I do not wish to create a problem."

"Okay, well, we can talk about it more when it's time to leave." Another huge yawn from Jahira caused Krnar to yawn as well.

"Goodnight, Krnar."

"Sleep well, Jahira."

The next morning, just as they were finished with breakfast, Arkan burst through the trees, running full tilt toward Jahira's tent.

Krnar stood. Arkan slowed, scanning the ground. Krnar realized he must be looking for the stones that would mark the boundaries of the hearth. Krnar waved him forward, saying, "What is it, Arkan? What's wrong?"

Arkan pulled air into his heaving lungs and said, "It's Ulletta. She woke this morning bleeding and said she couldn't hear the baby."

"Couldn't hear it?"

"Its mind, she couldn't connect with its mind. She sent me to find you. We thought, maybe..." Arkan's eyes cut toward Jahira, then back to Krnar.

"The healer!" Krnar exclaimed.

Arkan nodded.

Krnar turned to Jahira and said, "It's Ulletta, something is wrong with the baby."

Jahira's eyes widened. She'd already started moving when she said, "Medic, I'll get Medic."

Krnar nodded and Jahira raced toward the silver mountain.

"She is going to find the healer. I'll wait here and bring them to you. Go back to Ulletta and tell her we're coming."

Arkan turned and ran.

CHAPTER 14

Jahira stood back while Medic kneeled beside Ulletta. Her entire body clenched with worry. She twisted the cuff that once belonged to her sister, Zarya, around her wrist, hoping the baby would be okay, hoping Medic wouldn't unknowingly do something to offend the entire race of Leroni who stood watching from a distance.

With his usual forethought, he'd asked Krnar to hand the scanner to Ulletta and showed her where to hold it without ever touching her.

Arkan sat on Ulletta's right side. Ellall squatted on Ulletta's left. Krnar knelt beside Medic, interpreting Medic's questions and Ulletta's responses.

"I think the baby's heart rate is too slow," Medic said. "It is too slow for a human fetus at this stage. I would like to get Ulletta to the ship to get some pictures of the baby and its surroundings."

Krnar tilted his head. "You can see inside Ulletta? You can see the baby?"

"Yes."

Krnar relayed this news. Arkan looked apprehensive. Ellall trilled in disbelief.

Arkan and Ulletta exchanged words too fast for Jahira to follow. Arkan seemed hesitant, Ulletta insistent.

Finally, Ulletta turned to Medic and nodded.

"Should I bring a stretcher?" Jahira asked.

"I don't think we have time for a stretcher," Medic replied.

Jahira's heart rate spiked.

Krnar watched the exchange.

"Fast," Jahira said in their language, waving for them to follow her.

Arkan scooped Ulletta into his arms and followed Medic and Jahira through the grove. Krnar followed with Mrkon and Ellall.

Eyes followed them through the human settlement. Few Leroni had ventured past the alara trees since they'd arrived. The bright red blood trailing down Ulletta's legs, and now Arkan's arm and side, probably didn't help dampen the curiosity.

More stares greeted them from the staff and patients already in the medical wing.

Medic led the way to an empty exam room. He gestured for Arkan to place Ulletta on the covered table in the middle of the room. With fingers dancing across screens, he booted up the room's computers and pulled a mechanical arm along its track in the ceiling until it hung suspended over Ulletta.

"Do you feel any pain in your belly or back?" Medic asked, while his hands pulled something that looked like a small microphone from the end of the mechanical arm.

Krnar translated then said to Medic, "She said yes, she has pain in her belly and everything feels tight."

Medic nodded. "May I touch this to her belly?" he asked.

Krnar asked and Ulletta nodded.

With one hand Medic placed the tip of the device against Ulletta's fur. With his opposite hand, he tapped a light on the mechanical arm and a larger than life image appeared on the wall screen opposite the bed.

"My baby," Ulletta breathed.

Medic moved the tip slowly back and forth, then around the edge of Ulletta's swollen abdomen. "The placenta, that dark mass on the right, has detached from the uterine wall. It's called a placental abruption."

Krnar shook his head.

"*This*," Medic said, shining a red light on the placenta, "gives the baby food and helps the baby breathe, but it's torn off."

Krnar frowned but nodded and then translated.

Ulletta responded.

"She asks, 'What does this mean?'"

"It means the baby is in serious danger, and she might be as well." Medic paused to give Krnar time to interpret. "The pain and tightness she's feeling is the baby getting ready to be born."

As soon as Krnar finished, Ulletta began to shake her head and repeat the same phrase over and over.

"It's too early, she says," Krnar replied.

"I know, but the baby won't survive without the placenta. It's coming now."

Medic went to the sink and scrubbed his hands and arms.

"Jahira, go get me someone to assist."

Jahira nodded, dashed from the room, and grabbed the first staff member she saw.

"Can you help deliver a baby?" Jahira asked.

"Uh, yes," the startled woman replied.

"Great." Jahira pulled the woman back into Ulletta's room.

Ulletta moaned and clung to Arkan's hand.

"Bree," Medic acknowledged the assistant. "Scrub up. Placental abruption."

Bree's eyes widened before she hurried to follow Medic's instructions.

"Should I wait outside?" Jahira asked.

Medic nodded. "Take the boy," he said.

Jahira had forgotten about Mrkon. The boy stood still and silent, eyes wide. Jahira remembered he was Ulletta's nephew. He'd lost his parents not long ago. He must be terrified.

Jahira walked over and explained to Ellall that Medic wanted her to take Mrkon and wait outside.

Ellall nodded, spoke to Mrkon, and then nodded to Jahira.

The Akaruvel moved to stand near Ulletta's head, out of the way but able to provide what support she could.

Jahira opened the door and gestured for Mrkon to step outside with her. He glanced back at the scene behind him. His shoulders sagged, but he complied.

The light blue cushions of the chair in the hallway formed around her back and buttocks when she sat. She patted the chair beside her, inviting Mrkon to sit as well.

Krnar had told her the boy had been born during the last "Season of Ice," but that could put him anywhere between two and eight years old. He didn't look much smaller than Zarya had been at twelve, so she guessed he must be closer to eight.

She wished she had something with her that might distract him from what was happening on the other side of that wall he stared at so intently. "Krnar said you like fishing," Jahira said in her best Leronese.

The boy didn't respond.

She tried to picture the boy with a baited hook, tossing a line in the river with a smile on his face. Focusing on the image, she held it in her mind for a few seconds and repeated the Leroni word for *fishing*.

Mrkon looked down at his hands.

"I hope Ulletta and the baby are okay," she said.

She had no idea what else to say, and Mrkon was clearly not in a conversational mood so they sat and waited.

The rooms were soundproof. There were no windows. It was impossible to know what was happening.

Restless energy made her legs bounce until Mrkon glanced over at her jittery limbs.

Finally, what felt like days later, Krnar stepped out and shut the door behind him.

Jahira and Mrkon both jumped to their feet.

"Is she okay? Is the baby okay?"

Krnar looked down at his hands and Jahira's heart sank.

"Oh no, what happened?" Jahira instinctively reached out and took Krnar's hands.

Mrkon glance at their hands, and then back to Krnar's face.

"The baby did not live," Krnar said.

Hot tears filled Jahira's eyes and fear twisted her heart. "Ulletta?" she asked.

"Ulletta lives," Krnar said. "She lost much blood, but somehow Medic stopped more from coming. Ellall says Medic saved her. If we had not come, she would have died also."

Mrkon sank to the floor.

Krnar squeezed Jahira's hands then released them. He knelt in front of Mrkon and spoke softly to him. Mrkon didn't fall into Krnar's arms, but his shoulders began to shake.

The door opened again. This time Medic, Bree, and Ellall stepped into the hallway.

Ellall spoke to Mrkon and he jumped to his feet and bolted through the open doorway.

Medic shut the door behind him.

"We'll give them some time," he said. Fatigue and sorrow deepened the lines around his eyes. "I want Ulletta to stay here for a few days. I'll need to monitor her and I don't want her moving any farther than the bathroom. She can't lose any more blood. I'd like to give her a transfusion but I have no blood to give her and I know nothing about Leroni blood types to attempt to find a match."

"Is she doing okay?" Jahira asked. "How's Arkan?"

"I think they're both still in shock. They need some time. The loss and how it happened...they need some time."

Ellall spoke to Krnar and Krnar turned to Medic.

"She said to tell you thank you. Thank you for trying, and for saving Ulletta. If we had been at our cave, we would have lost them both."

Medic nodded in acknowledgement. "I wish I could have done more," he said.

"Medic," a male attendant came up and touched Medic on the arm. "The patient in room six would like to see you."

Medic nodded. "I'll be right there," he said to the attendant.

The young man nodded and left.

"I'll be back to check on her when I'm done," Medic said, then bowed to Ellall.

Ellall returned the bow.

Once Medic had disappeared into room six, Ellall spoke to Krnar.

"Ellall wishes to return to the grove. She must tell everyone what has happened. I will walk her back and then return."

"I'll wait here," Jahira said. "If they ask for you, I'll tell them you'll be right back."

Krnar nodded, his face relaxing. She realized he'd wanted her to stay but didn't want to ask. She was glad she'd offered.

After Krnar and Ellall left, Jahira sank back into the chair and dozed off.

A light nudge against her shoulder brought her instantly awake. Several long blinks brought the world into focus. "Krnar, you're back."

"Ulletta wishes to see us."

"How do you—oh, the mind thing."

Jahira swallowed the lump in her throat. She took a deep breath, trying to prepare herself to be strong.

Krnar opened the door. Jahira took in the sight of Ulletta cradling a tiny, silent bundle and Arkan's grief-stricken face. Tears began to stream down her cheeks.

"Ulletta, Arkan, I am sorry," she said in their language.

Ulletta nodded and said, "Thank you for helping."

Jahira's throat constricted, making it impossible to respond. She simply nodded.

Ulletta spoke to Krnar and, in an unLeroni-like display of affection, she put her arm around Mrkon's shoulders, pulled him close, and rested her forehead against his.

Krnar turned to Jahira and said, "She would like us to help care for Mrkon while she is here."

"Of course!" Jahira replied without hesitation. "Whatever she needs."

CHAPTER 15

The following sun, rumors spread through the Leroni like cracks through thin ice.

Ellall had returned from the silver mountains and told them the story of the human healer saving Ulletta's life, but not the baby's.

Without Ulletta or even Arkan there to confirm the account, everyone speculated. With Ellall adding that Ulletta needed to remain inside the mountain, but they could not visit because she needed her rest...well, no one felt at ease with the situation.

Frmar went from hearth to hearth, soaking up the doubts like a seed takes in water. Tllomell watched them feed his fear and inside she cringed when he came to speak to her.

"Tllomell, I am gathering some of those with like minds on the issue of The Marked. We will meet at the edge of the alara grove, outside the ring of trees that way," he said, nodding his head to the north. "You must join us. Put out your fire and come. I will go first. Perhaps go into the trees in a different location, and then circle around. We don't want it to be too obvious."

Without giving her a chance to respond, he rose and left, stopping at two more hearths before heading into the trees.

The fire hissed in protest and steam rose in a thick white cloud as she poured water over the flames. A part of her wanted to ignore the request, to stay at her hearth and enjoy her meal in peace. Another part of her burned with curiosity. What did others think had happened? What would they have to say when they knew Ellall would not overhear?

Curiosity won.

She packed some dried fish and fruit in her pack, looked around to make sure no others were leaving at the same time so as not to draw attention, and then headed for the trees.

"This is not the way of The People," Frmar's voice rose to greet her when she stepped into the long grass of the northern field. "To do things in secret and not allow anyone to see them. This is the influence of The Marked. They lure us in with their knowledge and then steal our souls."

Trills of agreement rippled through those who'd gathered.

"They will start by changing our way of life, little by little. It will be so subtle we will barely notice, until we've become the same as them." Frmar paused. "We cannot allow them to continue to tell us their lies, to awe us with their magic, or to change who we are."

"What will we do?" Erknok asked.

Tllomell was surprised to see Arkan's closest friend at the meeting.

Frmar paced in front of the crowd. "I have given this much thought and I believe the alara grove is not the place for us."

Trills of alarm sounded all around.

"What do you mean 'not the place for us'? This is the place of our ancestors."

"Where else would we go?"

Tllomell watched Frmar assess his audience. He exuded confidence; she felt pulled by his calm assurance. "Krnar spoke of mountains, near the shore of the sea where he came to land. We crossed over them on our journey here. It is a place of snow and caves, a place still in the warm land, but away from the influence of the humans, away from the oppressive heat, a place where we would have shelter...a place that we are adapted to live in."

No one spoke but Tllomell could see the longing in many faces. In her mind's eye she could see the strong stone walls, feel the solid rock beneath her feet. She could almost smell the chill mountain air. Her heart ached with homesickness.

What about Ellall?

She would never agree. There were many who would vehemently oppose the idea. It would lead to arguments, division. "Ellall would never allow it," said Tllomell.

Frmar turned to face her. "Ellall doesn't have to."

Tllomell's eyes widened. *What is he suggesting?*

Frmar pulled back his shoulders and faced the crowd again. "I have been trained to become the next Akaruvel. We would not need Ellall's permission, or her presence."

A few people nodded, others squirmed, clearly as uncomfortable with the idea as Tllomell.

"You are suggesting we divide The People?" Tllomell said.

"We won't force anyone, but those who wish to remain pure, untainted by The Marked, or these *humans*, can leave this place and start over. We are no longer trapped by the ice and sea. We are free, Tllomell. Free to go wherever we wish. Free to be whoever we want to be." His blue eyes blazed.

Her reticence made the light in his eyes dim.

"We don't have to decide today. We will talk, we will see if there are more who feel this way. We will see how Ellall handles the situation with The Marked. There is time."

The night insects began to screech.

People rose and brushed the dirt from their fur. They left alone or in pairs, taking slightly different routes back into the inner field.

When only the two of them remained, Frmar stood before her with pleading eyes. "You will support me in this, won't you, Tllomell?"

"I don't know, Frmar. Leave the grove? This is the place we've dreamed of. We've been trying to get back here for generations. We've barely given it a chance."

"For generations we've been chasing a dream, Tllomell, a dream of who we used to be. I think it's time we started to appreciate who we are."

Tllomell didn't respond.

"Think about it. I hope, in time, you'll see things the way I do." Frmar bowed low and took his leave.

Tllomell did think about it. She thought about almost nothing else for a restless sleep and another full sun. Her brain hurt from thinking about it, and yet she remained as torn as she had been from the beginning.

CHAPTER 16

Krnar's heart bled for his brother, Ulletta, and Mrkon. He did not allow himself to grieve, however. He didn't deserve to cry with them.

Medic had explained that what happened to Ulletta was usually caused by physical trauma, such as a blow to the abdomen. It must have happened, or started to happen, when she fell while crossing The Great Ice.

It is my fault.

Across the fire, Jahira taught a game to Mrkon that involved stacking small sticks and then removing them one at a time until the stack fell. It didn't require much talking, and Mrkon hovered over the stack like a predator eyeing its prey.

When Arkan and Ulletta had asked them to watch over Mrkon, Krnar had assumed the boy would want to return to his family's hearth inside the ring of alara trees. Instead the boy had insisted they stay as close as possible to the ship.

Jahira's cry of consternation pulled him from his thoughts. Jahira had pulled a stick from the pile and caused its collapse. Mrkon's eyes lit with humor and his lips twitched in an almost-smile.

"Play again?" Jahira asked.

Mrkon shook his head. He stood and approached Krnar. "May I go and pick some fruit, Uncle?" he asked.

"Yes, of course."

Mrkon walked over to the nearest tree and scanned the branches for the best fruit. After spotting his prize, he scrambled up the smooth trunk and disappeared into the branches.

"Do you think he'll be okay?" Jahira asked. "He's so quiet."

"He is a good boy, he will be okay."

Jahira twisted the silver cuff on her wrist. "You saw the baby, right?" she asked, not making eye contact.

"Yes," Krnar answered slowly, wondering where she was going with this.

"Could you carve a likeness of the baby?"

Krnar's brow furrowed. "I could, but why would I do that?"

"I would like to give it as a gift to Ulletta and Arkan, as a reminder of their baby."

Now Krnar's eyebrows rose. "They are not going to forget their child."

"No, I know they won't forget, but...it's like this," she said, holding up her wrist. "It reminds me every day of my sister, my family. I'll never forget them, but seeing this, touching this, it helps me to think of them more often. Sometimes it hurts, but it also helps. I thought, maybe, it might help Ulletta, to have something to hold once in a while."

Krnar thought for a moment and finally nodded.

"Thank you," Jahira said, and squeezed his hand.

Krnar glanced over to check on Mrkon, and then took a deep breath. "I have something to ask you, also."

"Shoot," Jahira said.

Krnar tilted his head, not understanding the word.

"Sorry, go ahead, ask."

Krnar nodded then said, "What do you do, with your dead?"

When Jahira didn't answer right away, he feared he'd crossed some line. "I am sorry. Should I not ask this?"

"No, it's okay. It just made me think. On our big ship, in space, it was different. We would cremate, uh, burn the bodies into ashes, and then release the ashes into space, or some people buried the ashes under a tree, others kept them." Jahira paused to make sure he understood what she'd said. He nodded for her to continue. "Here, I don't know. The ship that crashed, there were no bodies." Jahira cleared her throat and blinked rapidly. "What did you do, with your dead?"

"In the caves, we would give the bodies to the krska." Krnar saw Jahira flinch. "It seems bad, but we had to survive. In order for us to survive, the krska had to breed, and eat. It was necessary." Jahira nodded. "Here, I do not know. This will be our first death in the warm land. As the closest kin, it would have been my job to take the body to the other side of the caves. I do not know what to do."

"Wow. Well, have you asked Ulletta what she wants to do with the body?"

"No."

"I guess you need to ask."

Krnar closed his eyes briefly, and then nodded.

"I'm going to gather some more firewood," Jahira said.

Krnar nodded.

Once she'd left, he picked through his supply of bone pieces until he found a flawless, bleached-white piece that would fit in the palm of his hand. An image of his niece filled his mind, and tears filled his eyes. He blinked the tears away and held the picture in his head of the impossibly small infant, and began to carve.

The image began to come to life on the bone canvas, and Krnar became so absorbed in his task that he didn't realize Mrkon had returned. The boy stood watching over his shoulder.

"Is that for Ulletta?" Mrkon asked.

The voice made Krnar jump and he nearly sliced his thumb. "Yes," he replied once he'd settled. "It was Jahira's idea.

She thought Ulletta would like to have something to remind her of the baby."

Mrkon nodded and continued to watch as Krnar resumed his work. "It looks just like her," Mrkon whispered.

Krnar swallowed around the sudden lump in his throat and nodded. "You gathered a lot of fruit," he said, tipping his head toward the hide the boy had filled.

"I'd like to take it to Ulletta and Arkan," Mrkon said.

"That's a good idea. Do you want to take it yourself?" Krnar asked.

"No, I'd like to wait." Mrkon tipped his chin toward Krnar's carving.

At first, Krnar felt a bit self-conscious under the boy's scrutiny. Soon enough though, he lost himself to the act of creating. He did not stop until the last piece of bone had been scraped away and a tiny, perfect infant lay in his hand.

"It's beautiful," Jahira breathed. She, too, had returned unnoticed.

"Can we go see Ulletta now?" Mrkon asked.

"I've brought water," Jahira said, pointing to a string of water bags near her feet.

"And Mrkon collected fruit," Krnar said.

"Let's take them their gifts," Mrkon said.

Krnar nodded. He rose, stretching the ache from his back and shoulders, which had not moved since he'd begun his carving.

"We should trade," he said to Jahira, holding a hand out to take the water bags.

"But you made it," Jahira said.

"It was your idea. I think she will like you giving it to her."

Reluctantly, Jahira held out the water and took the carving. She cradled it in her palm and ran a finger over the tiny features. "It's perfect," she said.

When she looked up, her green eyes shimmered with unshed tears.

Krnar trilled softly in acknowledgement. He still felt apprehensive, wondering how Ulletta would feel about it, but he was proud of the likeness, as well as Mrkon and Jahira's reactions.

Allorkan hung just above the dancing trees on the horizon. Another sun was nearly gone. In this warm climate, something would have to be done with the infant's body soon. Krnar dreaded having to ask, and dreaded the task, but he would do his duty for his family. It was the least he could do.

Ulletta had been moved from the medical area to a private room just down the hall. They had privacy but were close enough that Medic could check on her frequently, or Arkan could find someone quickly if he needed them.

Once they stood outside the door, Jahira reached up to knock, but Krnar caught her wrist.

She frowned at him.

He reached out with his mind and pushed gently, until Arkan opened to him.

We are outside your door. May we come in?

Yes, of course, I'm glad you're here.

Krnar turned to Jahira and nodded. She pushed the button and the door zipped into the recesses of the wall.

Mrkon's eyes grew huge.

They stepped in and exchanged bows, Ulletta nodding her head since she was still required to lie down on the bed most of the day. "Thank you for coming," she said.

"We brought gifts," Mrkon announced.

Ulletta grinned at him and beckoned him forward. She trilled in delight at the hide full of fruit and nodded in thanks for the water.

"Jahira has something for you," Mrkon said.

The boy is very talkative suddenly, Krnar thought.

Ulletta trilled, the sound a mixture of surprise and curiosity, and turned to watch Jahira.

Jahira glanced at Krnar and he nodded, gesturing for her to go ahead. He could feel Jahira's apprehension and was sure that Ulletta could as well, if her mind was open.

After a deep breath, Jahira stepped forward and opened her hand.

For several heartbeats, Ulletta stared at the tiny carving. Dread crept up Krnar's spine and he felt sure he'd made a mistake.

Finally, she reached out and traced a finger over the tiny face. "Krnar, did you make this?" she asked, her voice thick with emotion.

"Yes, but Jahira asked me to make it. She thought you might like something to hold, to remind you of the baby. I told her you would not forget, but she insisted. She lost her family, her sister and her parents, and she said it helps her to have something to remember them." Krnar rambled, still not sure of Ulletta's reaction.

Ulletta lifted the tiny figure from Jahira's palm, turned it over and back, inspecting every detail. "It's perfect," she whispered.

When Ulletta finally looked up, she and Jahira were both crying.

"Thank you," Ulletta said.

Jahira smiled and nodded.

"Thank you, Krnar. It looks exactly like her," Ulletta said.

"What is her name?" Jahira asked in her language, and then looked at Krnar to ask how to say it to Ulletta. "Baby's name?"

Krnar shook his head.

"Just ask her," Jahira said.

Krnar cleared his throat and said, "Jahira wants to know if you named the baby."

To his surprise, Ulletta smiled. "Ullan," she replied, caressing the carving. "Our daughter's name is Ullan."

Arkan and Krnar looked at each other, both blinking back tears. Krnar decided it was time to face his responsibility.

"How do you...want me to...care for...Ullan?" he asked, pausing several times to find the right words.

Arkan and Ulletta looked at each other. "We have discussed this," Arkan said. "We don't know exactly what to do. It is different from the caves." He paused and swallowed, clearly not comfortable with the thought of sacrificing his daughter to the krska. Krnar nodded in understanding.

"We want her to remain in the light," Ulletta added. "It is how we greet each other, how we say goodbye. It is why we came to this place, to be in the light of Allorkan. This is what we wish for our daughter."

"But we don't know how to do this," Arkan finished.

No one spoke for several heartbeats, until Jahira asked softly, "What did they say? I heard Allorkan, but didn't catch everything."

"They wish for their daughter to remain in the light, but do not know how to do this," Krnar replied.

"Oh! I have an idea," Jahira walked to the shelf protruding from the wall and tapped the glowing disc. Krnar knew what would happen but heard Ulletta and Arkan hiss in surprise when a picture appeared in the air in front of Jahira.

"Krnar, what is this?" Arkan asked.

"It is how they keep their memories," he said. "In this *thing* instead of within an Akaruvel."

Arkan and Ulletta nodded, understanding the words, but frowns creased their foreheads as they watched Jahira with rapt attention.

After tapping the air several times and sliding through a series of images, Jahira stopped and moved to the side of the hovering picture. "What do you think of something like this?" she asked. "It was a ritual performed by some people far in our past. They would put their dead up on these scaffolds, out in the sun and the air, they could decorate them, visit them if they wished..." Her voice trailed off while Krnar continued to interpret.

Ulletta's eyes filled with tears and Arkan began to nod. They looked at each other, then back to Krnar. "Yes, this is what we want for Ullan."

Krnar nodded. "I will see to it, and then I will take you there when you are able to leave."

Arkan moved forward and placed his hands on Krnar's shoulders. "Thank you, brother," Arkan said. He shifted his gaze to Jahira and bowed. "Thank you."

Jahira smiled a close-lipped smile and nodded.

Yes, Krnar projected into her mind. *Thank you*.

He felt her empathy for him, for his family, her satisfaction at having been able to help in some way, and for at least the dozenth time since finding her in the mountains, he thanked Aruvel for bringing her to him.

CHAPTER 17

"Are you sure you don't mind if I go?" Jahira asked.

A bulging pack rested against her shin. Looking around at the flat, worn patch of ground that had been her home since they'd landed here, she began to have second thoughts.

"No. Go. This is something you need to do, and I need to stay with Arkan and Ulletta," Krnar replied.

Jahira nodded, reassured by his insistence but a part of her still felt like she was abandoning him in his time of need.

A week had passed since Ulletta's baby Ullan had died. Krnar and Jahira had built a raised platform and secured the wrapped body of the tiny infant on top. Arkan and Mrkon had taken turns visiting and decorating the platform with small offerings.

Yesterday, for the first time, Ulletta had been well enough to walk to the site, in the eastern field between the grove and the dancing forest. Today she would return to her hearth.

The last seven days had been a whirlwind of entertaining and caring for Mrkon, taking food to Ulletta and Arkan, trying to help when she could with the final stages of Magnar's boat, and gathering supplies for their trip to the southern continent.

A vacation sounded perfect.

Krnar planned to stay with Ulletta and Arkan so that he could continue to help with the hunting, cooking, and keeping an eye on Mrkon.

Jahira knew that, though she'd been able to provide some help, Ulletta would be surrounded now by friends and family and that she would feel out of place, or worse, useless.

This would give Krnar the time and space he needed to focus on his family, and his people, while they adjusted.

Her bicep muscle engaged and Jahira grunted when she lifted her pack off the ground and slung it over her shoulder. "Well, here we go then."

The air smelled different, Jahira noticed, like someone had removed the dirt and flowers and left behind pure, clean air. Two and a half months remained before the long winter and the world was changing. The grass felt dry and brittle when it rubbed against the backs of her hands on the way to the *Kepler Colonizer*. Their first task entailed picking up the crate of medical supplies that Medic had put together for Lusela and her followers.

The sleek silver crate waited, as promised, at the base of the entrance ramp. Jahira gripped the handle on her side and bent her knees in order to lift with her legs. With a nod, she and Krnar lifted together and Jahira almost fell over.

"Not as heavy as I expected," she said with a laugh.

Krnar smiled and his blue eyes sparkled with amusement. "I can carry it alone," he offered.

"No, no, I'll help."

Krnar shrugged, something she'd noticed him doing more of lately. She wondered if he'd picked it up from her.

Together they carried the crate to the river.

From the top of the embankment, Jahira could see Magnar hauling supplies from the shore to the boat on a dock that hadn't been there previously.

Carefully placing her feet in the loose rock and sand, Jahira sidestepped down the embankment, watching Krnar out of the corners of her eyes to make sure they stayed even.

"Magnar!" Jahira called once they'd reached the shore.

They set the crate down. Jahira waved when Magnar poked his head out of the hold.

Magnar waved back, then nimbly navigated along the deck and vaulted over the railing onto his temporary dock. "Hey! Everything's loaded up. Once we get this crate on board, we can be off." He nodded to Krnar and said, "Thanks for helping."

Krnar nodded back.

"Okay, I'll go up first, you hand the stuff up to me and I'll stow it," Magnar said.

Jahira gripped her handle and nodded to Krnar.

They lifted and followed Magnar onto the dock.

Once Magnar was up on the deck, Jahira and Krnar lifted the crate over the railing to hand it off to Magnar.

"Good thing you're here," Jahira said out of the corner of her mouth. The crate wasn't heavy to lift, but the awkward angle and the need to hold the weight with straight arms significantly increased the difficulty.

Krnar trilled.

Suddenly, the weight was gone and Magnar had disappeared with the crate.

"Well, I'll see you in about a month, uh, one moon? Maybe less if we make good time with the boat."

"A moon?" Krnar repeated, and then glanced over her shoulder where Magnar had reappeared.

Jahira smiled and placed a hand on his cheek. "Don't worry, Magnar is only a friend," she said, amusement coloring her voice.

The corner of Krnar's mouth twitched. "I thought you could not see into my mind," he said.

"Some things are universal," she replied. With her pointer finger, she reached up and traced a circle on his forehead.

Krnar closed his eyes briefly. When he opened them again, he leaned down and gave her a lingering kiss.

"Hey, come on, enough PDA!" Magnar called. "If we want to make the most of this daylight, we need to head out!"

"Okay, see you soon," Jahira said after reluctantly pulling away.

Smooth plaited fibers slipped through her fingers as she untied the ropes from the dock and tossed them onto the deck of the boat. Once the last rope had been released, Jahira vaulted over the railing and onto the deck.

Magnar perched behind the clear solar glass encasement surrounding the flying bridge like a king on his throne. "Time to see if she works!" Magnar called.

Jahira gave him a thumbs-up.

A soft whir like the fluttering of a large insect's wings rose up from the stern of the craft. They were moving.

The current caught the boat and began to carry it downstream. Jahira waved to Krnar's retreating form until he was no longer visible. Finally, she climbed up to join Magnar.

"Just like old times, eh?" Magnar said.

"Hmm, yeah, except you're sitting in the wrong seat." Jahira winked. "Speaking of seats, these are comfortable," she said, crossing her arms and leaning back into the cushion.

"Took them out of the control deck on the *Seyfert*."

"With permission, of course," Jahira said.

"Of course." Magnar grinned and kept his eyes forward.

Jahira grinned and rolled her eyes. "So, anything I should be doing?"

"Well, the biggest concern on the river is anything hiding under the water. Cholie installed an Enhanced Viewing System, just like we had on the *Eagle*, so there are cameras on the front, bottom, and back of the boat. You can keep an eye on this screen," he said, flipping a switch on the dash so that a picture popped up on a small screen in front of her. "Toggle up for front, down for back, middle for underneath. Watch for logs, rocks, sandbars…"

"Got it," Jahira said, happy to have something to do.

"Kato and Creed said there are two tributaries feeding into the river farther south, which will be good for depth, but might mean trickier currents."

"Aye-Aye, Captain."

The corner of Magnar's mouth lifted.

It's all part of the adventure, she thought and, truth be told, she longed for some adventure.

Other than her concern for Krnar and his family, she couldn't wait to get away from the settlement and explore a little more of this unique planet. "How far do you plan to go today?" she asked.

"I'm going to take it slow at first. We won't be breaking any records, but hopefully we won't be breaking any parts of my girl here, either."

"Your girl?"

Magnar nodded and pointed to the bottom corner of the glass in front of him. The name *Amara* had been etched in the glass just above the dash.

A sad smile pulled at Jahira's lips. Amara, Magnar's wife, had died in the crash with her family. "She would have liked that," Jahira said.

"Yep, I'm taking her with me everywhere I go." Magnar cleared his throat and asked, "So, how are Ulletta and Arkan doing?"

"They're okay, I think. It's hard for me to tell for sure, and I don't always catch everything they say, but they appear to be holding it together. I think, overall, the Leroni cope better, you know? They're used to dealing with loss, which doesn't make it easier necessarily, just less of a shock, maybe? And the people around them can help and empathize. They have a good support system."

Magnar nodded. "What about the rest of them?"

"What do you mean, the rest of them?"

"The rest of the Leroni. Grollon mentioned that some of the Leroni didn't believe Medic was trying to help, that maybe he hurt the baby somehow."

"*What*?" Jahira spine straightened and her fists clenched. "I hadn't heard anything about that. Are you sure?"

Magnar lifted one shoulder. "Well, it's secondhand information, but I don't know why Grollon would lie."

"Yeah, I suppose." Jahira released her clenched fingers and leaned back in her chair. "Crap. I had no idea. I would have said something, done something."

"Ellall was there, right?"

"Yes, and Krnar, too. I'm sure they've told everyone what happened."

"Well, no offense, but If they didn't believe their own leader, I doubt they'd believe you."

"What's that supposed to mean?"

"Come on, Jahira. You can't be that blind. Not everyone is happy with this situation. People are grumbling about Krnar still sleeping in your tent and Grollon has mentioned that some of the Leroni aren't happy with the match, either."

Jahira scrubbed her face with her hands. The news didn't come as a surprise. Cholie had mentioned it as well, and she noticed the looks some people gave them when she and Krnar were walking through the settlement. She'd just tried to block them out and hoped that the more people saw them together, the more they'd get used to it.

"Maybe I shouldn't have said anything," Magnar said, glancing at Jahira with a concerned frown.

"No, I'm glad you did. I want to know what's happening, I just feel guilty and worried. I'm leaving and I won't have any idea what's going on until we get back."

"Well, nothing you can do about it, so you might as well enjoy the ride."

She tried to take Magnar's advice. With her eyes closed, she focused on the warm sun penetrating the solar glass and soaking into her skin. Small vents built into the glass allowed the cool breeze into the flying bridge. The scent of cold water over wet rocks and warm sun-soaked earth filled her nostrils.

Like invasive weeds, the worry crept back in.

The fact that some of the Leroni were skeptical about Medic wasn't really that surprising, especially when she looked at the situation from their perspective. The humans wielded unfamiliar technology on a daily basis. For the Leroni, it must seem like magic. It was a historical trend for humans to fear anything they did not understand, so why would the Leroni be any different?

What bothered her more than what people thought of her and Krnar was the mistrust directed at Medic, the only person she could think of with absolutely no personal agenda. His mission was to help whoever needed his help, period.

"Jahira, look," Magnar whispered and pointed downriver.

Jahira squinted against the afternoon sun. Three medium-sized yellow bodies of an animal Jahira had not yet seen on this planet blended into the shore. Their snouts were buried in the cool refreshment, making it difficult to see their faces.

Not daring to breathe, she sat entranced while the boat encroached upon the drinking animals.

Seconds later, one triangular head lifted. Ears twitched and the animal trilled in alarm. The similarity to some of Krnar's trills struck her like a blow. Before she could give it much thought, the other animals raised their heads and, together, they bolted into the long yellow stalks of grain that lined these shores.

"Kato and Creed said the small game is more plentiful the further south you go."

"That should be interesting."

"Yeah."

"Did they record what they found?"

"A lot of it, yeah. Ryan already made maps." Magnar tapped her screen twice and pulled up a log of maps he'd loaded.

"They also took a lot of pictures of plants and animals but I didn't get a chance to study them much; figured I'd see it for myself."

Jahira studied the maps briefly before returning the screen to the EVS monitor. "I'm thinking another hour or so and we should call it a night. I don't want to risk waiting too long and then trying to navigate at night."

"Sounds good."

They settled in for a quiet ride until about forty-five minutes later, the boat rounded a bend, and Jahira pointed.

Ahead, the waning light lit a patch of sand on the right bank, making it glow orange-red.

Magnar nodded and used reverse thrust to slow the boat down before carefully guiding it to shore. "I'll climb down, you toss me the rope that's attached to that cleat there," he said, pointing to the tip at the bow of the boat.

Jahira nodded, climbed down to the deck, and waited for Magnar's signal.

Once in place, he nodded his head and lifted his right hand. The circle of rope uncoiled as it flew. Magnar caught a piece, but the knotted end struck him in the cheek.

"Sorry!" Jahira called.

Magnar gave her a thumbs-up, and then turned to drive a stake into the firmer soil beyond the sandy bank. He tied the rope around the secured stake and, finally, wove an intricate series of knots in the rope to keep it from working loose.

Once he'd finished that task, he walked back to the boat and stood on the ground looking at Jahira. "Hey," he called. "Toss down my pack, and watch the face this time!"

Jahira grinned, gathered up the supplies, and tossed his bag down to him.

After shouldering her own pack, she climbed down the ladder at the midsection of the boat. From the last rung, she jumped and her feet crunched against the cool, damp sand.

By the time they had a fire going and a temporary camp set up, an egg-drop sunset descended on the horizon.

"First day down, thirty or so to go," Magnar said, waggling his eyebrows.

"Aruvel help me," Jahira replied with a grin.

CHAPTER 18

Every living thing went still the moment Ulletta and Arkan stepped from beneath the canopy and into the inner field of the alara grove.

Tllomell noticed the way Arkan hovered, some part of him always in contact with Ulletta. Ulletta's hands fluttered, fingers fidgeting. Once she almost rested her hand on the smooth plane of her abdomen that had, only seven suns before, rounded with the life it held before pulling it away like she'd been stung.

Krnar and Mrkon followed close behind. The Leroni stopped what they were doing and bowed as the family passed. Outside the circle of stones that marked their hearth, gifts were piled.

Arkan stooped to pick up the offerings and carried them across the threshold. Soft noises returned like the first tentative bird calls returning to the forest once danger had passed.

Once the family had settled and started their fire, friends began to make eye contact, pushing against each other's minds and silently deciding who would be the first to visit.

Erknok and Tllakall went first. Ulletta waved them in, and Tllomell focused on the rip in her pack that needed mending. She waited most of the day before it was her turn to pay her respects.

After Plldoll and Krag left, Tllomell set aside her mending and made her way to the circle of stones. Apprehension flared in her gut when Ulletta waved her inside. With a firm block on her mind, she stepped into the family's home and bowed. She feared she would not be able to prevent her mind from drifting to the rumors she'd heard about the human healer, or Frmar's accusations and plans. She couldn't let any of that slip in front of the grieving family.

Tllomell sat across the fire and Ulletta smiled in spite of the fatigue and sorrow that shone from her eyes.

"I am so sorry for your loss," Tllomell said. She extended her offering, a small package of dried glow weed, which Ulletta accepted with a nod.

When Ulletta shifted to reach forward, a small amulet swung outward as well, catching Tllomell's eye. When she realized what it was, her breath caught in her throat. A tiny, perfect infant hung from a string of gut line that had been tied around Ulletta's neck.

Ulletta noticed the direction of Tllomell's gaze and placed her fingers on the carving.

172

"Krnar made it. Isn't it beautiful?" she said.

"Yes," Tllomell responded. "Is that—" Tllomell wasn't sure how to finish, and didn't know if the child was a boy or girl; fortunately Ulletta saved her.

"This is Ullan," she said. "It looks exactly like her."

"Ullan," Tllomell repeated. "You had a daughter."

Ulletta nodded.

Tllomell's tongue felt as if it had been tied into a knot and she had no ability to form proper words. None of the questions swirling through her mind were appropriate to ask right now. Every ounce of will went to making sure her face remained neutral.

A glance at Krnar told her she wasn't succeeding in controlling all of her body language. Keen blue eyes watched her, not bothering to look away when she made eye contact.

Tllomell cleared her throat and returned her attention to Ulletta. "Will there be a ceremony? To remember your daughter?"

"Yes, now that I am strong enough, we will meet when Allorkan rises again at the place where Krnar put Ullan to rest."

Tllomell nodded and then stood, brushing the dirt from her fur. *Impossible to keep clean here*, she thought. Aloud she said, "I'd better go; there are more who wish to pay their respects and I'm sure you need to rest."

"Thank you for your gift," Ulletta said.

Arkan bowed in thanks as well.

After a final bow of farewell, Tllomell stepped outside their hearth and returned to her own. Emotions warred for dominance inside her head: Relief that Ulletta and Arkan *seemed* okay, but also worry that if someone had altered their mind or changed their memories they *would* seem okay, even if things were not. Then there was Krnar. She found it difficult to concentrate with him around. She wondered what he was thinking, specifically of her, and wondered where he'd been. Had he stayed in the silver mountain with Ulletta and Arkan? Or had he stayed in the human settlement? If the latter, then where?

When she rose the next sun, Tllomell couldn't help but glance at Ulletta's hearth. Krnar had slept there. In fact, he still slept. His eyes were closed and one hand was tucked under the opposite shoulder, the other hand lying loose and open on the ground. Her mind started to imagine waking up next to him.

Stop, she commanded. To distract her mind, she set about starting a fire and then boiling water to which she added a few pieces of dried fish and a sprinkle of dried glow weed. Some of The People had stopped rationing their stores, confident in the abundance of the warm land. Tllomell found it harder to set aside a lifetime of survival training. She kept her meals small and count-ed her reserves every morning.

After everyone had risen and finished their morning meal, they gathered at the base of the oranlodi to remember Ulletta's baby.

Frmar came to stand beside her and pushed against her mind.

Opening to the connection, she allowed her mind to link with Frmar's. Wariness, mistrust, and curiosity tinged his thoughts.

You'd better keep that to yourself, Tllomell projected.

The emotions cleared just as Ellall began the familiar chants of the remembering ceremony and began to reach out to join the minds of all The People.

The still-raw grief of Ulletta and Arkan's loss sucked the air from her lungs.

Arkan shared one image, a vision of a small, perfect face, still and blue like the ice that covered their previous home.

Tllomell felt her throat constrict and her chest tighten.

Ulletta shared several memories. She began with the day she had told Arkan she was with child. His face radiated pride and joy. The vision merged with another, a small white hand placed tenderly over a distended belly that rolled with the movement of the life within. Finally, little Ullan, wrapped in a blanket and held close to Ulletta's chest as Ulletta's voice whispered, "My girl, my baby girl."

The People reached out with love, comfort, support, empathy. There were few here who had not experienced loss. In moments like this, it helped to know you were not alone.

The ceremony was brief, for the child's time in the world had been brief, and there were painfully few memories to share.

When the ceremony ended, The People began to drift away.

What happened on the ship was not revealed, but surely if there had been reason to worry, Ulletta and Arkan would have told them, wouldn't they?

Tllomell returned to her hearth, gathered her water bags, and headed to the stream.

A few steps into the shaded canopy, the soft *sush-sush* of footsteps alerted her to someone else's presence. Shortening her stride, she casually glanced over her shoulder and saw Frmar striding to catch up.

With a nod of acknowledgment, he fell in step beside her. "We need more information," he said in an urgent whisper. "I need you to go inside the silver mountain."

Her stride faltered. "Go inside the mountain? How am I supposed to do that?"

"It appears as though anyone can simply walk inside."

One eyebrow lifted and Tllomell glared at Frmar out of the corners of her eyes.

"You are close to Krnar, are you not?" Frmar asked, his voice tight. "Get him to take you."

"You are apprentice to the Akaruvel! Why don't you go?" Tllomell had grown tired of these games, the intrigue. She wanted a simple life, without complications.

"Grollon may already be influencing Ellall. And the other Marked, the human, he is often with Krnar and that human female. They may both be compromised. If The Marked takes control of my mind, we'll have no one to remember for us."

His paranoia really is getting the better of him, Tllomell thought. *This sounds like a coward's excuse.*

"Will you do this for me, Tllomell?" Frmar asked, leaning in close so that his breath tickled the fur that covered her ear.

"I'll see what I can do, Frmar, but I'm not making any promises."

CHAPTER 19

"See that place, where the water is dark and it swirls under the bank? In rivers, that is where the fish like to hide."

Mrkon flicked his wrist, in exact imitation of Krnar. The bait plopped into the swirl of water. Mrkon pulled in the line slowly, every now and then giving the line a gentle jerk.

"Good," Krnar said, once the bait had been removed from the water. "Now try again."

Mrkon obeyed. This time, the instant the bait hit the water, the line went taut. Mrkon trilled, tightened his grip, and began to wind the line around the padding on his forearm.

Huge eyes threatened to pop from Mrkon's head.

"You've got it. Take your time. The fish will fight. You have to learn when to give it slack and when to pull."

Mrkon focused, struggling against his prize.

After retrieving a net, Krnar moved with slow grace into the shallows of the river. When the fish drew close enough, he scooped the shimmering body out of the water. With a thumb and forefinger looped through the fish's gills, he held the prize aloft for Mrkon to see.

A peal of laughter echoed between the banks.

Krnar was so startled by the sound he nearly dropped the slippery body of the arm-length fish.

Mrkon laughed!

Once Krnar had recovered his grip, he held the fish out to Mrkon. "Well done, nephew! This will feed the whole family tonight!"

A joyous smile split the boy's face as he accepted his catch. He worked the bone hook from the fish's mouth, held the fish by its lower jaw, and slid the knife from his belt.

Krnar smiled with pride to see the boy efficiently gut and filet his prize.

Once he'd properly disposed of any parts they would not use, he wrapped the rest in a hide before storing it in his pack. Krnar had started this practice only recently, the wrapping of the filets. It had not been necessary, of course, on the third continent. Any moisture froze instantly. Here, however, the smell of fish lingered on the hands, fur, anything it touched really. Jahira had assured him of this fact.

With everything properly stowed, they climbed the bank to return to Arkan and Ulletta's hearth. Krnar could taste the fresh roasted flesh melting on his tongue. His mouth watered and his stomach growled in anticipation.

"Krnar," Mrkon said hesitantly.

"Hmm," Krnar replied, pulled from his daydream of a delicious meal.

"You know the carving you made for Ulletta of Ullan?" The boy paused and took a deep breath.

"Yes, of course," Krnar said, intrigued now.

"Do you think you could make one for me? Not of Ullan," he added quickly. "One of my parents."

The request shocked the words from his mouth.

"I can show them to you. I have memories of them."

"I have memories of them also," Krnar said. "Do you worry that you will lose those memories?"

"Sometimes," Mrkon said. "I mean, look what happened to our people. We lost all sorts of memories while we were gone. Even Ellall doesn't remember the names for everything, and I'm learning so many new things I feel like my mind is filling up. Sometimes I think it might push the old memories away. I don't think I'll forget them, but I am afraid I'll forget what they looked like."

Krnar turned his head and gazed at the boy. "That's the most I've heard you say for as long as I've known you," he said. "Who knew that underneath all that silence, you were so wise?"

Mrkon pressed his lips together and stared straight ahead. Apparently he'd used up all his words for the day.

"Of course I will do this for you, Mrkon. It would be an honor."

A huff of air burst through Mrkon's lips. He nodded, a solemn thanks.

"I'll start this sleep."

They continued the rest of the way in silence.

A few body lengths away from his family's hearth, Tllomell approached, stopped in front of Krnar, and bowed. "Krnar, may I speak with you?"

Krnar's eyes narrowed, wondering what she wanted to discuss, but he nodded his acquiescence and then turned to address Mrkon. "Go ahead and show Ulletta your catch. I'll be there soon."

Mrkon nodded, bowed to Tllomell, and closed the distance to his home.

Tllomell's jaw muscles worked as she clenched and unclenched her teeth. Her body looked rigid with tension, which piqued his curiosity.

"What is it, Tllomell?" Krnar asked.

"I was wondering...I'm curious, about the silver mountains. I would like to see more. I thought, perhaps, you could take me inside."

That is not what I expected, he thought. "Uh, I don't see why not. I would just need to...well...let me ask, and I will tell you when we can do this."

Tllomell nodded. For a moment she looked as if she might say something else, then she spun on her heel and walked away.

She's been acting odd lately, he thought, turning toward his family's hearth.

Krnar had no idea what might be going on with her, but the more he thought about her request, the more sense it made.

That night, during their meal, his mind wouldn't let the idea go. The humans and Leroni had done very little mixing other than their first night at the celebration feast. There were likely more Leroni who would want to explore the ships. Maybe it would help them to feel more comfortable around the humans if they had a better understanding of how they lived. It could help the humans get to know more of the Leroni as well.

Excitement built inside Krnar like a grass fire, until doubt doused the excitement. *I wish Jahira were here*, he thought.

It would be so much easier to approach her with this; to have her give the tours, or ask permission, or tell him if it was necessary to ask permission. He felt comfortable aboard the ships now, but he'd always had Jahira with him. He could not recall her ever asking permission to enter the ship or any of its rooms, but

Krnar thought, if he were to go alone, without a human present, he may not feel so confident.

He couldn't ask Magnar, either; the two humans he knew best were gone...together.

Deciding not to dwell on how he felt about that situation, his mind scrolled through the list of whom else he might ask. *Perhaps Medic or Ryan?* They had both been supportive of helping his people. *Maybe Tala*, he thought. Jahira's friend joined them for a meal at times. He would feel comfortable approaching her even though they didn't always communicate effectively.

I will think about it tonight, and ask in the morning, he decided.

The following sunrise, Krnar woke feeling invigorated. The prospect of a mission that needed accomplishing filled him with a sense of purpose, and it was one that might make an impact on both human and Leroni. They needed something to bring them together.

After loading his pack, he paused long enough to bite off chunks of dried meat and swallow them down with swigs of water.

"Chew, please," Ulletta said from across the fire. "It would be rather pathetic for the savior of our people to choke to death on a piece of srlen meat."

Krnar chewed his last bite twice, swallowed, and nodded his goodbye before setting off for the human settlement.

Trepidation slowed his steps the closer he got to the evenly spaced rectangular shelters.

How will people react when Jahira is not with me? he wondered. *Will they even recognize me?* He'd noticed that many of the humans had difficulty telling one Leroni from another. Some couldn't even seem to distinguish male from female, which he found completely absurd. True, he couldn't always tell the human males and females apart, but their bodies were covered. It was completely different.

Sweat prickled along his spine when he spied the first humans. He nodded in their direction when they noticed him. A huff of relief deflated his chest when they lifted their hands and waved.

The next residents were not so friendly.

Krnar lifted a hand in greeting, but the gesture was not returned. Instead, eyes followed him. His heart rate increased and he tried to ignore the urge to turn and look behind him.

The well-worn path curved around a tidy sod house. When Krnar rounded the corner, he stopped dead in his tracks.

Two men stood in his path, blocking the trail. Krnar opened his mind and his senses were flooded with revulsion and anger. His palms began to sweat.

"Where do you think you're going, *animal*?" one of the men asked. He was taller than Krnar, but leaner. His voice sounded normal, almost friendly—completely at odds with the expression on his face and the malevolence screaming from his mind.

"I am looking for Tala," Krnar replied.

"Oh yeah? One woman ain't enough for your kind?" the second man asked.

Krnar tipped his head in confusion.

"You need to go back to your own kind and leave our women alone," said the first man.

"I only want to ask her a question," Krnar said.

"Sure, maybe we can help you find her," the first man said this and his companion looked at him with a frown at first, and then grinned.

Krnar's mind reeled with the effort to figure out what was going on. Clearly these men did not mean well, and were not trying to help him. But what were their intentions? What could they do to him in the middle of the settlement?

"I think I can find her on my own," he said. Walking at an angle to the path, Krnar tried to go around the men, but they moved to stand in front of him again.

The hairs on the back of Krnar's neck stood on end and in one fluid movement, he drew his knife.

"Hey! What's going on?"

All three heads swiveled to the new voice, coming from the doorway of the house nearest them.

"Just helping our new neighbor find his way around," said the first man.

A dark-haired woman stepped out into the yard, followed by a tall, broad-shouldered man with dark skin like Jahira's.

"Take your trouble somewhere else, Mitch," the woman said.

The man's eyes narrowed but he tilted his head at his companion and the two of them walked away.

Krnar sheathed his knife and then flexed his fingers.

"You alright?" The woman asked.

"Yes, thank you."

"Steer clear of them—they were dropped on their heads a lot as kids." The woman smiled and winked.

Krnar wondered if that is really what happened to them. "Do you know where I can find Tala?" he asked.

"I think she's working on the greenhouse. See those tall silver beams right there?" she asked, pointing toward the center of the settlement. "You should find her there."

"Thank you," Krnar said. He bowed and then began to walk quickly toward the structure that the woman had pointed out.

Soon he stood near the heart of the settlement in front of the greenhouse. Jahira had explained that it would allow the humans to grow their vegetables all winter. His experience thus far with vegetables didn't make him eager to try more, but food was food. If it kept children from starving when the snows came, he could support it.

Krnar spotted Tala among the workers and he waved to get her attention.

"Hey, Krnar! What's up?" Tala jumped down from a small platform and walked over to him.

Krnar barely resisted the urge to look to the sky. He often had this difficulty when trying to communicate with Tala. She said things in a way that made it hard for him to tell if she meant what she said, or meant something else entirely. Pulling his shoulders back, he steeled his resolve.

"Hello, Tala," he said with a short bow. "I wish to take the Leroni into the silver mountain, the ship."

"Oh, um, okay. How many? When do you want to go?"

"How many?" he repeated.

"How many of the Leroni do you want to take on the ship?" she clarified.

"Oh, all of them."

Her eyebrows climbed up her forehead. "All of them? At one time?"

"No, not all at the same time. Two or three in and out, and then two or three more."

"Oh, like a tour," she said.

Krnar tilted his head and lifted one shoulder, unfamiliar with the term she used.

"I think it would be fine but I'll need to check with The General. We'd probably need to find someone to be your tour guide also." Tala turned and yelled, "Be right back!" to the others working on the greenhouse. To Krnar she waved and said, "Come on."

Staying an arm's length away from Tala, he followed along a well-worn path that took them between some of the older dirt and grass houses.

"General Thayer!" Tala called once they were in range of a second group of people working on a structure similar to the greenhouse but smaller in scale.

General Thayer turned at the sound of his name. When he saw them, he waved and walked over to greet them. "Tala. Krnar. What can I do for you?"

"Krnar is wondering if he can take the Leroni on tours of the ships. I thought we'd better check with you and also see if you could suggest someone to show them around, explain how everything works. What do you think?"

The General's eyes scanned the horizon before meeting Krnar's. He nodded slowly and then returned his attention to Tala. "I think it's a good idea. I'll talk to Ryan. He and some of his assistants have been studying the language." He focused on Krnar and asked, "When do you want to do this? How many people are you planning to take on board?"

Gratitude for Tala's earlier questioning filled him. His answers for the General were prepared. "I would take two or three at a time. I would like to start as soon as possible."

General Thayer nodded again. "I'll make some inquiries and get back to you." He nodded to Krnar, then addressed Tala. "Can I send you as a messenger once we've ironed out the details?"

"Sure thing," Tala replied.

"Excellent, thank you. And Krnar, I think this is a wonderful idea. I've been wondering how to get everyone to mingle a bit more. Maybe this will help."

Krnar nodded.

The General left them and returned to his task.

"Okay, well, I'll let you know when we can start. Hopefully, I'll see you soon."

"Thank you, Tala."

"Don't mention it," she said with a grin. Then she hit him on the shoulder.

Shock prevented him from reacting. Tala walked away and left him standing with his eyes bulging. *Sometimes I don't understand humans at all*, he thought.

When he recovered from his interaction with Tala, he realized that he was alone, that he would have to go back through the settlement by himself.

What if I encounter those men again? he wondered. He wasn't afraid to face them, if that's what he had to do, but he was afraid of what it would do to the relationship between the humans and the Leroni if word spread about a fight.

Hoping that the men had remained near their homes, Krnar took the long way around the settlement, near the river.

It was a strange thing to be suddenly wary in a place he'd always thought he would be welcome. He even began to second-guess his idea of showing his people around and taking them to the ship. What if they encountered more people like the ones he'd faced today?

Things were definitely different with Jahira gone.

Krnar didn't like it.

CHAPTER 20

The days on the boat crawled forward like an inchworm through long grass. Jahira wished she'd thought to bring a digital reader, but she'd been expecting an adventure, excitement, new places to see. She hadn't considered that most of the trip would be days sitting while floating down a river with occasional wildlife drinking at the banks before the approaching monstrosity scared them away. The tall banks blocked the view of most of the landscape to either side.

"It's kind of like that week we were stuck on the *Eagle*," she said to Magnar. "I'm starting to go a little crazy."

"Crazier, you mean?"

"Ha ha."

Magnar winked and then flexed his fingers on the wheel. "Not me. I'm feeling great. We've got fresh air, clean water, great scenery, and no *oranlo* in sight. What's not to love?"

"I'm really not great at sitting still," Jahira said.

"Well, you didn't have to come." A slight frown creased Magnar's brow.

"I know. I wanted to come. I still want to be here, I just expected a little more...excitement."

"Want me to sing?" Magnar asked, his brow smoothing again.

"Uhm, I think I'll pass."

"I did pack a handheld with some vids downloaded on it. It should be charged, I haven't used it."

"Really!" Eagerness straightened her spine. "Where is it?"

"Front pocket of my pack in the cabin."

Springing from her seat, she skipped down the stairs and ducked into the cabin. Her fingers fished through the pocket until they bumped against a hard rectangle. With a shout of triumph, she pulled the handheld free and turned it on. It took a moment to connect to the ship's comm signal, and then she was in business.

The mattress formed around her body while her thumb scrolled through the contents.

One eyebrow rose in irritation when most of the titles were instructional vids. Necessary, she supposed, to troubleshoot en route, but not very entertaining.

Her thumb stopped when she saw the vid titled *Amara in Garden*. Guilt settled like a stone in her stomach and fear of getting caught raised the small hairs along the back of her neck. Still, she couldn't stop her thumb from pressing the title.

Tears pricked her eyes when Amara appeared on the screen. She stood in front of a lemon tree in the former garden complex of the *Aquilo*.

"So, I brought you here today, to my most favorite place in all the galaxies, to give you a surprise," Amara's voice drifted from the speaker, as clear as if she were standing in the same room. Her face glowed and she grinned as she produced a small metal box, flipped the latch, and, with exaggerated slowness, began to open the lid.

"Okay, come on, what's the big surprise?" Jahira heard Magnar's voice, louder than Amara's. He must have been the one filming the vid.

Amara's hand reached in and, with a flourish, pulled out a tiny flight suit and held it toward the camera.

Jahira heard Magnar's gasp. Amara held the outfit against her still-flat belly.

"*What?*" Magnar yelled.

The picture became a nauseating blur of colors before it settled on a close-up of Amara's arm. Amara and Magnar laughed and cried. There were kissing sounds and then the vid cut out.

Tears welled and overflowed. Emotion tightened her throat. All the memories of everything they'd lost flooded her mind: their home, their families, their contact with anyone else in the universe...

"Hey, Jahira!" Magnar called.

Jahira jumped, nearly dropping the handheld. Like a teenager caught watching naughty movies, she closed out the screen, scrolled up to the top of the list, and stashed the device back in its pocket.

"Yeah," she called back, while rubbing her thumbs under her eyes to erase the trace of tears.

"Come up here and take a look!"

After placing the pack back where she'd found it, she made her way up to the flying bridge.

Magnar didn't have to say anything else.

Ahead of them, the river widened into a fanning triangle of water and sandbars that looked almost like the root system of a giant tree. Beyond stretched the open water of the channel that separated the two continents.

"We made it!" she exclaimed.

"Well, we made it to the channel. Now we have to cross it."

"Will that be hard? It seems like it would be easier to cross a channel than navigate down a river."

"In some ways, but I don't know the currents, and we can't control the weather. I also have no idea what lives in there."

"Oh, right. How long to get across?"

"Should be an hour at the most." Magnar slowed. Navigating through the delta with its various clumps of snagged debris, had beads of sweat running down his temples despite the cool evening breeze.

Like a sudden change in wind, Jahira felt the shift in current press against the side of the boat once they passed through the delta and entered the main channel.

Beyond the shifting sands of the river's deposit, the water was clear and deep.

Jahira moved from the flying bridge to the bow of the boat in order to hang over the edge and watch the water. With narrowed eyes she stared into the depths, trying to discern changes in shape or color that might indicate marine life.

The water darkened suddenly. Jahira's eyes adjusted their perspective and she gasped. "Magnar," she called in a whisper-shout. When he looked, she pointed down to the water.

He waved her up. Reluctant to leave and miss seeing more of whatever swam beneath them, she hesitated. "I'll give you a better view!" Magnar called down.

After one last glance over the edge, Jahira dashed up to Magnar's side.

"Here, put this on," he said, handing Jahira a virtual reality headset.

"Why?" she asked even as she began to fit the device to her head.

"Cholie installed the EVS system," he said.

Jahira nodded, not making the connection.

"Well, she connected it to the VR units."

"Awesome!" Jahira exclaimed. "Okay, fire it up!"

In the next breath, she found herself submerged in the clear salt water. She could feel the weight of the water pressing against her body. Sunlight filtered through the rippling surface, but what drew her eye and made her grin until her face hurt were the torpedo-shaped bodies moving all around her.

Dark blue on top and lighter underneath, some were massive, easily longer than their boat, and some were not much bigger than her. Thick triangle-shaped fins undulated on either side of each creature's body, reminding Jahira of the Leroni's water wings.

Some of the smaller animals swam up toward the bottom of the boat and darted around, like curious children. An eerie whistle filled her ears and the small creatures zoomed away from the boat and back into the middle of the group.

Entranced, Jahira remained motionless, barely daring to take deep breaths. It wouldn't matter of course; her physical body did not float there among them, but the image was so real, the emotion so intense, she dared not do anything to disturb or shatter the illusion.

She watched until the last creature had disappeared out of sight. With a sigh somewhere between joy and regret, she removed the headpiece.

"Now, wasn't that better than some vid?" Magnar asked.

"Definitely," Jahira replied, though she didn't meet his eye, afraid that he would be able to tell what she had been watching.

"Hey, maybe we should record all of this, to show everyone back at the settlement, and we'd be able to load it into the VR simulations on the ship!" Jahira suggested.

"Hey, great idea! Too bad you didn't think of that twenty minutes ago," Magnar replied.

"Ha ha."

The corner of Magnar's mouth quirked upward. "Don't worry, I've got it covered. I've been recording bits and pieces of the whole trip."

"Oh," Jahira said, the air leaving her lungs in a huff of defeat. He'd beat her to the idea.

After a few minutes of silence, Magnar asked, "So are you nervous?"

"About what?" Jahira asked.

"Facing Lusela."

"Oh, no, not nervous. Definitely curious, and a little wary about how we'll be received."

"Well, they'd better be pretty damn happy to see us, considering all the supplies we're bringing them after they *stole our food and broke our ships*."

"Very true, however, you and I are *mostly* sane, rational people. I'm not convinced that Lusela sees the world in the same way."

"Ain't that the truth."

"I did want adventure and excitement, right? It definitely won't be boring."

"Never that," Magnar agreed.

CHAPTER 21

Anticipation sizzled through Tllomell's veins. Today was her day to visit the silver mountain.

She hadn't expected Krnar to take to the idea quite the way he had, and she definitely hadn't expected him to announce to the entire world that he would be giving tours of the ship. Excitement rippled through The People with the announcement and almost everyone had voiced their desire to see more of the human's marvels. All of this meant Tllomell had to wait her turn.

She hated waiting.

Elders first, of course, and only two at a time, but today the secrets of the humans would be revealed to her...she hoped.

Those who returned from the ship seemed firmly divided into two camps. There were those who fell under an even deeper thrall with the humans and their marvels, on the verge of worship. Others feared the things these humans had made, the things they could do, and wanted no part of it. Frmar continued to sow seeds of discontent among those who were ripe for the planting.

"Tllomell, are you ready?" Krnar asked, interrupting her thoughts.

Swallowing the lump of fear lodged in her throat, Tllomell nodded, checked to make sure she had all she needed, and then stood to join Krnar.

"Where is Plldoll?" Tllomell asked.

"She is not feeling well, and requested to see the ship another day," Krnar replied. A thrill of emotion curled through her insides. She couldn't tell if it was excitement or anxiety. She would spend the day alone with Krnar.

Her feet seemed to float above the ground, her senses so heightened that she felt as if she might burst right out of her skin.

When they exited the outer ring of trees, Tllomell stopped and scanned the scene before her. Worn footpaths wove through strange-looking structures twice her height. Many of the walls glinted in the early morning light, in the same way the sun reflected off the silver mountains. Others were clearly made of dirt and grass, some with freshly torn ground surrounding the outer walls. Bright colored garments flapped on lines strung between the walls. They reminded Tllomell of the dancing leaves, always moving, almost as if an invisible body still inhabited the fabric.

The human settlement had expanded to take up the entire field in both directions. To her right, dancing trees dwarfed the human dwellings. To her left, a few of the structures looked as if they were going to slide down the embankment into the river below.

Rising behind the chaos, the four silver mountains pierced the sky, true to their namesake, in spite of the inaccuracy of the label.

A human waved from the edge of the settlement and then walked toward them.

"Tala will take us to the *ship*," Krnar said.

Tllomell nodded, thankful that it was not the female Jahira. She bowed when Tala greeted her, but otherwise remained silent.

Feet firmly grounded now, Tllomell followed behind Krnar, aware of the stares of the humans who watched them pass. She kept her mind firmly blocked, as Krnar had instructed. She had only briefly experienced the tidal wave of emotion that had hit her the first time she dropped her shields at the welcoming feast. It was an experience she had no desire to duplicate.

Only one of the mountains boasted the hundreds of tiny captured flames which Krnar called *lights*.

"This is the ship that brought us here," Krnar said. "It is named the *Kepler Colonizer*. The humans usually refer to it as *KC*."

Another human waited at the base of the opening, which reminded Tllomell of the gaping maw of a hungry beast, waiting patiently for its next meal to stroll inside. He or she, Tllomell couldn't always tell with the humans and their strange clothes and their wild hair of every different color and length, waved.

Krnar waved back then, when they were no more than two body lengths away, he stopped and bowed his head. "Ryan, this is Tllomell," Krnar said with a gesture toward her. "Tllomell, this is Ryan. He has been studying our language and volunteered to show us the *ship* today."

Ryan bowed to Tllomell and said, in a heavily accented attempt at their language, "May Allorkan shine on you this day."

Tllomell bowed and replied, "You, also."

Ryan straightened and grinned.

Tala and Ryan exchanged words and then Tala departed.

The man, Ryan, talked constantly as they walked through what he called the cargo hold. With ears buzzing from his nonstop chatter, she looked around. Tllomell remembered this place well. This is where the humans had first greeted The People after they'd crossed The Great Ice. Her mouth watered with the memory of her first taste of alara fruit.

Ryan made an effort to include Leroni words into his continuous monologue, but Tllomell rarely understood even these words. Instead of listening to him, she focused on Krnar's translations, which he sent to her via mental link since he couldn't have gotten a spoken word in if he'd tried.

We are going to take the elevator, Krnar projected. One white furred finger pointed to the wall straight ahead.

What is an elevator?

It is a small room that moves up and down inside the wall to take you to different places inside the mountain. It is faster than climbing.

Curiosity bubbled up, and when the wall in front of her opened to reveal the aforementioned tiny room, it burst into heart-pounding anxiety.

You expect me to go inside? Tllomell projected.

Yes, it is safe.

Safe, Tllomell scoffed. There would be barely enough room to maintain a proper distance from one another.

Krnar and Ryan both stood, staring at her expectantly.

Sweat trickled down her spine, but she stepped forward. Her heart hammered against her ribs when the two men stepped in with her and the door zipped closed. Inhaling and exhaling through her nose, she thought she was prepared, and then her stomach dropped to her toes. An involuntary trill escaped her lips. She barely had time to regain her balance before the door zipped open again.

Silver tunnels curved away in either direction. She remembered these as well; she'd walked through these tunnels to get to her room during the flight here.

No revelations so far.

When they stepped out of the tiny room and began walking through the tunnel, Tllomell realized the rooms were different than the one she'd stayed in, much larger, some with what Krnar called *tables* and *chairs*, other rooms with strange-looking devices that the humans used to *exercise*.

What is exercise? Tllomell asked.

Running, walking, that one is called a bike. *They use them to stay strong and healthy.*

Why do they not do these things outside? Run, walk, hunt, swim...

They had them on their big ship because they could not go outside. They were in the sky. And now, I think, they do not always like to be exposed to the elements. Few humans go out when it is too cold for them, or sometimes even when it rains.

I see, Tllomell responded. The thoughts of how weak the humans must be she kept carefully blocked.

Ryan then showed them to the *control room*. Tllomell stood in awe of the clear walls that surrounded her, making her feel as if she were floating. The whole world outside could be seen, but no breeze slid along her fur.

How do they do this? How do they create all of this?

Krnar shook his head. *I don't really know. Many of the explanations I do not fully understand.* Krnar paused. *But I might be able to show you.*

Krnar spoke to Ryan in the human language. His eyes were alight with excitement and he gestured to his head and hands, trying to convey some message that Tllomell couldn't hope to understand.

Ryan's face lit up in response.

The human waved them forward, out of the control room. "Come, this is something I have seen, but I have not shown to any of the other Leroni. I thought it might be best to save it for another time, but since you are here alone..."

The excitement rolling off Krnar infected her. She bounced on the balls of her feet while they waited outside another door. When they entered what the human called his *lab*, Tllomell's jaw dropped. Her feet froze to the floor and her eyes must have grown as large as a sea worm's.

Images covered every wall, and others hung suspended in the air. The images moved, and boasted a riot of colors that made her eyes ache.

"These," Krnar said, tapping one of the pictures, "are called *data screens*. There are many of them. Every human has one. Ryan has many. They hold all of the humans' memories."

Her brain stretched with the effort of trying to wrap itself around the idea. The explanation, by itself, made some sense. She could see this *data screen* before her and see the picture in front of her nose. But how did it work? How did the humans put their memories into this screen? Was there one screen for every memory? No, he'd said each human had *one*, so one screen for each person, to hold all the memories from that person? Then why did this Ryan have many?

"This is Leron," Krnar said, moving to stand beside a hovering sphere. With the tip of one finger, he spun the sphere and then tapped. The sphere disappeared and was replaced by a very detailed and tiny image of the human settlement. He slid his finger along the picture and the land began to speed past until Krnar tapped again. Now she could see the Leroni, inside the circle of the alara grove. She looked down on her people as if she were Aruvel, floating in the heavens above the oranlodi.

The sensation made her dizzy.

She squinted and leaned forward to get a closer look and immediately jumped back and gaped at Krnar. "They're moving!" she exclaimed.

"Yes! The humans have screens in the sky. They can see all of Leron at different times. Isn't it amazing?" Krnar smiled, apparently thrilled with the idea.

Tllomell felt a knot of fear form in her gut. "They can watch us?"

Krnar frowned and said something to Ryan. "Not exactly," he said, once his attention returned to Tllomell. "He said they don't have enough screens in the sky to see everything all the time. These are pictures from two suns ago."

Tllomell's mouth felt dry and she found it hard to swallow.

"There is more," Krnar said.

He walked to a corner of the room and returned with a mass of thin black threads and black strips of material. "You wear these like this." He projected an image of her with these strips of material wrapped around her fingers and toes, black lines trailing from her body.

"Why?"

"It allows you to be in the memory."

Tllomell frowned.

"May I?" he asked, holding up the items in front of her hands.

Her entire body had gone numb. Her heart raced and she felt light-headed. *I wanted to learn the humans' secrets*, she told herself. *I can't back down now.* After a deep breath, she nodded.

"Hold out your hands."

Krnar began to wrap the strips around her fingers. The thrill of his touch against her fur mingled with her anxiety to send her into a state of extreme overstimulation.

"Stay calm. It is okay. I have done this," Krnar reassured her. He did not even need to connect with her mind to see that she struggled to remain in control.

Tllomell fought to slow her heart, to steady her breathing.

When he'd finished with her fingers, he moved to her toes. Next, he placed something on her head, pushed what felt like wads of hide into her ears and, finally, a pair of clear circles descended in front of her eyes.

"Are you ready?" Krnar asked.

Afraid to nod for fear of upsetting the strange crown, she trilled softly. She blinked and found herself back on the solid rock of her former home. The sea stretched out before her, more silver than blue under the cloud-covered sky. When she turned her head and saw the community cavern, a spear of longing pierced her heart.

She wanted to be there, so desperately; to leave this strange, hot, scary place and return to her home. She longed to be surrounded by the familiar solid walls of the cave, to see the fire-light dancing on the walls and the glow of bodies dotting the dark like stars in the sky.

Tears burned the corners of her eyes. She blinked rapidly to keep them from falling.

"Okay, now it's going to change."

She heard Krnar's voice so close it was like he'd pressed his lips against her ear.

The cave and sea disappeared. Tllomell's heart howled. She held out her hand, as if she could physically hold on to the image.

She trilled when she saw her hand, without the black strips that she knew were there. Beyond her fingertips stretched infinite darkness. Her trill rose an octave.

"It is all right, Tllomell. It is only a memory. This is the sky around Leron. The humans call it *space*. And that," he said holding a fingertip in front of her eyes, "is where they came from."

A huge gray sphere hung in the darkness, spinning toward her, covered with their captured flames, growing bigger, drawing closer...

Tllomell closed her eyes and dropped to the ground. Her hands covered her head as it curled into the center of her body. Her limbs shook.

The sound of alarmed voices barely registered. She felt hands pulling off the straps and lines but she did not move, only pressed her eyelids together more tightly.

"I'm sorry, Tllomell, it was too much. I'm sorry." Krnar's voice. Krnar was somewhere out there, but she did not dare look.

Time passed. It could have been a moon; Tllomell had no idea. She tried to block out what she had seen while simultaneously clinging to the image of home.

When she had recovered enough that she could follow Krnar out of the mountain, one thought drove her forward.

She had to tell Frmar.

CHAPTER 22

Well, that didn't go as planned, Krnar thought.

An arm's length to his right, Tllomell walked with her back stiff, limbs rigid, and eyes staring straight ahead. She hadn't said a word since her collapse in the lab. When he attempted to touch her mind, he encountered a solid wall.

Ryan called it *shock*. He said it happened sometimes when a person experienced or saw something that their brain couldn't comprehend.

Why didn't that happen to me? he'd asked.

Ryan didn't know for sure, only that every person has a different capacity for new ideas and that Tllomell had reached her threshold.

Thank Aruvel I didn't try that with anyone else, he thought.

They continued through the grove in silence. Krnar paused when Tllomell stopped to take a drink from the stream, and then resumed walking when she continued, with never a glance in his direction.

When they reached the inner field, trampled flat now from the Leroni's habitation and constant movement, he felt a thrill of surprise when Tllomell did not return to her own hearth, but went straight to Frmar's and waited for him to motion her inside.

Before he could consider the reason for this, he heard a familiar voice calling his name.

"Krnar! Krnar!"

Mrkon raced toward him, holding a sizeable *brnada* by the hind legs. "I set the snares, like you showed me!"

"Very impressive," Krnar said. "Well done. Where did you set the snare?"

"At the edge of the forest, beneath the dancing trees."

"Which direction?"

Mrkon pointed.

Krnar looked and nodded. "Did you take someone with you?"

Mrkon cast his eyes to the ground.

"Mrkon, what have I told you? Even Arkan and I take a hunting partner. If anything happened to you, there would be no one there to help."

"I know. I'm sorry."

"Well, you made it there and back this time." Mrkon looked up with hopeful eyes. Krnar smirked. "Let's go show that catch of yours to Ulletta."

For the rest of the evening, Mrkon's retelling of his hunt and the peaceful company of family pushed the day's disasters from his mind.

The next morning, the memory crashed over him in a wave of worry. He looked around for Tllomell, hoping to ask her how she felt this morning and to try to talk to her about what she had seen.

He could not find her.

During his second circuit around the field, he noticed that Frmar was also absent. *Interesting*, he thought. They are sure spending a lot of time together. They seemed an unlikely couple to Krnar, especially with the added complication of Frmar's apprenticeship to the Akaruvel.

"Krnar, are you looking for someone?"

After turning toward the speaker, Krnar bowed low. When he straightened he said, "Ellall, yes, I am looking for Tllomell."

"Ah, I heard there was some trouble during her tour of the mountain."

Krnar wondered where she'd heard this. "Not trouble exactly. I showed her something, about the humans, something that she was not ready to see. It...affected her in a strong way."

"Hmmm, and she went to Frmar with this information?" She voiced it like a question but Krnar felt certain she already knew the answer.

He nodded and said, "I believe so. I saw her go to his hearth when we returned, but I do not know what was said. Now, this morning, they are both gone."

Ellall's eyes narrowed.

"Is everything alright?" Krnar asked.

"I'm not sure," Ellall replied. "I know that Frmar is...less than satisfied with his place and with our current relations with Grollon and with the humans."

Krnar trilled in concern. "Has he talked to you about this?"

"Not directly, no, but I know him well. Also, when we share memories, he must open his mind to me. He cannot hide everything, no matter how hard he tries."

"What does he plan to do?"

"That is the part I am unsure of. He's been talking to others, those who feel the way he does, but I have not heard of any plan. Perhaps they gather only to complain." The tightness around her eyes and mouth told him that she did not believe this.

"Talked to others? What others? What are they talking about?"

"This has all been a great upheaval, Krnar. It has changed everyone's life. Some are afraid. Normally, I would trust that, together, we would get through it."

"Normally?"

Ellall sighed. "Grollon told me something, that first day we met…" Her voice trailed off and Krnar waited in a fever of anticipation. When Ellall did not continue, he broke down.

"What did he say?" he asked, unable to stand the suspense.

"He said that his visions showed him that history would repeat itself."

Momentarily stunned into silence, Krnar could only gape at his Akaruvel. When he finally regained the ability to speak, he peppered her with questions. "What part of history? What did he see? What does he think is going to happen?"

"I don't know," Ellall replied. "He would not share these memories with me because he feared how it might change, or hasten, the outcome."

"How it might change," Krnar repeated. "If the memories can change, then what he saw happen might *not* happen. We can do something about it."

"Perhaps," Ellall said. "Or we might set into motion something worse."

Krnar had heard enough.

"I need to find Grollon."

Chapter 23

The southern continent.

Jahira took her first steps onto the sandy beach and inhaled. It smelled different here, like hot rocks and sweet smoke.

She and Magnar had anchored the boat as close to shore as they could manage.

After stripping down to their undergarments, they'd walked the rest of the way with their packs balanced on their heads. They left the crates of trade supplies aboard the boat. It was more than the two of them could carry alone. They would have to return with some of the southern colonists to make the final trade.

Now the hot sand burned the soles of her feet, sending Jahira hopping up to a grassy patch where she dug her toes in to the cooler sand beneath the surface.

"Let's dry out up here in the grass," Magnar called from his patch of grass several meters away.

Jahira gave a thumbs-up and then steeled herself for a final sprint across the burning sand. She leaped over the last stretch of sand onto the grass and immediately placed her shirt on the ground to stand on.

Magnar joined her.

"Well, that was a new experience," Jahira said.

"Maybe we should have put our shoes back on first," Magnar replied.

"Live and learn, live and learn."

While she waited for her feet to recover, Jahira scanned their surroundings. Ahead and to the right were the familiar yellow stalks of grain, similar to those on the second continent, but much taller, and with thicker, sturdier-looking stalks.

Ahead and to the left, a forest of gnarled black trees twisted toward the sky and then erupted in vibrant red, orange, and yellow foliage.

"Like a forest on fire, permanently," Jahira said.

"The tracker's telling us to go straight ahead, right between the forest and the grain field," Magnar said, glancing up from his blinking handheld.

"Sounds easy enough."

Jahira stepped off her shirt, placed her pack on the ground, and began to dress. The silky blue pants and shirt would help regulate her body temperature in the heat, and she didn't want grass cuts all up and down her legs. She had to sit down to get on her socks and boots and then she was ready.

Magnar had pulled on his pants and boots, but left off his shirt.

"The straps are going to chafe your shoulders," Jahira said.

"I think I'll be okay," Magnar replied, complete with an eye-roll.

Jahira shrugged and let him lead the way through the long, fibrous "grass" that divided the forest and the grain field. Her ears tuned in to the sounds around her. Some were similar enough to the creatures in the north that she thought she could categorize them into bird, insect, or small game. Those she didn't recognize she attempted to memorize in order to identify later.

Maybe I should be a zoologist, she thought, *or a botanist. I could go exploring, discover new animals and plants, name a few. That could be fun and satisfying.*

After about an hour, and at least thirteen new animal calls to investigate, she heard a sound that stopped her in her tracks. "Magnar," she said.

He stopped and turned.

"Do you hear that?"

They both squinted and leaned. A distant, eerie wail floated through the trees, like discordant music.

"What do you suppose that is?" Magnar asked.

"I don't have a clue, but it definitely doesn't sound like an animal."

"Want to check it out?"

"Absolutely."

A knot of apprehension tied around her chest and tightened as they headed into the forest.

The dark and mildly creepy trees became menacing when combined with the haunting notes that drifted on the breeze.

Patches of the dark trunks glistened where the light hit them, as if they were slick with moisture. Her fingers reached involuntarily to touch the shimmering surface.

A spike of panic pierced her gut when her fingers stuck.

When a gentle pull didn't work, she yanked—skin be damned—and the tree released its hold. Her action, thankfully, did not remove the skin from the pads of her fingers, but a sticky residue remained where she'd contacted the tree.

"What is it?" Magnar asked.

"I don't know. Maybe some kind of sap?"

"Look at all the bugs caught in it," Magnar said, pointing to the tiny wriggling bodies interspersed along the trunk.

"Huh, do you suppose the tree absorbs them or something?"

Magnar shrugged. "Maybe we'll find out while we're here."

Dry leaves and a dry moss-like substance crunched beneath her boots, boots which, Jahira noticed, were wearing thin at the toes. *What am I going to do for the winter?* she wondered.

The sound that had initially drawn them into this wood grew louder. Now Jahira could hear rushing water as well as the unnerving whistle.

"It's a river!" Magnar called, having moved ahead of her.

Breaking into a brief jog, she joined him at the bank of a wide, shallow river. Interspersed evenly along the river's meandering path were tall rocks protruding from the current. Each rock bore at least one hole straight through. The holes were all different sizes and different distances from the water.

The breeze picked up, shifting Jahira's hair so that she had to brush it from her eyes. Then the tune changed.

"It's the wind blowing through the rocks," Magnar said.

"A song played by nature," Jahira said. "How cool is that?"

"Makes it easy to find water, anyway."

Jahira slid off her pack. The sweat-soaked fabric clinging to her back cooled instantly, sending shivers down her spine.

Fingers rummaged through the contents until she found her target. Extracting the thumb-sized device, she pressed the release button causing a soft synthetic tip to protrude from the small tube. She placed the tip in the water and watched tiny numbers scroll along the side of the tester. When the numbers disappeared after a few seconds, Jahira waited for the final verdict.

The screen glowed green.

"Says it's good," Jahira stated.

"Excellent." Magnar squatted beside her and then dipped his hands into the clear current. A blissful smile spread across his face when Magnar tossed two handfuls of water over his head, then scrubbed his face.

"I think this is a perfect time for a break," Magnar said. He filled his canteen from the river and then found a good rock to sit on. He slid his pack off and pulled a wrapped package from the top.

"Want some?" he asked, holding up a stick of dried meat.

"Sure," Jahira replied. She caught the tossed jerky and found her own rock to sit on. "Do you want to try to make it today?" she asked, glancing at the sky, now a light purple-blue in the waning afternoon light.

"Nah, let's take our time. I'm not in that big a rush to see Lusela." Jahira's lips quirked in response. "Besides, I've still got my sea-legs. All this walking on flat unmoving land is making me dizzy."

"Maybe we should follow the river, find a place to camp upstream," Jahira suggested.

"We can follow it for a while but we're going to have to move back to the grass to camp. I don't think I can sleep with that creepy noise all night."

"Fair enough, I just like the idea of being close to water."

"Yeah, I'll bet all the animals do, too."

"Fair point."

Once the last bit of meat rested in her stomach, they continued upstream for another couple of hours before turning back through the forest. They both wanted to make it past the dark trees before full dark descended.

The thick canopy muted the last of the day's light. The dark trunks absorbed what little light did make it through, creating an inky canvas.

Against the black background, Jahira noticed glowing dots beginning to appear on the sticky trunks.

Stopping to take a closer look, she leaned in toward a glowing circle about the size of her thumbnail, careful not to touch any part of the tree this time.

Encased in a glowing bubble, one of the tiny insects that had stuck to the tacky surface earlier in the day paced and flitted its wings, testing its beautiful prison.

"Magnar, check this out," Jahira whispered.

Magnar joined her and they leaned in, cheeks touching and noses centimeters from the trapped insect. "Crazy," he said.

"Yeah."

They watched in silence for a few more seconds then Magnar backed away and stood.

"Come on, it's getting really dark," Magnar said.

Jahira stood, stretched her back, and turned. Her mouth gaped open. All around her, glowing bubbles dotted the twisted trunks, creating a display like the holiday lights wrapped around the bunk bed poles that her parents used to make for her and her sister.

When they finally reached the grassy lane between the forest and towering grain stalks, they made quick work of setting up camp and clearing a circle to have a fire.

Full night descended while the smell of wood smoke and roasted fish soaked into Jahira's clothes.

Famished from the day's exertions, Jahira tucked in to her meal with single-minded determination. She didn't look up until she was licking sticky juice from her fingers and felt Magnar bump her leg.

Her head lifted to see what he wanted. His eyes were fixed on the forest.

She turned and her jaw dropped.

Climbing down out of the branches were hundreds of lizard-like creatures, each one about the length of Jahira's forearm from tip to tip. Their bright orange, red, and yellow bodies stood out against the dark trunks.

"They match the leaves," Magnar whispered.

Jahira nodded, staring in fascination as the lizards moved down the trunks from one glowing bubble to the next, popping them into their mouths with tiny webbed front feet. "I guess that answers that question," Jahira said.

They continued to watch until the lizards retreated back into the upper branches.

"We should have taken a vid of that," Magnar said.

"Great idea. Too bad you didn't think of that twenty minutes ago," Jahira replied with a grin, echoing his comment to her from the boat.

Magnar smiled. "Touché."

Jahira buried the remains of their meal a good distance from their campsite. Steam hissed and rose from the fire when Magnar poured half a canteen of water over the smoldering coals.

"Big day tomorrow. Let's get some sleep," Magnar said, and then crawled into the tent.

"Sounds good," Jahira replied. Her limbs felt heavy with fatigue, but her muscles twitched. Her mind buzzed, keeping her awake.

What's happening at the settlement? Is everything okay with Krnar? What is going to happen tomorrow?

CHAPTER 24

"Krnar took me to a room that the humans call a *lab*. There were pictures on the walls that moved, and more pictures in the air." Tllomell projected the memory to her audience.

Trills of disbelief rode on waves of fear and awe.

"Tell them what happened next," Frmar prompted.

Tllomell shifted her weight. She felt emotionally uncomfortable being the center of attention and physically uncomfortable with her butt bones digging into the hard surface of the log she sat on.

"Next, Krnar placed straps around my fingers and toes, another around my head. I blinked and then I was standing outside the community cavern. I could feel the cold, smell the sea. I was there." The final sentence came out barely more than a whisper.

Murmurs and tilted heads followed her confession. "How? How can that be possible?"

"They are descendants of The Marked. They have to be. They can control our minds and show us any memories they wish using this *lab*." The murmurs rose into angry mutterings in response to Frmar's words. "They can also watch us. Tllomell saw these pictures that they take of us."

More trills and murmurs.

Tllomell didn't believe the humans were descendants of The Marked, but she did not correct Frmar. She hadn't told him the whole story, and never intended to tell him or anyone else about her response to seeing that giant floating orb racing toward her in the pitch black.

She didn't believe they descended from The Marked. She believed they were something far more dangerous.

"What should we do?"

"Do you still believe we should go, Frmar?"

"Yes, I do," Frmar said.

"But what about those we leave behind?"

"Those who choose to stay may already be under the influence of The Marked. Tllomell has been following Grollon, watching him. So far he has done nothing suspicious, but I believe he is only biding his time."

"Is it true that one of the humans is also marked?"

"Yes, it's true," Frmar said.

Minds buzzed with silent communication and fearful glances were exchanged.

"When should we leave?"

Tllomell's head snapped up.

Thus far Frmar's idea of leaving the grove had received half-hearted responses at best. Some agreed with what he said, but did not wish to divide The People. Others said they were ready to follow, but none had been so bold as to suggest an actual timeframe.

Frmar pressed his lips together in a thin line, thinking. Eventually he said, "We would have to leave before the snows come. Ellall said this would be two more moons. We must leave in time to make it to the mountains that Krnar and Allnall passed through. It may take as long as a moon to travel there."

Tllomell watched the crowd's reactions.

Some nodded. Most looked to those around them, trying to decide how to respond.

"We should ask Allnall how long the journey took her once she crossed the mountains."

Frmar nodded. "Yes, but be cautious in asking. Do not make our intentions obvious," he said.

Someone is coming.

The mental warning from their lookout brought every head up.

Who is it? Frmar asked.

A pause and then: *Krnar.*

Tllomell's brow furrowed in confusion. Had he followed her?

What is he doing out here? Frmar asked the lookout.

Hunting most likely, the scout responded. *He has his weapons.*

He always has his weapons. He would not be hunting alone.

Tllomell thought she knew where he was headed. "I will intercept him," she said. "Lead him away from the group."

Frmar's eyes narrowed but finally he nodded.

Tllomell sprang to her feet and followed Krnar's mental signal. She had learned stealth during the past suns of attempting to sneak after Grollon. She'd learned where to step so that her footfalls made no noise.

Quickly but quietly, she chased his mind until she could finally see his body. A push against his mental block brought him to a halt.

Tllomell jogged the rest of the distance.

Surprise and impatience warred in his features. "Tllomell, what are you doing out here?" he asked.

"I might ask you the same question."

Krnar tipped his head, acknowledging her point. "I am looking for Grollon," he said.

A warm tingle of satisfaction filled her. She'd guessed right. Fighting to keep her expression neutral, she nodded.

"And you?" he asked.

"I was meeting with Frmar," she said. It would be easier to tell a partial truth than try to completely make up a story on the spot.

Krnar didn't look surprised. "You've been spending a lot of time together," he said. "Where is he?"

"He returned to the grove," Tllomell replied.

Krnar lifted his chin. "But you didn't?"

"I saw you and I wanted to talk to you."

Krnar's shoulders relaxed. "I've been wanting to talk to you also. I'm sorry about what happened on the ship, Tllomell. I only wanted you to know. I wanted to help you understand. I didn't mean to frighten you."

"I know. It's okay. I wanted to tell you that I'm okay."

Krnar nodded and then glanced over her shoulder.

"I think I might know where he is," Tllomell said. "Do you mind if I join you?"

Krnar's eyes clouded. "I don't think that's a good idea."

Tllomell crossed her arms and stared him down. She would follow him anyway, and he knew it. Finally he sighed, and then resumed walking. "Why do you seek The Marked?" Tllomell asked, keeping pace beside him.

"I must ask about a memory he alluded to, but did not share with Ellall."

Tllomell's interest was piqued. She didn't press, figuring that if she were present for the conversation, she would find out soon enough.

When they reached the place where Grollon normally sat, The Marked was not there.

Krnar spun in a circle, looking for any sign of the old man, and finally growled in frustration.

"It is important, then," Tllomell said.

Krnar nodded.

Tllomell hesitated before voicing her next thought, afraid she might be going too far.

"Perhaps the human marked could answer your question."

Krnar's head snapped toward her and he stared. She did not meet his eyes. "You and Frmar *are* getting close," he said.

Heat spread from her gut to the top of her head like an unpleasant rash. She didn't respond, only waited.

"He would not know the answer to my question."

"Why not?"

"He did not pass through the gateway. He does not have the Knowledge. He only drank the silver and went a bit mad."

She tucked this information away for later.

"Grollon sometimes visits Magnar, but Magnar is gone." Krnar seemed to be speaking to himself, but Tllomell deduced that Magnar must be the human marked.

"Gone? Gone where?" she asked.

"He went south, to the first continent," Krnar replied.

Thoughts of more marked, hiding on the first continent, filled her mind. "Why?" Tllomell asked.

"You have many questions," Krnar growled.

"Can you blame me?"

Krnar rubbed his face with his hands, an odd gesture, and not one she'd seen him use before. "There is a group of humans that did not want to help us. They destroyed parts of the silver mountains, to try to prevent those who did wish to help us from leaving for the Great Ice. Then they left for the first continent. The humans who remained fixed one of the mountains. The others never returned."

Tllomell's arms tingled, going numb as they fell to her sides. Her jaw dropped. "And this marked human went to see them," she said, her voice flat and cold.

"To trade with them, yes, bring them food and supplies."

235

Her shock melted and began to boil through her veins in a scorching rage. *"Trade with them?"* Her fists clenched, attempting to hold her together. "What else have you kept from us, Krnar?"

"It's complicated, Tllomell."

She hissed and turned her back to him. *Lies upon lies*, she thought. Her feet began to move of their own volition, away from Krnar.

He did not try to stop her.

The rip in her soul bled anew.

CHAPTER 25

A series of sharp whistles alerted Jahira to the presence of other human beings. Magnar stopped and held up a hand to wave. "They post guards around their camp. Kato and Creed said to wait for someone to come and greet us when we heard the whistles," he said.

"Guards? Do they expect us to attack them? Why do they need guards?"

"Who knows what they think, but I'm not willing to risk my life because they're paranoid."

With narrowed eyes, Jahira watched the tall, thick stalks of grain rustle and sway.

A young man emerged, held up a hand in greeting, and approached Jahira and Magnar with a wide, bright smile. "Hi! Welcome! I'm Samuel." He looked to be in his late teens. His white teeth stood out against a dark olive-toned complexion. Thick black hair hung in waves that reached below his ears and deep brown eyes sparkled in greeting.

He did not look like someone who would sabotage four colony ships and steal a winter's supply of food.

His smile faltered when he noticed Jahira giving him the once-over. He held his hand out to Magnar and his shoulders relaxed when Magnar shook it.

"Hi, I'm Magnar," he said.

Now it was Samuel's turn to stare. Several uncomfortable seconds passed during which Samuel could not tear his eyes away from Magnar's forehead. Jahira decided to intervene.

"Hi, Samuel," Jahira said, holding out her hand. "I'm Jahira. We've come to trade. There are medical supplies, food, and some other materials Lusela requested back on our boat."

"Your boat? Where'd you get a boat?" Samuel asked, finally shifting his attention away from Magnar's scars.

"I built it, with some help," Magnar said.

"Wow, cool! I'd love to see it!"

"Well, maybe you can come back with us to make the trade. I'm not exactly sure how it's all going to work," Magnar said.

"Great! I'd love to!" Everyone stood in silence for several seconds before Jahira gave Samuel a pointed look. "Oh, uh, I guess you want to see Lusela."

"Yes, please," Jahira replied.

"Okay, right this way." Samuel started off at the front of the procession, but soon fell into step beside Magnar, apparently one of those people who didn't like silence.

"So, how did you find us?" Samuel asked.

Magnar lifted his hand, which held the tracking device.

"Oh, right, kind of forgot about those. We didn't bring much of that kind of stuff with us." Samuel finally seemed to realize the awkwardness of the situation and glanced sheepishly out of the corners of his eyes.

"Yes, about that," Jahira said. Magnar gave her a warning look but she ignored him.

"You don't strike me as the type to destroy ships and steal food," she said, watching for Samuel's reaction.

A crimson blush stained his neck and the cheek she could see.

"Well, uh, the truth is not all of us knew about Lusela's whole plan. I found out after, what they'd done to the ships. By then it was too late, anyway." Samuel paused and cleared his throat. "I just don't like the cold. A year of winter didn't appeal, you know."

Jahira's eyebrows rose and she looked down her nose at him.

"So, it's not much farther."

239

Five long strides took them out of the tall grain stalks and onto the edge of a vast clearing. Jahira blinked in surprise.

"Wow, I guess we can't call them lazy," Magnar said.

Multiple dwellings rose from the hard-packed ground. Stalks of grain had been lashed together into large square panels formed walls and pitched roofs.

"Lusela is over here," Samuel said, waving them toward a cluster of houses to the right. He stopped at the doorway of a hut at the center of the cluster and knocked on the doorframe.

Pale fingers curled around the edge of the door panel and slid it sideways. Cold grey eyes regarded them impassively.

"Magnar, Jahira, what a surprise." Lusela's voice was as flat and cold as her eyes. She looked Magnar up and down, and then turned to Jahira. "Where's your pet?"

White-hot hate seared Jahira's veins. She felt Magnar squeeze her bicep. Her teeth clenched and her nostrils flared, but she managed to hold herself together and give Lusela a tight-lipped smile. Without taking her eyes from Lusela, Jahira said, "Remind me again why we're helping her?"

Magnar's jaw muscles bunched and relaxed. He had no love for Lusela either, but they didn't want the rest of the settlement to suffer because of her. "*Thank you* might be a more appropriate thing to say," Magnar said.

"Hmm, and what am I thanking you for?"

"We brought medical supplies, the materials you asked Kato and Creed to bring, and even some food. It's on my boat, anchored in the channel. Several people will need to return with us to get the goods, and we expect something in trade."

Lusela regarded them with narrowed eyes. "It will take a few days to get something together," she finally said.

"That's fine," Magnar replied. "We'll just pitch a tent and relax. Let us know when you're ready."

"Samuel can show you around and answer any questions. I'll send for you in a few days."

The door slid shut.

"Well, that was fun," Magnar said.

"She'll send for us?" Jahira hissed.

Samuel wisely remained silent, but he guided them to a campsite not far from his dwelling.

"Hey, once you get your tent set up, let me show you around," Samuel offered. "There are some really cool things to see."

"Sure," Jahira replied. "That would be great." She smiled, making an effort not to take her frustration out on Samuel.

"Great. I'm going to go grab my pack. I'll find you."

When Samuel left, Jahira scanned the surrounding area. People watched them from a distance. No one waved or walked over to say hello. Tingles of unease crawled up Jahira's arms and tickled the back of her neck. She tried to ignore the feeling, and the onlookers, but tension coiled inside her.

"Hey! You guys ready?"

Jahira jumped and turned at the sound of Samuel's voice.

Magnar brushed his hands against his pants and pulled his shoulders back to stretch the muscles. "I'm ready," he said. "You ready, Jahira?"

She pressed a hand to her hammering heart and nodded. "Sure, let's go."

After a surreptitious glance at their distant audience, she grabbed her pack and slung it over one shoulder.

"You're taking all that with you?" Magnar asked.

"Yep," Jahira replied without explanation.

Magnar shrugged.

"Lead the way, Sam," Magnar said.

"Okay, great!" Samuel headed toward the western edge of the settlement, where the yellow grain stalks formed a wall that rose a foot above Jahira's head. Pressed against this wall was a large rectangular enclosure formed from the thick stalks of the same plant. Inside the enclosure a dozen herd beasts watched them with large, impassive eyes.

"So, the rumor is true," Magnar said.

"Well, if the rumor is that we're taming the grain-eaters, then it's true," Samuel said. His confident gait took him right up to the edge of the fence, where he proceeded to stick his arm through the horizontal posts and offer a hand to the closest animal.

Apprehension tightened Jahira's muscles. "They're strictly plant eaters, right?" she asked.

"Yeah, they're really docile, actually," Samuel said. "They're strong enough to break through this fence pretty easily, but as long as we keep them fed and watered, they're pretty happy to stay here, as long as they have their family with them."

"Their family? How do you know which ones are related?" Magnar asked.

"They stick pretty close together," Samuel replied. "If you catch the leader of a family unit, the others in the family will follow. The rest of the herd gets spooked and runs away, but the family won't leave the one that you capture."

"That sounds pretty sad to me," Jahira said.

"Well, it would be if you separated them, but like I said, as long as the family's together, they seem happy."

"*Seem* being the operative word here," Jahira muttered. A sharp pain shot down her side when Magnar elbowed her in the ribs.

"You can pet them if you want," Samuel said.

Jahira and Magnar exchanged a glance. Jahira stepped forward and offered a sweaty and slightly trembling palm.

A small srlen, she preferred the name that Krnar used, walked over on spindly legs and bumped her hand with a soft snout.

"Aw, it likes you," Magnar said.

"It is pretty cute," Jahira replied. Her anxiety level lessened with each pat on the animal's nose. Then a long tongue extended from the animal's mouth and licked the full length of her hand and half her arm.

Samuel and Magnar both laughed.

"It thinks you have a treat for it," Samuel said.

With a grimace, Jahira pulled back her hand and wiped the sticky saliva on Magnar's sleeve.

"Hey!" Magnar said, jumping to the side.

Now it was Jahira's turn to laugh.

"Okay, I think I've had enough contact with the beasts. What's next?" Magnar asked.

"Next I'll show you the southern border. It's quite a view," Samuel said.

They began to walk along the western edge of the clearing.

"Do the srlen, the grain-eaters, eat anything besides grain?" Jahira asked.

"Oh sure, grass, leaves, the nuts from the trees to the east, but the grain is their main diet."

"You mentioned treats, what do you give them as a treat?" Magnar asked.

"There's this plant that grows by the river that they absolutely love."

"Hmm, wonder what it is?" Jahira said.

The ground began to change from hard, dry soil to solid rock, and they were climbing. The rise was subtle, but enough that Jahira felt her heart rate increase and her calf muscles strain.

When they reached the top of the rise, Jahira's stomach dropped. She backed up three paces and hugged her arms to her chest.

Before them, the land fell away. Beyond the cliff edge and out to the horizon, a rolling sea of orange, red, and yellow unfolded, interrupted here and there by sparkling strips of light where sun reflected off water. The tips of some of the distant hills were shrouded in mist.

"Come up closer, Jahira, the view is breathtaking," Samuel said.

"Thanks, but I actually really like breathing," Jahira replied.

Magnar snorted. "She's afraid of heights," he said by way of explanation.

"Really?" Samuel asked. "Aren't you a pilot?"

"Yes, but it's completely different," Jahira said. "When I'm flying I'm surrounded by walls and I'm strapped in to the vehicle that *I* am controlling. That," she said, waving her hand toward the open sky, "is suicidal. A strong wind could blow you right over."

Samuel grinned. "Well, then, you're really going to like this." He laid down on his belly and backed up until his legs dangled over the edge of the cliff.

"Samuel! What are you doing? Get back up here!" Jahira's voice rose an octave.

"Magnar, can you give me hand?" Samuel asked.

Magnar knelt on one knee and extended a hand. "What are you doing?" he asked. Even he looked a bit green around the edges.

"Collecting our dinner," Samuel replied.

Fighting down the bile that rose up in her esophagus, Jahira watched Samuel disappear over the edge.

"Okay, you can let go," Samuel called.

Magnar released his hand and Jahira wiped sweat from her brow.

Several minutes passed. Magnar lay down on his stomach so that he could peer over the edge. Jahira wished she could do the same. She wanted to make sure that Samuel was okay, but she was afraid she'd get dizzy and fall to her death, or puke on Samuel's head.

Eventually she sat, mostly because her legs didn't feel like they would hold her anymore.

What felt like hours later, Samuel's dirt-coated fingers gripped the top of the cliff and Magnar reached down to help.

Pieces of Samuel appeared one after the other. Jahira began to breathe easier when she saw that all of the pieces were still connected and none visibly mangled.

Samuel dusted off the front of his shirt and pants, and then reached around to a pouch he had slung over his shoulder. From the pouch he pulled out two fist-sized ovals, light grey in color and speckled with brown dots.

"What are those?" Magnar asked.

"Eggs!" Samuel announced, puffing his chest out with pride.

"Eggs," Jahira said, her voice flat with disbelief. "You did all of that for eggs?"

Samuel's chest deflated a little and Jahira felt a pang of remorse. "Sorry, Samuel," she said. "That's really great. I haven't eaten eggs in forever, and you climbing out over that cliff to get them, well, that was really brave."

"There are three more in here," Samuel said, patting the bulging pouch. "Let's head back."

Jahira smiled and stood, happy to be moving away from the edge of the cliff.

"Would you guys like to come back to my place?" Samuel asked. "My roommates are on watch tonight so it's just me, and this is more than I can eat."

Magnar raised his eyebrows at Jahira.

Jahira pouted her lips and shrugged.

"Sure," Magnar said.

They returned to Samuel's hut, a small, neat place with a fire-pit outside the front door. Samuel waved and called greetings to his neighbors. They waved back but their smiles died when their eyes moved past Samuel and saw who accompanied him.

"Pull up a seat," Samuel said in a too-cheerful voice. "I'll just get the fire going and scramble these up!"

Four large stumps surrounded the fire-pit. Jahira picked the one that looked the most level and perched on the edge.

With the efficient ease of long practice, Samuel started a tidy fire.

The *tock-tock-plop* of cracking egg shells sounded five times before the repeated clink of Samuel's camp fork against the mixing bowl. Finally, the runny, yellowy mass slid into the pan over the fire and began to sizzle.

"It smells amazing!" Jahira said.

Samuel beamed.

Jahira couldn't remember the last time she had eggs. They were a rare treat even in that previous life aboard the *Aquilo*. There were plenty of birds back at Empyrean, but the larger birds nested so high up in the dancing trees no one dared climb to such heights to gather eggs.

Maybe Samuel would, she thought. She shuddered at the memory of his climbing out over that drop with absolutely nothing preventing him from plummeting to his death.

"Here you go," Samuel said, handing her a plate of fluffy light yellow globules.

"Thank you," Jahira said. With a thrill of excitement, she inhaled the steam rising from her meal. The first bite melted on her tongue. Her eyes closed in bliss. "This might have been worth the effort after all," she said.

"Mmm-hmm," Magnar mumbled around a mouth full of food.

"I'm glad you like them," Samuel said.

"So, where were the birds who laid these eggs?" Jahira asked. "They must be pretty big."

"They are," Samuel said. "Huge! Their wingspan must be eight feet! The females have to leave once in a while to eat, so then I swoop in."

Samuel grinned into his eggs and glanced out from under his lashes.

"Ha ha," Jahira said.

Magnar snickered.

Before long the crackling fire grew steadily brighter as the world around them darkened.

"It's probably time for us to get back," Magnar said. "It's been a long day."

"Sure, sure," Samuel said. "Thanks for stopping by. It was nice to have company."

"Thanks for the meal," Jahira said.

They all nodded their goodbyes and she and Magnar retreated to their own campsite.

"That kid is really nice," Magnar said.

"Yeah, he is," Jahira agreed. "I wonder how he got mixed up in all this."

"Well, you heard him, he didn't know what Lusela was going to do."

"When he found out what she did, he should have high-tailed it back and told someone."

"He was probably scared, thought he'd get in trouble, didn't want to rat out his friends, you know."

"Yeah, I know, and I think he was a coward."

"A coward who climbs out over the edges of cliffs with no safety harness."

"True."

"And a very likeable coward."

Jahira sighed, "Fine. He's a very likeable, courageous coward."

Magnar grinned. "Goodnight, Jahira."

"Goodnight, Magnar."

CHAPTER 26

The next morning, Jahira stepped out of the tent and her stomach clenched. She stood face-to-face with a small handmade doll covered in white feathers and strung up by its neck. The thin piece of string around its neck was tied to a branch that had been driven into the ground. The white doll with blue pieces of cloth for eyes, swung and spun in the morning breeze.

Rage boiled through her, heating her skin and burning the back of her eyes. She untied the doll, set it gently on the ground, and began breaking up the branch with a bit more violence than necessary. She tossed the broken pieces into the fire pit to use to cook some breakfast.

Every fiber of her will worked to keep her eyes down. She knew if she looked around and saw someone watching her with anything even resembling a satisfied expression, she would take the stick and beat the person bloody. Probably not the best course of action considering she and Magnar were significantly outnumbered.

"What's that?" Magnar said.

She hadn't heard him leave the tent, probably due to the sound of her own blood rushing in her ears. "A gift from one of our lovely trade partners," Jahira said. "It was a hanging from that stick." She pointed to the pieces she'd tossed in the center of the bare circle of dirt where she planned to build their fire.

"What the hell?"

"I expected some grief, but that's…"

"Horrible? Childish? Hateful? Asinine? Ignorant?" Magnar supplied.

"Yes, exactly," Jahira agreed.

"Do you know who it was?" Magnar asked. "I have a very full bladder and I'd be happy to empty it out on the villain's house, or face."

Jahira snorted and then grinned. "No, I don't know who it was."

"Well, maybe I'll just take a guess." Magnar wandered off.

I hope he was joking, she thought.

Kneeling down, Jahira picked up the crude effigy and wondered what to do with it. It seemed wrong to burn it, like adding insult to injury somehow. Save it and give it to some kid to play with?

Maybe I should bury it, she thought.

Then she wondered what Krnar would think of it, which made her wonder how Krnar was doing. She missed him.

Every night since they'd left Empyrean, she'd tossed and turned, unable to get comfortable despite the fact that she'd brought her own sleeping mat and sleeping bag. Her frustration had grown to an inferno until it finally occurred to her that she'd grown used to curling up against Krnar's warm, solid body. Now, apparently, she couldn't sleep without him. That was an annoying discovery.

Last night, in her desperation for rest, she'd briefly considered spooning with Magnar but decided she'd likely get an elbow in the eye for her efforts. Resigned to her fate, she'd lain there in the dark until exhaustion finally took over.

Now her puffy gritty eyes were staring at this tiny symbol of someone else's huge problem, and it made her wonder if his people were giving him a hard time about their relationship.

"So, what are you doing to do with that?" Magnar asked, returning from his mission to mark his territory.

"I don't know," Jahira replied. "I was just trying to decide."

"Maybe you should hook it to your pack and wear it around. Show them you're not intimidated."

"Hmmm, maybe. Or maybe I'll be able to think more clearly after breakfast."

"Roasted veggies?" Magnar asked.

"Sounds good," Jahira replied. "I'll make some tea."

Each rifled through their pack for the necessary ingredients. Magnar opened a freeze-dried pack of vegetables and Jahira pulled out a wrapped bundle of dried leaves to steep.

Two flexible silicone "pots" of water were just beginning to boil when Samuel appeared, grinning, waving with one hand, and carrying a strip of bark in the other. "Good morning," he called. "It looks like I'm just in time!"

The hand that held the bark lowered and extended, revealing a small pile of round, yellow cakes.

"What is it?" Magnar asked.

"Smells good," Jahira said.

"This is my current version of bread," he said. "We've been experimenting with grinding the grain and cooking it in different ways. This is method four, and so far, it's the best."

"Have a seat," Magnar said, nodding to the empty place by the fire.

"Would you like some tea?" Jahira asked.

"Sure! Thanks," Samuel said.

Once everything was ready, they settled in to their meal.

Jahira accepted one of the small rounds of bread and took a bite. Her tongue sampled the unfamiliar flavor and worked the bolus around in her mouth, exploring the texture. "Not bad," she said.

"Tastes kind of nutty," Magnar said.

"You might change your mind after today," Samuel said.

Magnar cocked his head and frowned.

"What's today?" Jahira asked.

"We're organizing a work party to gather nuts from the forest. They're going to be part of the trade goods for you to take back. I thought you might like to join us."

"Yeah! We'd love to," Jahira said.

Magnar raised an eyebrow in her direction.

"I don't like sitting around, remember. I'm glad we have something to do."

"So we have to work for the goods we get in trade," Magnar said.

"We're not the only ones going, right, Samuel?" Samuel nodded. "And it's a lot better than sitting here sweating in this heat."

"Oh, yeah, instead we'll be breaking our backs and sweating in this heat."

"He's a grouch in the morning," Jahira said with a wink at Samuel. "Deep down he's excited."

"So deep down I can't even detect a trace," Magnar muttered.

Jahira smiled.

Three hours later, she was beginning to agree with Magnar.

The shade of the canopy provided a small amount of relief from the blistering sun. Their prize was scattered across the forest floor. Her lower back burned from the constant and prolonged bending. A raw patch had formed on the right side of her neck where the repurposed tarp rubbed against her skin.

"Having fun yet?" Magnar asked, moving to her side from where he'd been collecting several meters away.

Jahira groaned. Muscles groaned right along with her when she stood and pressed her stomach forward while her shoulders pressed back. The fire along her spine turned to cool prickles. "Snack break?" she suggested.

"I've been eating the whole time," Magnar said with a wink.

The "nuts," called that because of their semi-soft and edible interior surrounded by a hard shell, tasted nothing like any nut Jahira had ever eaten before. The initial flavor seemed mild and sweet, but after a few seconds of chewing a distinct spiciness caused her nostrils to flare in anticipation of the heat to follow, but there was no heat.

"They're like the perfect snack, sweet and savory all in one," Jahira said.

"If I die in the middle of the night from some crazy allergic reaction, at least I'll die happy," Magnar said, patting his belly.

"They've been eating these for weeks, right?" Jahira said, a sour feeling taking over her stomach.

"Yeah, don't worry, I'm kidding. Okay, back to work," Magnar said. He downed a swig of water and then chucked her on the shoulder.

Jahira waved a hand back and forth past her ear in an effort to drive away a few hundred insects, which swarmed around her head now that she'd stopped moving. Thankfully they didn't seem to be the biting kind of insects, or they didn't like her smell. Ryan had mentioned something about the humans not giving off the right scent for the bloodsuckers on this planet. Either way, Jahira was grateful for small favors because what they lacked in viciousness, they more than made up for on the sheer annoyance scale.

Remembering the lizards that must be resting above her in the bright leaves, she pushed a handful of the tiny pests towards the sticky trunk of the nearest tree.

"Ten down, ten million to go," she muttered. A long pull of cold water soothed her dry throat.

When she resumed the backbreaking work of collecting the forest's bounty, she began to wonder what else Lusela's group might offer in trade.

CHAPTER 27

Seventeen sleeps since she'd left. Seventeen sleeps alone. Krnar did not like it. He'd spent most of his life feeling like an outsider, and though his status had elevated, he still felt restless inside the confines of his daily life as a Leroni.

With Jahira, there was always something new; new things to learn, new things to see, to think about, to talk about. She'd shown him a new life and he, in turn, was able to share what he knew and see it from an entirely different perspective. With her he didn't feel restless; he felt invigorated.

He missed that feeling.

The end of the stick he held caught fire. He pulled it from the flames and blew it out, rubbed the excess char from the tip, and then returned to practicing the human letters on the surface of a flat rock. Jahira had been teaching him before she left, in exchange for the mind-communication lessons he'd been giving her.

The concept fascinated him. The Leroni had never had a need for creating a written language. They'd had a living vessel full of all of their memories, their stories, and all of their people.

"What are you doing?"

Startled, Krnar rubbed his hand over the symbols, smearing the black char across the rock as well as all over his hand. Relief filled him when he looked up and saw Allnall standing just outside the hearth circle peering over his shoulder.

"Uh, writing," Krnar said. "Jahira has been teaching me the symbols for their words."

"Hmm." Allnall stepped over the stones and squatted beside him. He hadn't waved her in and, had it been anyone else, he'd have been shocked by the rude behavior. Allnall, however, had never been one for propriety.

"Where have you been?" Krnar asked. "I've hardly seen you lately."

"Aw, did you miss me?" Allnall grinned but continued talking, obviously not expecting an answer. "Honestly, I've kind of been hiding."

Krnar trilled and then began to laugh. "Hiding? Hiding from what?"

"From Ellall, the elders, my family...everyone."

"Okay, so why did you come out of hiding today?"

Allnall shifted to make herself more comfortable and helped herself to some fish broth that had been set to cool by the side of the fire.

"Why did you enter the trials, Krnar?" she asked.

Krnar paused, surprised by the question and taking a moment to consider his answer.

"To prove myself," he said.

Allnall nodded and sipped her broth.

Curiosity ate at him. "Seriously, Allnall, say what you have to say."

She tipped her head and pushed against his mind. Krnar let down his mental wall and connected with her thoughts.

I entered the trials to get away, she projected. *Do you remember our conversation outside the cave? I would have left even if I hadn't won. I needed to get away. I expected to die, Krnar. I didn't believe. I never expected to make it back and now, here we are, with more room to move, but still constrained by all the same rules and traditions.*

And that's a bad thing?

Yes! she shouted inside his head and he flinched.

Sorry, she said, much softer. *I can't do it. I want things to be different.*

But they are *different and they will continue to change the longer we are here. In fact, things are so different that there are some who wish we'd never come.*

Yes, I've heard some rumors. They're crazy.

But you're not?

Allnall gave him a look that made his lips twitch with amusement.

Does this mean you're stepping down from The Circle? Krnar asked, half-teasing, half curious.

This means I want to keep moving. I want to see what's out there, not sit in meetings all the time.

Krnar trilled softly. A part of him agreed with this sentiment. Another part of him had come to feel responsible for making all of this work. He wanted to help his people adjust to their new world. Bridging the gap between the humans and Leroni had also become a very personal mission.

What are you going to do? Krnar asked. *Are you leaving?*

I haven't decided exactly. I'm not leaving *leaving. I want to come back, see everyone, tell the stories of the places I've been...I just don't want to be stuck here.*

Krnar nodded. *I can understand that.*

You can?

Yes.

Allnall sighed and her shoulders relaxed.

You were worried about what I'd think? he asked.

I thought you'd be angry if I disappeared and left you with all the responsibility.

Krnar waved his hand in dismissal. *I'm not mad*, he said. *I guess that's part of this new life, you know, being free to make our own choices. We're not physically trapped anymore. That will take some getting used to.*

Allnall trilled in agreement.

Krnar waited while Allnall swallowed another sip of broth then asked, *Where are you going to go?*

I'm not sure, she answered. *Anywhere. Everywhere.*

You should avoid the humans on the first continent if you can. I don't think you'd find a warm welcome there.

Allnall nodded.

Will you go alone? How will we know if you're okay?

I'll probably go alone at first. I don't know of anyone else who wants to just wander the way that I do. I thought, for a while, that you might, but I see you're a little...tied...to this place. Her eyebrows rose above the rim of her bowl.

The word she'd used had more than one meaning in their language. It could mean literally, physically tied to another, or it could mean mated, depending on the context.

Krnar cleared his throat.

That's what I thought, Allnall said. *So, where is Jahira?*

She traveled with Magnar to the first continent. They went to exchange items with the humans there.

Will they return before the snow comes?

They are supposed to be gone one moon. Half of that has passed already.

Why didn't you go?

I needed to be here for Ulletta and Arkan. I've been helping with Mrkon.

Allnall nodded and then tilted her head. *One moon? How can they travel that quickly, and cross the channel?*

Magnar built a boat, Krnar projected an image of the vessel to Allnall. *This carries them on top of the water and they are able to travel much faster than if they walked.*

Boat, she repeated, filing the word away in her mind. *This is something I would like to see.*

Krnar smiled. *Well, when they return, I could show it to you. Do you think you can stick around that long?*

Allnall hissed at him. *Are you trying to trick me?*

Krnar just grinned.

I might be able to tolerate it here for half a moon.

You know where to find me, Krnar said.

Ah, but you don't know where to find me, Allnall replied with a wink. *Thanks for the broth*. She placed her bowl by the fire and was gone once again.

Surprises at every turn, Krnar thought. *What will be next?*

266

"What are these?" Jahira asked, peering into one of the ten full gathering bags Samuel and his friends had brought to their campsite.

"Well, they're leaves," Samuel began.

Jahira looked up and cocked one eyebrow.

"That much I could tell," she said.

"Right. They are, or they contain, a stimulant," Samuel said.

The second eyebrow joined the first near Jahira's hairline.

"Chew 'em or brew 'em! That's what we say!" One of the friends, Mike, she thought he'd said, chimed in.

"Are you dealing drugs?" Magnar asked.

"No," Samuel replied. "More like tea, but stronger. It's almost like coffee."

A quiver of excitement shook Jahira's insides. "Coffee?" she repeated. Her fingers itched to start stuffing leaves into her mouth.

"It doesn't taste much like coffee, but definitely perks you up."

"What do you think?" Magnar directed his question to Jahira.

"Definitely worth a try. We should have Ryan test it—"

"Oh, it's safe," Samuel assured them. "We've been drinking it for weeks. One person did get an itchy throat, but no major reactions."

"As reassuring as that is," Magnar said, rolling his eyes, "I think we'll make sure before we kill off the entire population of Empyrean."

"So, nuts and tea," Jahira said. "Is there more, or is that it for now?"

Samuel shuffled his feet and glanced over his shoulder at his friends. "I think that's it for now. Sorry it's not more. You could double-check with Lusela."

Magnar shrugged.

"I think this is fine for a start. Especially if the tea is safe, and effective, it could become a very popular trade item," Jahira said.

"And the nuts are a perfect supplement for the winter stores," Magnar added.

"I think we have a deal," Jahira announced. "Are you the lucky crew that gets to help us haul all of this to the boat?"

"I volunteered," Samuel said. "The rest of the guys have work."

"Great. We'll head out at dawn tomorrow," Magnar said.

"See you then!" Samuel waved goodbye and then ushered his friends away from the campsite.

Dust filled the air as their departing steps disturbed the dry ground. The cloud of red-brown enveloped Jahira, making her eyes water and irritating her lungs. She coughed and then pulled the collar of her shirt up over her mouth.

"How are we going to carry all of these bags?" Magnar asked.

Six bags of nuts and ten bags of leaves were clustered outside their tent.

"We'll have help, and the leaves are light," Jahira said. "Should we pay a visit to Lusela, let her know we're heading out in the morning?"

"Do we have to?" Magnar asked in his best petulant child voice.

Jahira smiled. "My only consolation is that I'm sure she doesn't enjoy our visits any more than we do," she said.

"Fine. Let me eat something first. I'm pretty sure I won't feel like it after our visit."

Jahira laughed. "Good idea."

They shared a quick meal of eggs wrapped in Samuel's fifth version of flat yellow bread. Jahira banked the fire and then they headed to Lusela's tent.

Many of the inhabitants were sitting around fires outside their huts. The smell of roasting meat and baking grain filled the air. If she closed her eyes, she could have imagined a cozy, welcoming village where everyone smiled and invited them to share a meal. The reality was a sea of staring eyes. No one waved; no one greeted them. A few people had the decency to look abashed, but didn't have the courage to stand out in the crowd of hostility.

"What is up with this?" Magnar whispered out of the corner of his mouth. "Kato and Creed didn't say anything about people acting this way toward them."

"Maybe it's just us," Jahira said.

"Yeah, maybe."

"I'm going to be glad to leave this place behind," Jahira whispered back.

They stopped outside Lusela's doorway and Magnar knocked. The door slid open with a squeak as grain stalks rubbed together.

When Lusela saw them, she crossed her arms over her chest and leaned one shoulder against the door frame. No greeting. No invitation to come inside.

"We wanted to let you know we'll be leaving first thing in the morning," Magnar said.

"Good," Lusela replied.

Magnar and Jahira exchanged a look.

Anger bubbled under the calm surface she struggled to maintain. *Why does this woman always get to me?* Jahira wondered.

"We have six bags of nuts and ten bags of the tea leaves. Was there anything else?"

"Isn't that enough?"

"Holy mother of—"

"It's plenty," Magnar said, cutting off Jahira's curse. "We only wanted to make sure. We're trying to be polite."

"Fine. Samuel and the rest of the crew will meet you in the morning. You can send your trade items back with them."

"Fine."

With a jerk of her opposite shoulder, Lusela pulled her body away from the door frame. Long pale fingers gripped the edge of the door.

"There is one more thing," Jahira said.

Lusela paused, her eyes narrowed.

Magnar's eyes darted from Jahira to Lusela and back again.

Reaching across her body, she pulled the strap of her pack off her shoulder and slid it in front of her. The ripping sound when she opened the top pocket filled the silence. Dark fingers reached in and pulled out a white feather-covered figure.

Flashing green eyes met Lusela's confused stare before Jahira tossed the doll.

Lusela uncrossed her arms and caught it. The line between her brows deepened.

"You can tell whoever left that hanging outside our tent that if anything like this happens again, your little colony can say goodbye to any help from us."

"You don't have the authority to make that kind of threat," Lusela hissed.

"Oh no?" Jahira replied with a tilt of her head. "There's a year-long winter coming up, if you recall. I doubt anyone will be walking to the coast in hip-deep snow, let alone swimming across the channel. Thanks to you, there is no *Falcon* to make a supply run, we had to use the two undamaged solar coils from the smaller ships to keep the *KC* running. That leaves a boat, one boat, and I happen to be pretty tight with the one and only sailor on this entire planet."

Lusela's lip curled before she slammed the door. It bounced off the frame and rebounded so that it stood a quarter open, but Lusela had disappeared into the dark interior.

Jahira's nostrils flared and her temper simmered. Magnar tugged on her upper arm.

"Let's go," he said.

With a nod she shouldered her pack and turned on her heel.

"So, am I staying up all night to make sure she doesn't set fire to our tent while we sleep or are you?" Magnar asked. "I vote you."

"We'll be fine," Jahira said. The combination of adrenaline, anger, and apprehension coursing through her veins made her voice harsher than she'd intended.

"That woman brings out the worst in me," Jahira said. "I shouldn't antagonize her. Look what happened last time I confronted her. I just can't seem to keep my temper in check around her."

"Oh, I don't know. I think righteous anger looks pretty good on you," Magnar said.

One corner of Jahira's mouth quirked upward.

When they returned to the campsite, Jahira busied herself with tidying up the site, rearranging the bags of trade goods, packing and then repacking her backpack.

Finally, Magnar placed a hand on her shoulder. "We'll be fine, Jahira," he said. "Go to sleep."

"You go ahead, I'm not tired."

Magnar sighed but retreated to the tent.

A million thoughts buzzed through her head, all fighting for her attention but none winning the battle.

Take a deep breath, close your eyes, and focus on one thing, one image, until it is perfect in every detail.

She could hear Krnar's deep, calm voice instructing her. Settling on an image of him, she focused, she thought of every detail of his form, posture, expression, clothing, until she had a perfect picture of him glowing slightly behind her eyelids.

Happiness replaced the press of anxiety in her chest.

The fire dwindled and soon the smoke was not thick enough to keep the insects from lighting on her face and search-ing for a home inside her nostrils, ears, or corners of her eyes.

After a crazy flailing dance outside the door to rid herself of the pests, she ducked into the tent and scrambled into her sleeping bag. Magnar's deep breathing, and her detailed image of

Krnar, helped her mind to calm long enough for her body to escape into sleep.

"Time to rise and shine, sleepyhead!" Magnar's voice followed vigorous shaking of the tent walls until Jahira rolled over and slapped the material. "Time to go home!" he called again.

Jahira groaned.

Her eyelids were made of lead and grit coated her eyelashes. When she did finally pry the lids of one eye apart and peek through the crack, she could barely tell which eye was open and which was still shut.

"Is the sun even up yet?" her voice croaked and then she coughed. Every cell of her body protested its removal from the warmth of her sleeping bag. Too tired to do more than shuffle a few steps from the entrance, she might have had half a cheek hidden behind the tent when she squatted to pee.

Magnar smiled and waved.

Jahira flipped him off.

"Maybe we should try that tea," Magnar said, nodding toward the leaves in the nearby bags. "You could really use some caffeine. You're barely tolerable as it is, but first thing in the morning..." Magnar raised his eyebrows and shook his head as if she were a lost cause.

A fire already popped and danced in the fire-pit and Magnar, curse him, bounced around like it was the morning of his birthday party.

"What's with you?" Jahira asked, her voice still raspy with sleep.

"I'm anxious to get back to my boat. She's been sitting there for three days, at least I hope she has. What if the tide pulled her out or some huge sea creature gnawed through the anchor line?"

Magnar's energy proved infectious. After a few minutes of watching Magnar bustle around, Jahira forced herself to get up and help. She wasn't too worried about the boat, but she was eager to get back to the settlement, and to Krnar.

As Jahira collapsed their temporary shelter, the filmy material of the tent wall slid beneath her hand. The sound of approaching footsteps brought her head up. Her eyes narrowed and a rocket of apprehension shot through her when she saw a rough looking group stop beside their fire.

"Can I help you?" Magnar asked.

"Lusela sent us to help," the man in front answered.

"Oh, you're the crew," Magnar said. "Do you have everything you need? It'll be about a three-day trip for you to get there and back."

The man half turned and hooked a thumb at the pack on his back.

"Okay, great, well if you could all help carry these bags that'd be a big help." Magnar gestured toward the sacks of nuts and leaves. "Looks like two each, including Jahira and I...oh, by the way, I'm Magnar," Magnar held out his hand.

The first man took it and shook. "Ted," he said.

Magnar nodded and moved to the next person.

"Ron."

And he continued down the line.

"April."

"Lane."

"Oren."

"Nice to meet all of you," Magnar said. "This is Jahira."

After brushing her hands on the thighs of her pants, Jahira took her turn moving down the line, shaking hands and nodding.

"We just have to finish packing up the tent and we'll be ready to go," Jahira said.

"While you're finishing with the tent, I'm going to harness my grain-eater," Ron said before glancing at Ted who nodded.

"You're bringing a herd beast?" Magnar asked.

"To carry the stuff," Ron said before turning and walking away.

"Oh wow, you can get them to carry loads for you?" Magnar said. "That will sure help on the way back."

Jahira resumed breaking down the tent while Magnar doused the fire.

Steam rose in a hiss. Light began to creep up the horizon. The world remained eerily quiet until a familiar mop of black hair bounced onto the scene.

"Hey, great, you're still here!" Samuel bounded into the camp, beaming white smile and sparkling brown eyes fully alert.

"Someone had their tea this morning," Jahira grumbled.

Samuel either didn't hear her or wasn't fazed by her muttering. "I was afraid you'd leave without me!"

"You're coming, too?" April asked.

"Of course! I wouldn't miss it!"

"You have work to do here, Samuel," Ted said.

Samuel frowned at Ted. "I switched watches with Tandy, I'm good for a few days," he replied.

A look passed between Ted and April that sent a tendril of unease crawling through Jahira's stomach.

Ted shrugged and tossed a bag of leaves to Samuel. "Make yourself useful then," Ted said.

Samuel grinned and winked at Jahira.

Jahira had to admit, she felt relieved to have at least one friendly face in the group.

A distinct musk preceded the return of Ron and a medium-sized srlen.

The crew burst into action, hauling bags, tying them together, and draping the connected sacks over the animal's back. The creature shuffled its feet and bumped Ron in the shoulder with its nose a few times, but otherwise remained unbelievably placid.

Eight bags hung suspended on either side of the grain-eater's back, leaving one for each of the humans.

"Well, hey, that worked out well," Magnar said.

Eyes shifted, but only Samuel smiled.

The uneasy feeling in the pit of Jahira's stomach clenched tighter, making her feel nauseated.

Why hadn't Samuel's friends been chosen for the job?

CHAPTER 29

Frustration exploded through Tllomell's body. She growled and kicked a fallen log, then immediately regretted her choice when pain shot up her leg.

She couldn't find Grollon anywhere.

The Marked had been eluding her for a handful of suns. She'd even grown desperate enough to sneak up close to one of the silver mountains and peer into its cavernous mouth.

"Where is he?" she yelled.

"Who?"

Tllomell jumped and turned toward the sound of the voice. "Krnar," she said in surprise.

"You were looking for me?"

"No, I was looking for Grollon."

"Oh, me, too. Any luck?"

"No, none at all." Tllomell's fists clenched and she eyed the log, considering another kick despite the lingering pain.

A low growl rumbled from Krnar's chest and Tllomell felt a moment of satisfaction that he sounded as frustrated as she felt.

His eyes scanned the horizon before landing on hers. "I guess I'll check my snares then," he said. "Care to join me?"

Tllomell's mind itched. She wanted to link with him, to know what he was feeling, to determine his intention in asking her. Was it simply because she happened to be here and it was more convenient than returning to find Arkan? Did he actually *want* her company? The trouble was, if she could feel *his* emotions, he would also be able to feel hers.

"Okay," she finally said.

"Great, this way," Krnar said, waving her into the dancing forest.

Light and shadow chased each other over roots and dried leaves. Day birds cheeped and hooted, insects whined past her ears and tickled her fur. The air held a hint of the familiar smell of cold, teasing her like bait in the sunlight.

An animal skittered through the underbrush, startling her. She trilled and shifted closer to Krnar, bumping his arm accidentally. "Sorry," she mumbled, the heat of embarrassment flushing her face.

"It's okay. I understand. My first time in the forest to the north, I had to stop and close my eyes, even plug my ears, many times. It was too overwhelming. You are doing very well."

The heat from her face crept downward toward her middle.

"Not much farther now," Krnar said.

Without warning, Krnar stopped in his tracks. He drew his spear.

The hackles on Tllomell's neck rose and she imitated his action but saw no threat.

"What is it?" she hissed.

They naturally moved to place their backs to each other and began to circle.

Too quiet, Krnar projected.

Tllomell's ears twitched. Silence dominated where, typically, there was an annoying level of noise.

What does it mean? Tllomell asked.

I don't know, but I don't think it's good.

A thump to Tllomell's right brought them both around to face the threat.

"Mllkallo," Krnar whispered.

Bright yellow eyes pierced them. Dark fur with patches of deep purple where the light hit allowed the creature to blend perfectly with the canopy overhead. Muscles bunched beneath the sleek coat when the animal sidestepped. Paws the size of Tllomell's face were tipped with wicked-looking claws.

How many times have one of these creatures been watching me without my knowing? she wondered.

She and Krnar instinctively stepped away from one another and began to slowly circle the mllkallo in opposite directions.

The mllkallo took a step backward, momentarily unsure when one target turned to two.

With her free hand, Tllomell drew her belt knife. Krnar mirrored her action.

The mllkallo's head swiveled from one hunter to the next. A deep growl vibrated through the animal's chest, followed by a sharp-toothed snarl.

Krnar slowly drew back his spear, getting his arm into a throw-ready position. When he was in position, Tllomell would distract the animal, just like hunting a krska.

The animal belted out an ear-splitting yowl that froze Tllomell's blood.

A second thump drew her eyes to the left.

Another mllkallo, she projected.

Pllat, Krnar said. *I'll focus on this one. You take the second.*

She didn't dare turn her back to the first animal, but she did open her stance so that both were visible.

The second mllkallo began to circle outside the range of her peripheral vision.

Taking a step back to keep both in her sights, her palms began to sweat and her heart stuttered an irregular rhythm.

A snarl tore through the air and the first mllkallo pounced. Flashes of dark and white fur rolled out of her line of sight.

Chest tightening with fear, she faced the second animal. *I am on my own.*

She sidestepped until one of the tall roots scraped against her back.

Her mllkallo paced, eyes shifting from her to the struggle that Tllomell could hear but not see.

Tllomell tested the weight of her spear and flexed the fingers that wrapped around the hilt of her knife.

Krnar's scream tore through her like a wound. Without thinking, she looked. The mllkallo's jaws clamped down on Krnar's shoulder, blood soaked his fur.

The small hairs on the back of her neck tingled, alerting her to her own predicament.

Her animal had stopped pacing. Its muscles bunched and lips curled back from long pointed teeth.

The mllkallo leaped. Claws extended, aiming for her face.

Tllomell ducked, thrust her knife upward, and then rolled. Her mind registered the resistance when her knife caught some part of the animal then slid away.

White-hot pain seared down her back. The mllkallo had caught her as well.

Jumping to her feet, she faced her opponent again.

It growled and then whined. Its eyes turned to the first mllkallo.

Tllomell took advantage of its distraction. She aimed her spear and loosed, piercing the animal in the left flank. It mewled and then turned to her with death in its eyes.

The animal charged, bowling her over. Knives pierced her thigh in a dozen places. For a heartbeat she felt nothing, as if her body couldn't bring itself to register the level of pain she knew would come.

Her next breath came out in a scream when searing fire dove into her flesh and spread through her entire body.

She felt like she might throw up. The knives released, but the pain didn't stop. In fact, it seemed to intensify.

Blinking through hazy vision, she watched as two huge yellow eyes moved up the length of her body.

Years of training kicked in, fueled by a hefty dose of not wanting to die. Fingers gripped the hilt of her knife.

Her predator sniffed, pawed her, and finally opened its mouth to bite down on her throat.

The blade of her knife drove into the center of one large yellow eye. A yowl of misery blew out her eardrums.

The mllkallo backed away, thrashing and pawing at the knife protruding from its eye.

A second spear thunked into the animal's side. Seconds later it fell to the ground and all noise ceased.

Tllomell's chest rose and fell in rapid succession. Cold crept up the length of her body and her limbs began to shake.

"Tllomell, can you hear me?"

Tllomell blinked and looked toward the voice. A white head floated above a red body.

"Krnar?"

"You have to get up. We have to get to an oranlo."

"Can't walk," she groaned.

"Of course you can," he said.

A ripping sound preceded more pain jolting through her leg.

Tllomell hissed but couldn't move. When the pressure on her wound escalated, a scream ripped her throat.

"Remember the Great Ice?" Krnar's voice was low and calm. "Remember when you fell? You had a broken ankle, yet you climbed out of the crevasse and walked back home. You are incredibly strong. This is nothing."

"Doesn't feel like nothing," she said through gritted teeth.

"Well, then get up and help me, or I'm going to bleed out."

That triggered something inside her. Forcing her torso upright and ignoring the tears that streamed from her eyes, she focused on Krnar.

"What can I do?"

"I need you to bind my shoulder."

Tllomell took the hide he held out and then looked at his shoulder.

Bile rose in her throat but she forced it down. Flesh had been ripped from bone and flaps of skin hung from his arm. "Aruvel have mercy," she breathed.

"Yours doesn't look much better," he said. "Can you wrap it?"

She nodded. Tllomell used his knife to cut the hide she held into strips. With gentle fingers, she did her best to hold the skin in place while the opposite hand wound the bandage. Once she reached the end of the wrappings, she pierced several layers with a lizard claw from her belt and finally, wound a length of gut line over the top of the wrapping, and tied off the ends.

"That should hold until we get back," she said. "Can you make it?"

Krnar didn't respond. Tllomell's eyes traveled to his face. His eyes were closed and his nostrils were flared. His throat convulsed in an effort to hold down the contents of his stomach.

We'll never make it, she thought.

She forced herself to stand, and then paused to ward off the stars that whirled behind her eyes. "Come on, Krnar." With both hands together she pulled his good arm until he rose beside her.

She slid his knife into the sheath on his belt. Together they hobbled over to the fallen mllkallo and took turns supporting each other while they drew their weapons from its flesh.

"What do we do with them?" Tllomell asked.

"We'll have to leave them for now," Krnar said. "We'll come back as soon as we're able."

"Do you think they'll still be here?"

"Unless there's another mllkallo waiting to drag them off and feast on their remains, most of them will still be here. Either way, we can't afford to wait."

With a grimace of pain and determination, Tllomell supported as much of her weight as possible with her spear and took a quick hop-step with her bad leg.

"We'll never make it in time that way," Krnar said. "May I?"

Tllomell nodded, giving him permission to touch her.

After crouching and sliding her arm around his neck, Krnar lifted her weight on his good shoulder. Like a post-apocalyptic three-legged race, they made their way. Their pace wouldn't win any contests; that was certain. Tllomell tried to keep her mind off the pain searing up her leg and spreading fire across her back by contorting her wrist to be sure not to brush against Krnar's injured shoulder.

Ragged breaths intermingled and an occasional involuntary trill escaped from one or the other of them. Tllomell had no idea where they were, only a vague idea that, through the haze of pain and fatigue, they were aiming for the river.

Sweat rolled through her fur, tickling her cold, clammy skin. Her good leg shook like a dancing leaf and her heart felt like it might explode. She almost wished it would, so this torture would end.

Krnar grunted.

Tllomell blinked hard two times, making a serious effort to focus. "The river," she hissed.

Krnar grunted again.

They stumbled and half slid down the embankment. When her foot hit a rock and stopped her forward movement, the pain doubled her over. Tllomell dry-heaved over the lapping shore of the cold clear water while Krnar collapsed beside her.

Not going to make it, he projected.

Once the convulsions stopped, Tllomell sipped handfuls of water and then eased her body back against the rocks.

Seems like a nice place to die, she replied.

A rumbling chuckle preceded a harsh cough from Krnar and then silence.

Half a day, or half a moon, later Tllomell felt a push against her mind. At first she thought it was Krnar, but then the push came again. She opened to a new link and felt curiosity, then concern.

Tllomell?

Plldoll! Where are you?

Krag and I are fishing upriver. I think I see you both. What's wrong?

We need help.

Heartbeats later, trills of worry surrounded her. "What happened? Are you okay? You're both covered in blood!"

Tllomell didn't respond. Every particle of energy she'd been clinging to dissipated. Her muscles relaxed. She literally could not move if she tried.

"Krag is going back to get help. They'll bring some of Aruvel's soul to heal the wounds. Try to drink this."

Tllomell felt cold water dribble over her lips. The tip of her tongue peeked out to lick the moisture away. Her body craved more but it hurt to swallow. It hurt to breathe.

Is Krnar okay? she asked.

He'll be fine; we're going to get help. You're both going to be fine.

Tllomell drifted in and out of consciousness. Cool water filling her mouth would wake her, and then the world would disappear again.

Sudden blinding pain jolted her awake and she screamed in protest.

"It's okay, Tllomell. I'm here. Krag has you. We're carrying you back to the pools. You're going to be okay." Plldoll's soothing voice continued to ramble all the way to the grove.

With her last thread of awareness, she felt warm liquid encase her body. She sighed in pure bliss until the soothing warmth became searing fire burning through leg and up her back until she passed out.

When consciousness returned, she was lying in an oranlo, body hidden by opaque silver fluid. Her head rested on soft grass. A single white puff floated in the blue sky above her.

The throbbing pain in her leg had subsided to a subtle second heartbeat and she could not feel her back. She hoped that was a good thing.

"You okay?"

Tllomell tilted her head to the side. Two arm lengths away, Krnar's head protruded from the still, mirrored surface. "Yes, I think so. You?"

"Sore, but alive."

Tllomell rolled her head upright.

"Thank you for wrapping my shoulder," Krnar said. "I think I will still have use of it."

"You're welcome," Tllomell said. "Thank you, too. I wouldn't have made it back without you."

"That's what partners do," he said.

The word *partners* sent a shock through her system.

"Partners?" she echoed.

"We were today," Krnar said. "We worked well together. Arkan organized a group to retrieve the mllkallo. Tonight we will feast and tell the story of our hunt."

"Tonight," she said. "Is it still the same day?"

Krnar's deep chuckle sent a ripple through the water. "Seems like much longer, doesn't it?"

Lifting her hands from the pool and placing them behind her on the solid ground, Tllomell lifted her body up and back, pulling herself from Aruvel's soul.

Steeling herself for the first look at the damage, she took a deep breath and looked down at her leg. Stripes of furless, pale flesh stared back at her.

"Is my back the same?" she asked, turning slightly so that Krnar could see her back.

Krnar projected an image of her back.

Four stripes ran from her right shoulder to just below her last rib on the left side.

"Lovely," she muttered.

"Good thing we're not back at the cave. Your flesh would freeze and blacken where the fur did not cover."

"Thank you for that, Krnar."

She shifted forward and saw Krnar grinning.

"Can you move your thigh?" he asked, nodding toward the injured leg.

Tllomell bent and then extended the knee, flexing and relaxing the muscle. "It's sore, and the skin feels too tight when it stretches, but I think I will be able to walk."

"Good."

"I'm incredibly thirsty," Tllomell said.

Krnar tipped his head toward the grass behind her. "Food and water were left while you were asleep."

Taking the bowls in her lap, she forced herself to take small bites and small sips. Her stomach growled, begging for more, but her head knew better than her stomach.

"There is no meat," she said. "I need meat."

"Tonight," Krnar said. "You will have the choice pieces from your mllkallo."

"Tonight," Tllomell said.

Today they were partners, tonight they would be honored together and tell the story of their hunt. She carefully reviewed the details of the morning while she took slow sips of broth and water to regain her strength.

She savored the moment and tried to make it last.

Who knew what tomorrow might bring?

Nicole L. Bates

By the end of the first day of travel, Jahira felt completely wrung out. Samuel hadn't stopped talking the entire day. He seemed determined to get Jahira and Magnar interacting with the group from Lusela's settlement. She'd answered direct questions and tried to be polite, but honestly, they made her uneasy.

Ted had a tendency to draw his gun every time a bird squawked, which made everyone else jump and cower.

Simply the fact that he had a gun added to her jittery nerves. She'd gotten out of the habit of carrying a gun. She always had her knife, but she wanted to learn to live off the land, not blow it to pieces. Krnar taught her to pay attention to the world around her, like he did, to hunt and fish and be able to survive without the technology that wouldn't be around forever. Whenever she brought a gun hunting with him, she felt like a kid who'd brought a fire hose to a squirt gun party.

Ted clearly had a different philosophy.

"So the Leroni just sleep outside? No shelter or anything?" Samuel asked as part of his ongoing interrogation.

"Well, they used to live in caves, a cave, so I think they would like shelter, but there are no caves in or around the silver trees," Jahira explained. "We offered our extra tents, or to help them build sod houses, but they declined. They're well adapted for the elements, so I don't think they're suffering—maybe just inconvenienced when it rains."

"Right. Hmmm. And they eat fish and meat, no vegetables?"

"They eat, or ate, a lot of sea weed, *kllugall* they call it, but that was really the only thing even close to a vegetable that grew where they were. They're not used to them. I'm sure they'll come around."

"And they can read minds and talk to each other with their minds, right?"

Ted, Ron, April, Oren, and Lane had fallen silent when Samuel began asking about the Leroni. Now she was sure they'd moved closer as well.

"They can communicate telepathically," she said. "But they can block each other out as well."

"Can we block them out?" Samuel asked.

"Not yet, but I believe we can learn to."

April's eyes cut to them and then straight ahead.

"So, Samuel, do you have family here or did they stay behind at Empyrean?" Magnar asked.

Jahira shot him a *thank-you* look.

Samuel, however, clammed up for the first time in three days. "No," he said, and then lengthened his stride. "I better check ahead and make sure it's clear."

Magnar raised his eyebrows at Jahira. She quirked the corner of her mouth and shrugged one shoulder in a *you got me* expression.

About half an hour later Samuel came bounding back, grin restored. "I saw it! We're almost there!"

Without a word, everyone picked up their pace.

Jahira kept her eyes on the horizon. An exhale of profound relief blew from her lungs when she saw the last of the day's light glinting off the boat's solar panels like a signal mirror.

"Thank goodness," Magnar breathed.

"It's so awesome!" Samuel yelled and ran ahead.

Magnar was right on his heels.

By the time Jahira and the southerners reached the shoreline, Magnar and Samuel had already waded out to the anchored boat and scrambled aboard. Samuel waved from the deck.

"How are we going to do this?" Jahira called.

Magnar hoisted a plank over the railing and Samuel helped him extend the layers until they melded together to form a smooth ramp down to the sand in front of Jahira's feet. With an audible snap, Magnar attached his end to the railing, then he and Samuel disappeared.

Moments later they reappeared with one of the four crates.

Jahira adjusted the base of the ramp in order to reduce the angle and, hopefully, slow the crate's descent. After taking off her boots and socks, she rolled her pant legs up to her knees and waded into knee-deep water so that she could stand at the half-way point.

Ted joined her on the opposite side of the ramp. Lane and Oren waited at the base of the ramp, which rested in the sand.

"Go ahead!" Jahira called.

The first crate came sliding toward her face. Jahira held her hands out, caught the front and side, and then she and Ted sent it on its way to Lane and Oren.

"Heads up!" Magnar called before sending the next crate their way.

Once all four were safely on the sand, Magnar and Samuel climbed down the ladder and joined the rest of the crew on the beach.

Jahira's stomach growled loud enough that Magnar could hear.

"We should camp here for the night and transfer the rest in the morning," Magnar said.

Jahira nodded and Magnar moved to open the crates.

Lavender streaks shot through the sky, lighting the tops of the clouds. The reflection off the water doubled the brilliance.

Jahira stood staring, soaking in the view and the cool breeze sliding over the water from the north.

"Hands up and you'll get to see the next sunrise."

Chills raced up the back of Jahira's arms. Slowly, she lifted her hands, fingers spread, stopping next to either ear.

Out of the corners of her eyes she saw Magnar, knees in the sand and hands also raised. Lane held a gun to the back of his head.

Their guns didn't use bullets like the old-fashioned weapons of the same name. They were laser guns that shot concentrated balls of heat. The wounds were typically cauterized as they were made. Death had more to do with the location of the shot than the amount of blood lost afterward. Right now, Lane's weapon was aimed to kill.

"Hey! Stop! What are you doing?" Samuel, who was standing between April and Oren, started forward.

April's leg shot out and tripped the boy. Oren brought the hilt of his knife down on Samuel's temple.

"Samuel," Jahira breathed.

"It'll be better this way, more believable, if one of our own goes down, too."

Jahira's heart slammed against her ribs. *"Goes down,"* she repeated. "What are you planning to do?"

By this time she'd deduced that Ted was the one standing behind her. Trigger-happy Ted. Fantastic. He didn't bother to answer her question.

"Who do you think will bring your supplies from the settlement for the next year—"

"We will," Ted interrupted. "We'll have the boat, we'll decide when we get supplies."

"So, Lusela talked you into sabotage, stealing, and murder." She was scrambling, trying to buy some time while she figured out how to free herself and Magnar while outnumbered and outgunned.

"Lusela doesn't know anything about this."

A small kernel of relief bloomed, but quickly died again. If Lusela didn't know, they'd come up with the idea themselves, which meant they were less likely to feel guilty about their actions, and less likely to be talked out of following through with whatever it was they had planned.

"Lusela might not be happy that you destroyed relations with Empyrean. You're going to need their help."

"We don't need help from anyone and we aren't destroying anything. You and your friend had a tragic accident. We'll tell them all about how we tried to help but couldn't save you."

Adrenaline spiked, making her feel antsy with the need to do something. "And how will you drive the boat without us?" she asked.

"Your friend there is going to teach us, or we kill you."

She thought she heard a smile in Ted's voice. Sand crunched when Ted moved around to stand face to face with her. The barrel of his gun pointed between her eyes.

Rough hands forced her wrists down and behind her back, and then bound them with thick, flexible cord.

"Ron will stay here and keep an eye on you while the rest of us get our boating lesson," Ted lowered his gun.

Jahira dared to glance to the side.

April had a knee in Samuel's back, her fingers tied off a series of knots in the cord that bound his wrists and ankles.

Magnar's wrists were also bound, but not his feet. Lane and Oren each gripped one of his biceps. Lane kept a gun pointed at Magnar's temple.

"I'm going to need my hands to climb up and to show you how everything works," Magnar said, casting a glance in Jahira's direction as he passed.

"I'm sure we can figure it out," Ted said. "We fixed the ships for a living. I think we know more about the parts than you do."

The four men waded into the shallows. Several minutes passed as they tried to figure out a way to get Magnar up the ladder with his hands tied behind him. They finally devised a system of ropes under his arms that Lane and Oren could pull from the top while Magnar stepped from rung to rung. Ted climbed up last.

The men disappeared into the flying bridge.

If I'm going to do something, now's the time, Jahira thought.

She could definitely take Ron, maybe even with her hands tied. What about April, though? By the time she took Ron down, April would have plenty of time to intervene. Even if she got lucky and knocked them both out, what would she do against three guys with guns? They might shoot Magnar before she could take them all down.

Her planning came to a halt when a fingertip traced the skin on the back of her neck.

"You sure are a pretty one," Ron said.

Shit, Jahira thought. *One of* those *degenerates*. Her mind quickly switched gears to how much pain she could inflict on Ron before April shot her.

"Too bad you went and spoiled yourself with one of those furry freaks," Ron whispered against her ear. "Who knows what kind of diseases they're carryin'?"

And...chalk one up to interspecies relations, she thought, tensing in an effort to prevent contact in any form.

April eyed them from her station over Samuel's motionless body.

While she focused on a plan and tuned out Ron's muttering about "mind-controlling alien abominations," Magnar and his three guards appeared at the railing.

She and Magnar locked eyes. She'd never wished so hard to have the ability to connect with his mind.

Did he have a plan? Watching for any signs of impending action, she tested her bonds.

"Move," Ron said, shoving her toward the fire that April had started.

Jahira stumbled, caught herself, and continued across the sand, seething.

"Sit," Ron commanded.

She lowered her body to her knees and rested on her heels, a better position for quick movement than sitting. She was close enough now that she could see Samuel's back rising and falling. Little puffs of sand stirred when he exhaled.

I'm sorry I said you were a coward, she thought. *Please wake up.*

Magnar dropped to his knees beside her.

They were back several feet from the fire. Ron remained on guard in front of them while Ted, Lane, Oren, and April took seats around the fire and opened packs of the vegetables from the crate they'd just taken off the boat.

"Kind *and* selfless," Magnar whispered.

"Hey! No talking or I'll shut you up for good!" Ron threatened.

Once he'd turned his attention back to the fire, Jahira rolled her eyes.

Over a fine meal of dried meat and roasted vegetables, their captors discussed their fate.

"We need to ransom them," April said. "We'll get a lot more in trade goods for *them* than we will for a few bags of nuts."

"True, but then they'll never trade with us again," Ted replied.

"I thought we were just going to shoot them and make it look like an accident," Lane said.

"What if someone finds the bodies?" April argued.

"Who's gonna find the bodies?" Lane replied.

"I don't know, someone might," April muttered.

"These continents are huge and there aren't that many people wandering around. No one's ever going to find them," Oren chimed in.

"I agree with April—we'll get a lot more for ransom *and* we'll have the boat. After that, I say we never visit those traitors again," Ron said.

Jahira's innards clenched. It was strange to listen to someone plotting your murder, by far the most surreal thing she'd ever experienced.

Samuel groaned.

Leaning forward, Jahira tried to position herself close to his head without falling on top of him. "Samuel, can you hear me?"

"I said *no talking!*"

Jahira sat up to see Ron's face looming in front of her.

Before she could react, pain exploded across her face. Hot liquid gushed over her lips. She gagged, and then spit. Gobs of red blood hit the sand.

Magnar yelled and surged to his feet.

A body rose from beside the fire and moved toward Magnar.

Jahira tried to yell a warning but couldn't get any words past the mouth full of blood.

A gun slammed into the back of Magnar's head.

Magnar pitched forward, but instead of lying inert in the sand, he rolled and came up on his feet.

Lane's gun pointed at his face.

Lane and Magnar stared each other down.

Cold fear sent shivers through Jahira's body. This was it. She was going to see her friend die right in front of her face.

"You're no better than she is," Lane hissed. "Best friends with one of them furred freaks. Even went and got matching tattoos." Lane pressed the tip of his weapon against Magnar's scars.

"He doesn't have fur, he has wings, you idiot."

Lane's weapon dropped and his opposite fist rose, flying toward Magar's jaw.

Magnar dropped to one knee and then sprang up, ramming his shoulder into Lane's torso, knocking him on his back in the sand.

The second Jahira saw that Magnar was going to take the offensive, she pushed upward and knocked Ron to the sand.

While her weight held him down, she pulled her bound hands under her butt, behind her legs, and around her feet.

Ted, Oren, and April stood frozen with indecision. Eyes darted between the two skirmishes, trying to decide who needed help.

Ted began to move toward Lane and Magnar.

April moved toward Jahira and Ron.

Using her bound hands together, Jahira pulled her knife from her belt and sliced through Samuel's bonds; his eyes were wide open now. He rolled to his back as soon as he was free.

April charged. Samuel intercepted April, but he'd hardly had time to recover; he wasn't moving too fast.

Jahira slammed her forehead into Ron's nose to keep him down.

While he howled and thrashed, she rolled off, thrust the tip of her knife in the sand, and braced the hilt with one knee.

Jahira pushed the cord that bound her hands against the blade of her knife, slicing through, and then grabbed the hilt with her right hand.

Three to five, those aren't terrible odds, Jahira thought. *Too bad they have guns.*

Magnar had been holding his own against Lane, but Ted had joined the fray and now had Magnar pinned.

Ron continued to cry like a little baby, and Oren had finally made a decision. He started toward her. She guessed she had five seconds.

Without giving it too much thought, Jahira flipped her knife so her blade was in her hand, drew back and threw.

The blade spun through the air until the tip sunk into Ted's hand.

With a yell somewhere between pain and fury, Ted lost his grip on Magnar.

Magnar shoved a shoulder into the man's gut and stepped away.

Jahira dove and tackled Oren. Then fire ripped through her leg. She came down on top of Oren, groaning. A body slammed into her back. Sandwiched between two sweaty chests, she was actually thankful she couldn't smell at that moment. Moving her hips, she tried to shift her weight to throw the top person off.

Something pounded against the wound on her leg, making her gag as cold sweat covered her body.

She couldn't see Magnar or Samuel.

This cannot be how I die, she thought.

CHAPTER 31

Her shoulders were wrenched up and back. Thankfully the weight lifted from her body as well. Jahira inhaled through her mouth, tasting fresh blood on her tongue.

Oren scrambled up and away from her while someone, Ron, she guessed, since April had Samuel once again pinned in the sand, bound her briefly free wrists.

This time he didn't stop with the wrists. Cord bit into the flesh of her ankles and her back bowed when the cord between her wrists and ankles tightened.

"Can we kill them now?" Lane asked. "I told you they would be more trouble than they're worth."

Lane and Ted dumped Magnar on the ground beside her. His bindings matched hers.

"Sorry," Magnar whispered.

"No apologies," Jahira replied. "I would have done the same."

"Shut up," Ted said.

He'd come to a stop in front of Jahira. The tip of her knife dripped with his blood. The blade moved toward her. Jahira swallowed a lump in her throat and her nostrils flared.

The flat of the blade swiped along the arm of her shirt. Ted flipped it and cleaned the other side. Finally, he slid the knife into his belt and spit in the sand in front of her.

Jahira's shoulders sagged when he turned and joined the rest of his crew. They huddled several feet away, arguing in hissed whispers. Jahira couldn't make out any words, but felt confident that she knew what they were discussing.

One and a half of the planet's moons lit the sky tonight. Waves gently lapped against the shore. A northern breeze kept the worst of the bugs away. It would have been a really pleasant evening if she weren't contorted into an unnatural position that had every fiber of her body screaming in protest. The blood on her face dried and hardened. It itched like a thousand bug bites and she couldn't get any part of her body close enough to rub her face against.

Maybe she could rub the blood off on Magnar.

Before she had a chance to ask, the group broke apart.

They sat back around the fire and resumed their interrupted meal, or, in Ron's case, finally got a chance to eat.

So they're going to torture us before they kill us, Jahira thought.

Exhaustion pulled at her eyelids but pain, thirst, and hunger fought back with a vengeance. She tried shifting her position to ease the aches all over her body that were threatening to tighten into painful cramps.

"Quit moving," Ted said around a mouthful of food.

"Go to hell," Jahira hissed back.

Samuel's eyes widened and darted between her and Ted.

Sorry, kid, she thought.

Ted stood and walked over until he loomed over her. "I really don't think you're in a position to speak to me that way," he said, his voice unnervingly calm. "My hand hurts and pain makes me grouchy."

Magnar flashed her a warning look but she couldn't stop herself. It wasn't in her nature to go down without a fight.

"Yeah, well, my entire body hurts and pain pisses me off," Jahira replied.

Ted chuckled. He drew her knife and crouched down in front of her, blade twisting in front of her eyes. "We decided to ransom you," he said. "The General will pay well to see you two safe. The bonus is we have a couple of weeks to play before we arrive."

The blade inched forward until Jahira could feel the cold metal against her cheek. "I think they'll still pay even if you're missing a little skin," he said.

A stripe of fire bloomed along her jaw.

"Leave her alone," Magnar hissed, struggling to roll up to his knees.

"What are you gonna do about it, freak?"

Ted's eyes went wide before he doubled over. The knife fell from his fingers and his body fell against Jahira's chest, knocking her to the ground.

Ted rolled and curled into a fetal position. The heels of his hands pressed against his temples.

"What's going on?" Jahira asked. "Did you do that?"

"No, not me," Magnar said. "No idea."

"Look," Samuel whispered.

His chin jutted toward the fire where Lane, April, Oren, and Ron were all curled up like Ted.

Jahira scanned the dark and caught a glimpse of a faint blue-white glow.

"Krnar?" she said with mingled hope and disbelief.

"No," Magnar said. "Grollon."

The old man's wings were spread wide. He approached the fire like an avenging angel with blue eyes burning.

Jahira glanced back over at Ted. He continued to grip his head while his body writhed in the sand.

Ice-blue eyes appeared above her. Grollon picked her knife up out of the sand. "Are you well?" Grollon asked as he cut her bonds.

"I'll live," Jahira replied.

Her limbs went limp once the tension of the bindings released. Everything hurt so much that she just lay there in the sand, breathing through the pain. But now, at least, it was a good hurt.

Grollon moved to Magnar and cut him loose, then stood over Samuel.

"This one?" he asked.

Samuel's mouth gaped and the whites were visible all the way around his dark eyes.

"Him, too," Magnar replied. "He helped us."

It took several minutes before Jahira could force her body to cooperate. Pins and needles tingled through her arms and legs, making each movement an agony of sensation.

"What are you doing to them?" Samuel asked, standing on unsteady legs and staring at the contorted figures around the fire.

"I have them incapacitated for now," Grollon said. "I will give you time to get your things and leave before I release them."

"How did you know to come?" Magnar asked. "How did you even get here in time?"

"I flew," Grollon replied, flexing his shoulders in a way that made his wings spread.

"Those things still work?" Magnar asked.

"Not as well as they once did, but well enough."

Magnar clapped Grollon on the shoulder. "Thank you, my friend."

Grollon nodded.

"Is this part of that atonement thing you were telling me about?" Magnar asked.

Jahira's brow furrowed.

"Yours is the first life I have saved, instead of taken," Grollon said. "And they," he added, nodding toward the downed crew, "are the first I have spared when I wanted to kill. That must count for something."

"We can't leave you here," Jahira said to Grollon.

"Wait across the channel," Grollon said. "I will meet you there."

Jahira nodded and began to gather her things.

"What about you, Samuel?" Magnar asked. "Are you coming with us?"

Samuel shuffled his feet and cleared his throat. "As much as I'd like to, I think I need to stay," he said. "If I start now I can make it back before they do, and tell Lusela what happened."

"Not tonight," Magnar protested. "You need to rest."

"There's no way I'll be sleeping with them anywhere near me," Samuel said. "I think it's best to just get back."

"You know they're going to spin this to make us look like the bad guys, right?" Magnar said.

"Not everyone there is evil," Samuel said. "They might be more afraid of...them," Samuel tipped his head toward Grollon, "but they won't think it's okay, what they did to you, or what they planned to do, stealing the boat and ransoming you two."

Doubt filled her, but Jahira didn't voice it. She decided Samuel wasn't a coward, just naïve. There was no way Lusela would forgive this.

"I'll take the grain-eater and the supplies," Samuel said.

"Alright," Magnar said, nodding and clapping the boy on the shoulder. "Let me help you load the supplies.

"Grollon," Magnar said, turning to the old man. "How long can you hold them? Can you give Samuel a head start?"

"Yes." Grollon sat in the sand cross-legged and closed his eyes.

With the speed of adrenaline-infused systems, they packed the grain-eater and sent Samuel on his way.

"That's a very brave young man," Magnar said.

"Yes, a very brave, very likeable young man," Jahira said.

317

A flash of white teeth in the dark greeted her statement when Magnar grinned at her before they hauled their trade goods onto the boat. "See you on the other side!" Magnar called.

Grollon raised a hand in farewell.

Suddenly Jahira's limbs felt like lead weights and her eyes begged to close.

"You said you were shot, too," Jahira said, trying to talk to keep herself awake. "Are you okay? Where were you shot?"

"Just grazed my thigh," Magnar said. "I'm fine."

Jahira fished through her pack until she found some dried meat. Bolts of pain shot through her nose every time she chewed. "I'm going to need you to reset my nose," Jahira said reluctantly.

"Yeah, it's awful," Magnar said. "It can't wait until we get back to Medic?"

"You know it can't," Jahira said. "In two weeks it will have grown crooked."

"Yeah, but Medic will have pain meds and...doctor stuff."

"There are pain meds in the emergency kit I packed."

"Crap."

"It's going to be a lot worse for me, I promise."

Magnar nodded. "As soon as we cross the channel."

Jahira meant to nod but her chin decided to stay on her chest. She didn't bother to lift it until Magnar bumped her shoulder.

"We made it," he said. "I need you to help me with the anchor."

Forcing her body to move, she shuffled to the bow and released the anchor. Turning, she gave Magnar a thumbs-up. He cut the engine and joined her.

"Alright, let's take care of that nose," he said.

Jahira winced, just thinking about the coming pain.

Magnar had already retrieved the medical kit. He opened it and rifled through the contents. "Okay, here you go." He held out a pill that Jahira placed on her tongue and swallowed with a swig of water from his canteen.

In seconds the fire in her leg disappeared and the throbbing, eye-watering ache that was her nose lessened to a tolerable level.

"You ready?"

Jahira nodded.

"Bite down on this," Magnar said.

He placed the rubber-wrapped hilt of his knife in her mouth. She clenched it between her teeth.

Magnar prodded the sides of her nose, causing tears to leak from the corners of her eyes. "It's so swollen I can hardly feel it," he said.

"I know you know how to do this," Jahira said between her teeth, her tongue bumping the knife handle. "Just do it."

His fingers pressed down hard, one side pushing while the other pulled. More tears streamed down her cheeks.

"Done," Magnar said, stepping back. "Feel better?"

After several hard blinks, Jahira scrunched her nose. It hurt but it felt like everything was back where it was supposed to be. "Not really, but I can breathe," she said.

"Breathing is good," he said.

"Yes, I'm a fan," Jahira replied.

"Good. Go wash up please, you look terrible."

Moonlight played over the water.

Jahira climbed down the ladder and stepped into the trail of light. Bending at the waist, she scooped salt water into her hands. With gentle fingers, she washed the blood from her face. A sudden sting along her jaw reminded her of the least of her wounds. Once her face felt clean and no longer itched from the dried blood, she braced herself and stepped into deeper water.

Salt water entered the wound on her leg. Jahira sucked air through her teeth and squeezed her eyes shut. A chunk of her calf had been sliced away but should heal cleanly.

Beside her Magnar hissed as gentle fingers cleaned out his own wound.

They carried their packs to the shore and rolled out their sleeping mats.

"Help me patch this up?" Magnar asked.

With one arm extended, he held out some antiseptic salve and a second-skin patch. Jahira took the items, slathered on the salve, and then covered it with the patch.

"Now it's your turn," Magnar said, motioning for her to lift her leg onto his lap. He administered treatment with deft hands.

When he was done, Jahira gently placed her foot on the cool northern sand. Her entire body ached and sleep threatened to knock her over. She barely had time to close her eyes before blessed unconsciousness cradled her exhausted mind.

Nicole L. Bates

We found them, Arkan projected to Krnar. *We will wait at the edge of the grove. Come and claim your prize.*

Rising from his seat by the edge of the fire, Krnar rolled his injured shoulder. The muscles ached and his skin rose in bumps when the cool breeze hit the strips of bare flesh.

He sent a thread of his mind out to Tllomell and pushed against her shields.

Once he felt the connection with her mind, he said, *They have returned with the mllkallo. They wait for us at the edge of the grove. Can you make it?*

Of course, she replied.

They stepped out of their respective hearths and Krnar used long strides to catch up to Tllomell.

Once he reached her side, he slowed his pace. She walked with her back straight and her face neutral, but he could tell by her flared nostrils and clenched hands that this was not easy.

Arkan, Ulletta, Erknok, and Tllakall waited in the shadows of the trees. They had already gutted the animals, but the weight still caused his shoulders to stoop, and Krnar wondered if he had the strength to carry the burden across the field. Arkan smiled as he slipped his head under the ribs and held the animal's front legs.

"You didn't think I'd let you have all the glory, did you?" Arkan asked. "After all, I did carry it all the way here."

Krnar grinned, thankful for the help and appreciative of his brother's ability to deflect the conversation away from Krnar's weakness, even if they both knew the real reason Arkan helped.

Tllakall supported the other half of Tllomell's mllkallo and, together, they stepped into the light.

Krnar felt like a child again, returning with his first krska.

Everyone stopped what they were doing and all eyes fixed on the hunters. Before they'd made it halfway across the field, they were surrounded. People trilled in awe and admiration. White fur mixed with the dark hides as people stroked the animals.

They entertained a constant audience as they stripped the hides and cleaned them, then began to section off the meat.

Eager hands carried the pieces away to waiting fires.

Tonight they would feast, tasting the first flesh of the mllkallo that The People had eaten in generations.

Arkan informed them that one was a male and one a female, likely a mated pair.

Krnar hoped they had not orphaned any young cubs.

Once all of the meat had been partitioned, Krnar returned to the staked-out hide.

His good shoulder ached. His injured shoulder throbbed and sent jolts of painful tingles down to his hand.

Pausing frequently to flex his fingers, he was able to examine his work as he went. He took great care with the process, already having decided he could make a gift for Jahira from the dark, silky fur.

Perhaps something to keep her warm when the snows come, he thought. *A gift worthy of a mate.*

In the time that she'd been gone, he'd come to realize how important her presence was to him. He wanted her by his side, always, and he was prepared to tell her as soon as she returned.

By the time Allorkan once again bled across the horizon, Krnar's very bones felt weary.

Blood and dirt matted his fur. Sweat, a new and highly distracting phenomenon for the Leroni, created garish white streaks through the mess.

There would be no rest though, not tonight. He and Tllomell would be the center of attention. They would be called upon to tell their story under the light of the stars. They would be expected to feast and laugh and dance.

He longed for sleep.

After dragging his exhausted body to the stream, he lay down in the center of the gurgling creek. Cold water rippled over his body, swirling and pulling his fur in every direction. The cold and stimulation helped revive him enough so that he just might survive the night.

The current carried away the grime that had accumulated during his harrowing ordeal and subsequent labor. His fur began to glow.

The spade-shaped leaves overhead blocked most of the light from the moons and stars. Though the dark here didn't compare to the complete and utter lack of illumination in the underground caves, it was dark enough for his body's dark-adapted instincts to take over.

Krnar dreamed of falling asleep in the cool water, for the first time in forever he did not feel too hot.

They'll be looking for us soon.

Krnar heard the words inside his head. Slowly, reluctantly, he peeled his eyelids apart.

Tllomell stood above him, fur cleaned, oiled, and glowing. The light from her fur made her eyes sparkle like ice in the sunlight.

His eyes traveled down to the new scars across her leg. They made her look fierce. It suited her.

With awkward movements when his shoulder didn't work as expected, Krnar eventually pushed his torso out of the water. "I guess we'd better get back then," he said. When he rose from the water and stepped onto the bank, heat covered him like a warmed hide. "I think I'm actually looking forward to the snow," he said.

Tllomell trilled. "I cannot wait," she said. "I never in my life imagined I could be too warm."

Krnar watched her with a furrowed brow. "Tllomell, are you glad we came here?" he asked.

Tllomell didn't answer immediately. Krnar's curiosity heightened. "Sometimes yes and sometimes...no," she replied.

"What would make it better?" Krnar asked.

Tllomell's body stiffened and her eyes would not meet his. Finally, without saying a word, she began to walk away.

Krnar followed, not sure of what to say.

The bubble of tension thinned once they returned to the central field and were greeted like returning heroes. Fires blazed and drums sent vibrations through the ground and up through the soles of his feet.

He and Tllomell stepped together into the circle formed by the glowing bodies of The People. Bowls of food and hot tea were pressed into Krnar's hands.

His stomach growled in anticipation and his mouth filled with saliva. His body craved the meat. After the blood loss and the day's exertions, he desperately needed to replenish his energy.

Smiling and nodding his thanks, he moved to the log where he would sit to eat and then tell his story. Tllomell sat down beside him.

Their eyes met and, simultaneously, they lifted a piece of the roasted meat and tasted the first bites of mllkallo.

The rich juices coated Krnar's tongue and slid down his throat. Strong molars worked the tough meat, extracting more juice and eliciting another growl of hunger from his waiting stomach.

It tasted carnivorous, no hints of grass or leaves in the flavor like he'd found with the srlen. It reminded him of krska meat but somehow more...satisfying. "It is good," he said once he'd finally swallowed the first piece.

"Mmmhmm," Tllomell mumbled around a second mouthful.

The People trilled and then quieted as their mouths also filled with the rich, wild game.

Eventually the feasting slowed, and the drums quieted.

Krnar and Tllomell relived their adventure, each telling their version of the event that had brought down two mllkallo. They shared images of the memory, leaving the audience open-mouthed in fear and awe.

When the last of their words drifted into the night, the drums resumed, pounding a steady beat that beckoned The People.

Krnar blinked heavily and yawned into his hand.

"Care to dance?" Tllomell asked.

Indecision tore him in two. He didn't feel he had the energy for dancing, but he knew he would not be allowed to sleep. If he didn't dance, he might collapse on the ground in front of this log. "Sure," Krnar said.

Tllomell grinned and led the way.

As they made their way to the patch of beaten down grass in front of the drummers, Frmar's eyes followed them. Hooded and narrowed, those eyes pierced Krnar with malevolence. Frmar gripped his stone bowl like he wanted to choke the life from it.

Is he jealous? Krnar wondered. *He has no reason to be. Maybe I should talk to him later.*

A jolt of sensation traveled up his arm and all thoughts of Frmar fled from his mind.

Tllomell's fingers wove through his as she pulled him into the center of the throng.

Smiles and trills of encouragement greeted them.

Krnar allowed himself to drown in sensation. The beat of the drums vibrated up through the soles of his feet, the constant stimulation of fur brushing against fur, and the steady stomp of feet grew like a collective heartbeat.

Newfound energy coursed through his system, reminding him of Jahira's touch. He missed her.

A brush against his mind interrupted his thoughts. He opened to Erknok, his brother's best friend. *Thank you for your help today*, Krnar projected. He turned his head and looked for Erknok, finding him a body length away on the dance floor. Krnar nodded.

You did well against the mllkallo, Erknok said. *It is good to have you back. It is also good to see you with one of our kind.*

Shock froze him in place.

Before Krnar could respond, Erknok broke the connection and spun away to the rhythm of the drums.

Krnar? His attention returned to Tllomell and, slowly, he began to dance again. His mind reeled with hurt, confusion, anger, and he was ashamed to admit, a kernel of pride. He had always looked up to Erknok. He was Arkan's best friend, and he had always been good to Krnar. Erknok's praise meant a great deal to him, but his clear indication about his dissatisfaction with Krnar's relationship with Jahira stung.

How many others feel this way?

The trills of approval when he and Tllomell joined the dancers took on a new meaning. Krnar tried to read the looks of those watching, wondering what went on behind the calm masks.

When the sky began to lighten for a new day, he was finally allowed to return to his hearth or, more accurately, Arkan and Ulletta's hearth. His eyes closed and he was asleep before he even lay down.

Drool leaked from one corner of Krnar's mouth. He could feel it, the annoying tickle against his lip and fur, but he didn't have the strength to wipe it away. It felt like the weight of the entire sea pressed him down against the ground, preventing even a twitch of movement.

A few heartbeats, or maybe half-a-sun later, he worked up the willpower to move one hand enough to brush the side of his face.

The tantalizing smell of roasted fish filled his nostrils. His stomach rumbled like the warm land's thunder.

"Morning, Krnar." Ulletta's voice drifted over his shoulder. "Or should I say evening?"

Krnar rolled to his opposite side and felt the warmth of the fire heat his face. "How long did I sleep?" His words rasped out of a dry throat, not sounding like his voice at all.

"A full sun," Ulletta replied. "Allorkan is nearly ready to hide from us again."

Krnar groaned. More than anything he wished to close his eyes and return to the oblivion of sleep. Nature had other ideas. An uncomfortable weight pressed against his bladder, rivaled only by the gnawing of his stomach.

After shuffling to the trees, he returned to his family's hearth and accepted the fish that Ulletta offered.

"Thank you," he said, pleased to find that his voice was almost his own again.

Ulletta grinned and nodded. "You've had quite the adventure these past suns."

Krnar attempted to respond but all that came out was a muffled grunt.

"I'm not sure I've ever seen you dance so much," she said. Her eyes very pointedly remained fixed on her food.

"I had to, or I would have fallen asleep," he said.

"Ah, I see. You might not want to admit that your dance partner."

Krnar's head snapped up.

Ulletta's eyebrows rose.

"It was only dancing," he said.

"Mmmhmm." Ulletta's eyes flicked over Krnar's shoulder.

He turned and found Tllomell watching him from her hearth. Her eyes quickly shifted to her fire. Krnar scanned the surrounding hearths and saw Frmar watching Tllomell.

A soft hiss escaped his lips. "It was only dancing," he repeated.

"For a woman it's never only a dance," Ulletta said.

"Now you tell me," Krnar grumbled.

Did Ulletta disapprove of his relationship with Jahira as well? Was she secretly hoping he would mate with Tllomell?

The sudden sour feeling in his stomach ruined the remainder of his meal.

He wanted to be with Jahira, no one else. What if he had given Tllomell the wrong impression?

How am I going to fix this? he wondered.

CHAPTER 33

Sand clung to Jahira's eyelashes and coated her lips. Bright sunlight beat down directly overhead, warming her clothes while a cool breeze raised goose bumps on the back of her neck. Raising her fingers to her face, she brushed the sand from her mouth. Tears sprang to her eyes when her fingertips bumped her swollen nose.

The events of the previous evening rushed to the forefront of her mind.

Where's Magnar? she thought.

Her shoulders screamed in protest when she pushed her torso up to scan the beach.

Relief flooded her system. Magnar lay on his mat a few meters away, still asleep.

Grollon! she remembered. They'd left him behind to keep their attackers incapacitated. Had he made it across?

I'm here.

The message in her head startled her. She began to scan the beach. It took several seconds to find him; the mental voice gave no indication of location.

Sitting cross-legged far down the sandy shore, Grollon looked the same as he had when they'd left him on the opposite side; serene, still, as if meditating.

After emptying her bladder in the shelter of the tall grass beyond the sand, she gathered her pack and canteen and then headed for Grollon.

The loose sand shifted beneath her boots, which she hadn't bothered to take off before collapsing the night before. Walking in the shifting sand with heavy boots sapped her energy. She stopped to remove her boots and socks, leaving them in the sand, and then continued.

The sun-warmed grains massaged her bare soles. She wiggled her toes down into the cooler sand beneath the surface, smiling at the unfamiliar but wonderful sensation.

Grollon's eyes were still closed when she reached him.

Not knowing exactly what he was doing, or what would happen if she interrupted, she took a seat beside him and pulled a package of smoked fish from her pack.

The blade of her knife sliced through the vacuum-sealed envelope. The heady aroma of rich smoke and salt wafted into her face.

"What is that?" Grollon asked.

Jahira glanced over to find piercing blue eyes trained on the packet in her hands.

"Smoked fish," she replied. "Want some?"

"A small bite," Grollon said.

With her thumb and pointer finger, she broke off a choice section and handed it to Grollon. He examined it from every angle before his tongue darted out and took a small lick.

Blue eyes widened and he smiled before taking a good-sized bite. "Mmm, this is delicious," he said.

"I agree," Jahira replied, popping a morsel into her own mouth.

"You must teach me how to prepare this," Grollon said around a second mouthful.

"Sure! I'd be happy to, or I can just make it for you whenever you'd like. We owe you pretty big."

"You owe me nothing," he said, his face suddenly serious. "I owe both of you everything."

"Owe us? For what?"

"For finding me, for giving me a second chance with my people."

"Oh, well, let's call it even," Jahira said. She held out the packet of fish for Grollon to take another piece.

He peered into the packet, chose his piece, and then placed it on his tongue. "How do you feel?" he asked once he'd chewed and swallowed.

"I'm okay," Jahira replied. "A little sore, a lot tired, but I'm alive and not tied up with a knife in my face, so it's all good. How are you?"

"A lot sore," Grollon replied, rolling his shoulders. "And my head hurts."

"Yeah? Does it take a lot of...energy...to do what you did?" Jahira tipped her head and then added, "What *did* you do?"

Grollon didn't answer right away, he stared out at the rippling waves, perhaps trying to find the right words. "There is a certain amount of...*energy* is a good word, that most souls can stand. A little more and they shut down, too much and they die. I used a little more."

"Were they alive when you left?"

"Yes, they still live. I do not know if human minds recover that same as Leroni souls. Only time will tell." Grollon's eyes focused on a point behind her.

Jahira turned and saw Magnar walking toward them.

"He's alive!" Jahira said once Magnar was close enough to hear.

"Barely," Magnar groaned before he plopped down in the sand beside her.

"Smoked fish?" she asked, holding the package out to him.

"Thanks," Magnar said, breaking off a piece. "How long have you been up?"

"A few minutes," Jahira replied. "How are you feeling?"

"Achy but fine," he said. "Eager to get going. The more distance I put between me and those psychos, the better."

"So is that the end of your trading days?"

Magnar shrugged. "We'll see. Right at this moment, I have no intention of ever returning to that settlement."

"What about Samuel?" Jahira asked.

"I do want to know how Samuel is doing. Maybe Creed could ride along and be the emissary."

"Or maybe Samuel could come to you," Jahira said.

"Yeah, that might work, but I'd still have to get a message to him. I guess we'll see what The General has to say about the whole thing."

Jahira nodded. After handing the remaining piece of fish to Magnar, she stood, walked to the shore, and rinsed her hands in the clear, salty water. "I'm going to roll my mat and pack up," she said. "I'll meet you down there."

"I'm coming," Magnar said, rising and stuffing the last bite of fish into his mouth. He chewed twice and swallowed. "I'm ready to go."

"Are you ready?" Jahira asked Grollon.

The old man licked the last of the salty grease from his fingers and nodded.

Halfway back to the boat, Jahira stopped to pick up her boots but didn't put them back on.

There wasn't much to pack and they hadn't built a fire. In less than half an hour they were on board *Amara*, pulling up anchor.

Jahira stowed their packs in the cabin and returned to the deck to find Grollon staring at the bags of nuts and leaves that they'd left sitting out.

"Where did you get these?" he asked, pointing to the leaves.

"We traded for them," Jahira said. "The people in Lusela's camp found the leaves and they drink a tea made from them. Samuel said it is a stimulant, something that helps wake you up."

"This is *vllusta*," he said, making the word sound like a curse word. "It is poison to the Leroni."

"You're sure?" Jahira said.

"I am sure."

"Poison," she repeated. "Will it hurt you? Did you touch it?" Jahira began to move between Grollon and the leaves, thinking she might shield him from the effects as if the sight alone would harm him.

"Touching it hurts the skin, but doesn't kill," Grollon said. "Only eating it will kill."

Horror filled her as the possibilities flooded her brain. *What if Grollon hadn't been here, or they'd already put it away and he'd never seen it? What if she'd made it into tea and given some to Krnar?*

"What should we do? Should we throw it overboard? Will it kill the fish?" Panic reared as Jahira tried to figure out what to do.

"What's going on?" Magnar asked, joining them on the deck.

"These leaves are poisonous to the Leroni," Jahira said. "They'll hurt their skin if they touch them and can kill them if ingested."

"Are you sure?"

"Grollon is."

"Crap."

"Yeah."

"What do we do?"

"I don't know, that's what I was just trying to decide."

"Well, we certainly can't have people cooking it or brewing it and accidentally serve some to a Leroni."

"But the people in Lusela's camp are consuming it. Do you think it could be harmful to humans?"

"They apparently haven't had a reaction so far. I feel like we should tell them, but then they'll know that it could hurt the Leroni."

"I think we should still have Ryan test it, like we planned to."

"Definitely."

"Maybe, over time, we could create a salve or antidote or something in case the Leroni do come in contact," Jahira suggested.

"That's a good idea," Magnar replied.

"So, should we bring the whole batch? Maybe to keep in storage in the lab so they can test it?"

"I guess," Magnar replied. "Plus, if we dump it somewhere, it might start to grow and spread on this continent when maybe, right now, it's isolated to the first."

"Have you seen any growing near Empyrean? Near the grove?"

"I haven't noticed any, but I don't know. Now I'll know what to look for."

"Okay, so we take it back but take it straight to the lab."

"Which is what we were going to do anyway."

A deep breath helped to calm her quaking nerves. They had a plan. It would be okay. They just couldn't let any of this get near Krnar's people.

CHAPTER 34

"Well done, Dan!"

Ahead of them, on the left bank of the river, a permanent dock had been built while they were away. Dan was not actually standing there to receive his congratulations, but he had told Magnar he would finish it before they returned.

"Wow! That was quick work," Jahira said. "When did he find the time?"

"Oh, he's one of those people who never sits still. He's always working on something."

The boat drew closer, churning upriver in the final moments of what Jahira felt confident would be her last boat trip for a while.

"Would you look at that! It's perfect," Magnar said.

A long curve in the river wrapped around a larger-than-usual stretch of exposed shoreline. The dock had been built on the southern edge of this flat area. To the north of the dock the site looked perfect for a tent and a fire pit.

"Welcome to your new home," Jahira teased.

"*This* is my new home," Magnar replied, giving the steering mechanism a fond pat. "That's just a great resting point."

"Well I, for one, am thrilled to be back, and alive."

"Alive is good."

"Do you think Samuel is alright?"

"I'm sure he is. If Lusela really wasn't the mastermind behind the ransom plan, you can bet she's going to be pissed. They jeopardized the survival of that entire settlement."

"You really think she didn't know?"

"Yeah, I do. I mean, the crew couldn't decide what to do. If they'd had orders from her they wouldn't have been arguing."

"I suppose. I just can't bring myself to trust her."

"I didn't say I trusted her," Magnar replied. "I just don't think she was responsible for this particular crisis."

"Fair enough. So, how long do you think you're going to stick around?"

"Just long enough to restock. I want to get farther south before the snow hits."

"What do we have now, about a month?"

"I think so."

"Aside from the whole getting tied up and beaten part, I'd say the first trip when well," Jahira said. "I mean, the boat worked great."

"Yes, and the whole experience reinforces my belief that I will be much happier on the open water than I will on land." Magnar eased the boat forward at a crawl. They'd almost reached the dock. "When we get close, I'm going to need you to wait on the ladder and jump to the dock. Pull the ropes and tie her on so that we can ease her over without ramming the dock."

"Got it." Pushing herself up out of her seat, Jahira stretched and then hopped down the short flight of stairs, crossed the deck, and backed halfway down the ladder.

"Do you need some help?" Grollon's head appeared above her, jutting out over the railing.

"Yes, if you could toss me the ropes once I'm on the dock, that would be great."

Grollon nodded.

The old man had slept or meditated most of their return trip. He didn't seem big on conversation.

The engine barely whirred, nudging the boat against the current until Jahira was able to extend one leg out over the water and, with a small jump, make it to the dock. "Okay!" she called to Grollon.

A coil of rope arched over the railing and began to unwind as it fell toward her.

"Got it!" With rope in hand, she took three steps to the nearest post and pulled the hull in close before she wound the cord around the post and tied it off. She motioned to Grollon to follow her to the other end and then they repeated the process.

"All set?" Magnar called from the flying bridge.

"I think so," Jahira called back. "Two ties, one at each end. Do you want more?"

"That should be good for now."

Jahira climbed back on board and all three hauled their packs and goods to shore. Grollon kept a safe distance from the bags of leaves, and Jahira noticed, wouldn't even get close to the seats they'd been stored under.

Once everything was off the boat and resting on the shore, they stood staring at the mound of goods.

"We're going to need some help," Jahira said.

"Definitely," Magnar replied.

"I'll head up, find a few able bodies, and be back soon."

"Excellent."

After fishing her pack and sleeping mat out of the pile, Jahira climbed the bank and headed for Empyrean. Skirting the edge of the settlement, she took a quick detour to her tent. Disappointment tugged at her heart when she saw that Krnar was not there.

Not that she'd been expecting him to sit and wait for a month, but she really wanted to see him.

The grass had grown up and the fire pit looked neglected. It didn't look like Krnar had been there much at all while she was gone.

Probably taking the time to help his family, she thought. After placing her pack and sleeping roll inside the tent, she continued into the settlement to find help.

Several people waved, a few called greetings. She smiled and waved back, feeling happy to be around people who were friendly, and well, who liked her.

A grin spread across Jahira's face when she rounded a corner and saw Tala standing in her yard. Her expression looked angry and she shook her finger at something on the ground.

"Tala!" Jahira called.

Tala looked up, her scowl disappeared and a grin lit her features. "You're back!" she said once Jahira stood in front of her.

"Just arrived."

"And came to see me first? Don't I feel special."

"Well, we need some help."

"Of course you do." Tala's eyes narrowed and she asked, "What happened to your nose?"

"Long story," Jahira replied.

"That you will tell me in full detail."

"Of course."

"Leiko!" Tala called. "Come on out! Jahira's back!"

Leiko's fine-boned face and shiny black hair appeared around the edge of the doorway.

"Hey, Jahira!" Leiko stepped out of the house and rushed over to wrap Jahira in a hug. "Welcome back. How was the trip?"

"Eventful," Jahira said.

Her tone caused both women's eyebrows to rise. "I'll fill you in later. Magnar's waiting at the boat with all the trade goods. We need some help carrying everything to the *K.C.*"

"Sure," Leiko said. "I'll go next door and get Kato and Cholie. Cholie probably knows where Dan is, and he's going to want to know how the boat did."

"Great. Thanks, Leiko."

Once Leiko had disappeared around the corner of the dwelling, Tala fixed a stern gaze on Jahira. "So, spill. What happened?"

"Most of it went well. The boat worked great. The trip was fine. Lusela was her usual charming self, but just before we headed back home, the crew that came to exchange the goods tied us up, broke my nose, and plotted to ransom us. Oh, and planned to take the boat."

"*What?*"

"Yeah, one of them even shot me in the leg. Magnar, too."

"Are you kidding me? What did you do? Did you kill them? How are you here, not tied up and being ransomed?"

"Actually, Grollon saved us."

"Grollon? The old alien with wings?"

"That's the one."

"How? Did he go with you?"

"No, he flew there. I guess he had a vision, he knew something was going to happen, so he followed and did something to their minds. They were all curled up on the ground, incapacitated, and we got away."

"Incapacitated. Not dead?"

"No, he said they were all still alive when he left."

"Well, that's unfortunate."

"Not really. Can you imagine the backlash if we, or one of the Leroni, had killed five humans from Lusela's camp? Total disaster."

"Oh, and them deciding to tie you up, beat you, and sell you back to us was a real gesture of friendship."

"Yeah, well..."

"Hey!" Leiko called, running up to join them again. "Kato is getting Creed, Cholie went to find Dan, they're all going to meet us at the dock."

"Great."

The three friends made their way to the river where Magnar sat waiting.

Rocks skidded down the embankment and splashed into the water as they slip-stepped down to the small beach.

Magnar stood to greet them with a smile. "Tala! Leiko! It's good to see you." Magnar gave each a hug and then stepped back.

"It's good to see you, too," Leiko said.

"So," Tala said, cocking one hip. "You need our help, as usual."

Magnar smiled.

"Kato, Creed, Cholie, and Dan should be here any minute," Leiko said.

"Great."

"What did you bring back?" Tala asked.

"Some kind of nuts," Magnar answered.

"And a bunch of leaves," Tala said, peering into one of the bags.

Jahira and Magnar exchanged a look.

"What is it?" Leiko asked.

"Well, the leaves are apparently poisonous to the Leroni," Jahira said.

"What? Why did you bring them back?"

"We didn't know. The people in the south brew it into a tea and drink it. They said it's kind of like coffee, wakes you up but doesn't taste like it. They haven't had any reaction. But when Grollon saw it, he wouldn't even get close to it. He said it can kill a Leroni if they ingest it."

"Surely they wouldn't have known that," Tala said.

"I don't know how they could have," Jahira replied.

"And we don't want them to find out," Magnar added.

"But we do want to have Ryan's team test it and find out if we can make some sort of antidote, just in case."

"Oh, well, I suppose that's a good idea."

"The nuts are safe though?" Leiko asked.

"As far as we know," Magnar said. "We ate some while we were there."

Shouts and more skidding rocks alerted them to the arrival of the rest of their friends.

The story of their journey was forced out, piece by piece, and Jahira and Magnar got caught up on all the news from Empyrean.

Hours later, after they'd dropped off the trade goods and reported to General Thayer who, naturally, required a complete debriefing including their being-held-captive-and-saved-by-the-alien story...again...Jahira finally got to go home.

For the second time that day, her heart sank when no tell-tale glow waited by her fire pit. She felt torn between trying to go find Krnar and collapsing in exhaustion.

Exhaustion won. *Tomorrow,* she thought as she stretched out inside the familiar walls of her tents. *I'll definitely go look for him tomorrow.*

CHAPTER 35

Patches of white crystals rimmed the blades of grass and clung to the blood-red alara leaves. Tllomell felt comfortable, if still slightly on the warm side, for the first time since arriving in the warm land.

Allorkan hadn't cleared the horizon line yet. Its heat would soon burn away the frost but for now, she enjoyed the licks of cold against the bare stripes on her leg as she walked through the field to the east of the river.

This morning she would go fishing. The fish were less plentiful than they had been, so it had become necessary to walk a good distance downriver to bring home a decent catch. She would most likely be gone all day.

A small stab of guilt nagged at her. She knew Frmar would look for her and be frustrated by her absence. Ever since the feast he'd been pressuring her to decide if she would go north with him. What she didn't want to tell him was that ever since the feast, she'd been feeling less inclined to go.

Krnar had danced with her the whole night. He'd called them *partners*.

Tllomell! Wait up!

Tllomell stopped and turned, surprised to see Plldoll jogging toward her with that distinctive hitch in her gait. She'd been injured in the krska hunt during the trials. Tllomell breathed a prayer of thanks that the mllkallo hadn't broken any bones in her own leg.

"Mind if I join you?" Plldoll asked once she'd caught up.

"Of course not. I'd love some company," Tllomell replied.

"Great. I just made some new hooks and I collected some of those green worms that spin the webs in the trees. I'm going to try them for bait. What did you bring?"

"I've been using the *glluna*, those squishy creatures that live on the rocks along the riverbank. I usually find them as I go. I also have some fruit for back-up."

"*Glluna*? Can you show me when we get there?"

"Sure. I'm planning to go far downstream. Is that okay?"

"The farther the better."

Tllomell's lips twitched. "Trouble with Krag?"

"He's infuriating! He won't take me hunting, says I shouldn't go too far from the grove, and he won't let me go anywhere alone, especially since your encounter with the mllkallo."

"He's just trying to take care of you and his baby," Tllomell said, glancing meaningfully at her friend's barely rounded belly.

"I know, but I'm not an invalid."

"Yours will be the first Leroni child born in the warm land," Tllomell said.

"Not the first," Plldoll responded.

"Well, not the first birth, but still the first living child, and that will be significant. Are you excited?" Tllomell had to admit, jealousy ate at her every time Krag showered attention on Plldoll and patted her tiny bump.

"Very excited. Now that we're here, I'm not worried about running out of milk for him, or that he will starve during the Season of Ice."

"Him?"

"I'm pretty sure," Plldoll said, placing a hand on her abdomen. "I can feel his mind and the energy feels like a boy to me. Ellall says it's a little too soon to be sure, but I think so."

"What is it like? To connect with an infant's mind?"

"Well, nothing is really clear. There are moments where I feel suddenly hungry or really really tired, and when I really focus, I can tell the signal is coming from him."

"Interesting."

"So, when are you going to pick a mate?" Plldoll asked. "It looks like you have a few good choices." She wiggled her eyebrows suggestively.

Tllomell shot her an exasperated look.

"Seriously, Tllomell, you've been spending a lot of time with Frmar lately, so I thought maybe there was something there. But then you and Krnar..."

"Maybe I don't want a mate," Tllomell said.

"Hmmm, and maybe water doesn't freeze when it's cold," Plldoll retorted.

They walked several paces in silence before Tllomell glanced at Plldoll out of the corners of her eyes. "So, what would you say if someone suggested going north, to the mountains, and find a cave to live in there?"

"I would say, '*how hard did you just hit your head*?'"

"I'm serious. Have you ever considered it? There are caves, it's colder, there's plenty of water to drink..."

Plldoll stopped dead in her tracks and rounded on Tllomell. "Are you thinking of leaving?"

"No, of course not, I heard some people talking about it and it got me thinking, that's all."

"Who was talking about it?"

Tllomell trilled and said, "I don't know, just some people."

"Why would we do that? We just got here! Ellall would never allow it, and I guess it would be kind of nice to have some shelter, but I don't want to live surrounded by ice and rock. That's why we left."

"We left because there wasn't enough food and we had to live underground for most of a lifetime."

"So you do support this idea. Is it Frmar? Is that why the two of you have been talking so much?" Plldoll's words were stumbling over each other and her gestures became huge, threatening to knock Tllomell over if she got too close.

"No, never mind. Calm down or Krag will never let you go anywhere with me again." Tllomell smiled, trying to eradicate the tension that had sprung up between them. "Come on, let's head down into the river and I'll show you those *glluna*."

Luckily, Plldoll was easily distracted. Once they started searching for bait and pulling in fish, she never mentioned the conversation again.

They spent most of that sun following the river, tossing their lines into likely looking spots. A friendly competition emerged to determine whose bait the fish preferred.

It was the best day Tllomell had had in a very long time.

"What is that?" Plldoll asked, pointing downriver.

Tllomell looked and then squinted. "Something that belongs to the humans, obviously, but I have no idea what it is."

"Let's get a closer look."

Apprehension squeezed a fist around Tllomell's insides. *What if there were humans nearby?*

"Come on," Plldoll urged. She waded out into the water, and then lowered her body into the current until only her head remained above the surface.

With a hiss, Tllomell followed. The cool water curled around her thighs, and then her torso. The current pushed so that her fur swayed like tiny stalks of glow weed.

They floated with the pull of the river until they'd been swept underneath the structure which stood above the water and which the human creation had been tied to.

"It sits on top of the water," Plldoll said, reaching out to touch the smooth, hard surface.

Tllomell remembered her conversation with Krnar about the marked human going to trade with the humans on the first continent. "They must use it to travel on the water, like their mountains travel in the sky," she said.

Plldoll's soft trill expressed her awe. "How do they know how to make these things, Tllomell? Where did they learn? How do they have the tools, the materials?"

"I don't know."

"Do you think we could make things like this?"

Tllomell's eyes widened in surprise and her head turned toward her friend. "Do you want to?"

"Of course! It's amazing! Don't you want to fly? To ride on top of the water? We could see the whole world!"

No, no I don't, Tllomell thought, but she kept her feelings to herself.

The sounds of loose rocks shifting and splashing into the water made Plldoll's eyes go wide. Tllomell pressed her lips together, telling the other woman to be silent.

Voices drew closer. Tllomell's throat went dry and her heart hammered like she'd just swum in the trials.

Shifting scraping rock changed to the distinctive clomp of the humans' heavy foot coverings as they stepped onto the structure above their heads.

They're right above us, Plldoll projected.

Slowly, so as not to disturb the water, Tllomell tilted her head so that she could see the regular pattern of alternating bars and slits of light. Two pair of human boots blocked the light over her head.

Do you think they can see us? Plldoll asked.

I don't know. I don't think they will look down here if we stay silent.

Maybe we should just talk to them, Plldoll suggested.

Do you speak their language?

Well, no, but I thought some of them could speak ours.

Not many, and we don't know who it is. What if they're angry that we are here?

So they waited.

One voice had a low timbre, not as deep as a male Leroni, but most likely a male human. The other voice was higher, and Tllomell thought she recognized the sound.

She had to know. Tentatively, she reached out with her mind.

The human signals twisted and collided but, once she unraveled them and found the source of the female, her heart stopped. She knew this mind. From her very first sleep in this land, the night when Krnar had refused to dance with her, she'd learned this signal and memorized it.

The human voices cut off abruptly.

Panic surged through her veins and Tllomell pulled her mind back and threw up the walls around her soul.

"Krnar?" The human female's voice called for Krnar. She'd felt Tllomell's touch but did not recognize the signal. That was something at least.

Unfamiliar words passed between the humans. Tllomell concentrated, trying to find something familiar in the speech and wishing for the first time she'd made an attempt to learn some of the humans' language.

Brilliant green eyes set in a night-dark face appeared before her, upside down.

Plldoll trilled and Tllomell jolted backward.

Small waves splashed against the silver wall of the human creation and bounced back toward her.

"May Allorkan shine upon you this day," the female said in the Leroni language.

Plldoll grinned and responded, "The light of Allorkan warms us, today and every day."

"Come up," the woman said, motioning for them to climb up to where the humans stood.

Without hesitation, Plldoll reached up to grip the edge of the structure and kicked until her body lay on the platform. She got her feet under her, stood, and finally moved to the side to make space for Tllomell.

I have no choice, Tllomell thought.

With one hand in Plldoll's strong grip and the other pulling against the surprisingly warm platform above her, she kicked her body up and out of the water.

Feeling self-conscious, she slid her body forward until she could get her feet underneath her. She stood, and then with a deep breath to steel her resolve, she looked into the face of the human female. *Jahira*, she remembered, in spite of her repeated efforts to forget that name.

Jahira bowed.

Tllomell couldn't, in good conscience, refuse to return the formal greeting. She bent at the waist and when they both stood straight again, Jahira smiled.

"My name is Jahira," the woman said, still in the Leroni tongue, and then she pointed to her companion. "This is Magnar."

Tllomell had been so focused on Jahira that she had completely ignored the other human. She turned and had begun to bow when her mind registered the scars across his forehead. Her feet involuntarily stepped back and a hiss pushed through her teeth.

"Tllomell!" Plldoll reached out and grabbed her arm just in time to prevent her from falling backward into the water.

The two humans exchanged a glance. The male, the *marked* male, bowed.

Tllomell's hands shook. She remembered now, Magnar, the human who had drunk from the pools and been healed by Grollon. She stood face-to-face with him.

After forcing her breaths to even out and clenching her fists to stop the trembling in her hands, she nodded her head once, briefly. "What is your name?" Jahira asked. Her words were slow and deliberate, but only slightly accented.

"Plldoll," Plldoll answered, pointing to her chest. She glanced at Tllomell and then her finger shifted. "Tllomell."

Jahira's eyes flashed with recognition. The woman knew of her. Had Krnar told her stories of Tllomell? What did she know? "Why you here?" Jahira asked, trying to soften the very direct question with a smile.

Tllomell's tongue sat frozen in her mouth and her lips refused to move. Plldoll cut her eyes to Tllomell, pushing against her mind like a flick to wake her up, and then she smiled back at Jahira. "Fishing," Plldoll said, miming the actions in case the humans didn't know the word, and then pointed to the stringer of fish hanging from her belt.

"Fishing," Jahira repeated, nodding.

"We saw this," Plldoll said, pointing to the floating creation. "We wondered what it was."

Jahira said something to Magnar. The male nodded and smiled. "It is called *boat*," Jahira said, all in The People's language, save the unfamiliar human word. "It moves on water."

Plldoll trilled. "That is what we guessed!" She practically bounced on her toes, clearly delighted by the day's turn of events.

"You want see it?" Jahira asked.

"Yes!" Plldoll exclaimed.

Tllomell's heart sank.

Jahira smiled and then waved them forward.

After tying their catch to one of the metal poles so that the fish drifted in the current, they followed the human female onto the *boat*.

The entire experience proved excruciating. Jahira spoke in their language as much as possible, but most of the *things* on this *boat* had no name in their tongue. She pointed to objects, provided their human label, and Plldoll repeated every one of them, grinning and trilling like a child on the first day of Nall'Mrkellan.

When the tour finally ended, and everyone was saying goodbye, Tllomell backed toward the edge of the boat, trying to leave without turning her back and being rude.

Suddenly, Jahira's eyes widened and she held a hand out.

"Stop!" she yelled. "No!"

Tllomell opened her mind a fraction and felt fear pouring from the human female.

Adrenaline pumped through Tllomell's bloodstream. She glanced around slowly, trying to assess the danger, but could see nothing that would make the woman react with such vehemence.

Jahira crept forward, lowering her hands toward Tllomell's foot.

Tllomell shuffled backward, distancing herself from the woman's reaching fingers.

Jahira pointed to Tllomell's foot. "Bad," she said. "Lift foot, look. Bad."

With caution, Tllomell lifted her foot and looked underneath it. Seeing nothing, she tilted her foot so that she could see the sole.

A single spotted leaf clung to her fur.

Tllomell's eyebrows rose as she plucked the leaf off her foot and held it on the palm of her hand.

Before she could react, Jahira snatched the leaf from Tllomell's hand. "No! Bad! Wash in water." Jahira was waving her hands, trying to get Tllomell into the water, apparently.

"What is going on?" Plldoll asked.

"I have no idea," Tllomell responded. "I think she's going crazy."

"No, something about the leaf, she wants you to wash off in the water. She keeps saying bad, maybe you're not supposed to touch it."

"But she is touching it."

"Maybe she will wash, too."

The woman continued to wave and yell.

Tllomell backed out, stepping onto what the human had called *the dock*, and then dove into the water.

When she surfaced, Jahira stood on the dock watching. "You okay?" she asked. "Foot? Hand?"

"I am fine," Tllomell said.

Jahira's shoulders fell with relief. "Okay," she said, nodding.

Plldoll retrieved their fish and then lowered her body into the water. She waved before she and Tllomell swam to shore. They climbed the rise and, once at the top, Tllomell couldn't resist a last glance over her shoulder.

Both humans stood on the dock and watched them.

Shivers raced down her spine.

"Wasn't that amazing?" Plldoll said as they crossed the field heading back toward the grove. "That's the best thing that's happened since we got a tour of the mountain! I want to ride in a boat! Don't you want to ride in a boat?"

The tension in Tllomell's gut had long since curdled, leaving her feeling slightly nauseated. Her foot began to itch.

Plldoll kept up her one-sided conversation all the way to, and then through, the alara grove. Distracted by the itch on her foot, and a new one beginning to tingle against her palm, she didn't hear much of what Plldoll said until her friend yelled, "Krnar!"

Tllomell stopped in her tracks.

Krnar looked in their direction and raised a hand in greeting. Plldoll must have mentally beckoned him over, because he set the items in his hands carefully on the ground and approached.

"Krnar!" Plldoll exclaimed when he got close enough to hear. "We saw a human boat!"

At first Krnar frowned, and then excitement washed over his face like a wave smoothing the sand on the shore. "A boat! Was it coming up the river?"

"No, it was tied to a *dock*. There were two humans there and we got a tour! We met Magnar, and your friend Jahira—"

"Jahira! She was there?" His body coiled, suddenly restless and eager to move.

"Yes, she was very kind. She greeted us and spoke to us in our language..." Plldoll's voice trailed off once she realized Krnar was not listening.

"She's back," he said softly. His eyes focused again and he grinned at Plldoll. It was the happiest smile she'd ever seen on his face. "Thank you, Plldoll, for telling me." He bowed low and practically sprinted away.

"Well, I thought he'd want to hear more about it," Plldoll said, clearly disappointed.

"Plldoll!" From the base of the oranlodi, Krag sprinted toward them.

"Well, I guess that's all of my fun for a while," Plldoll said. "Thanks, Tllomell. See you later." Plldoll marched forward to meet Krag, whose expression went back and forth from relief to anger.

Tllomell remained rooted to the ground, frozen, afraid that if she moved she would shatter into a thousand pieces.

She's back, he'd said.

She had been gone. She must have gone to the first continent with the marked human.

Krnar had not decided to stay at his family's hearth because he'd finally realized his loyalty belonged to the Leroni. He hadn't danced with her because he thought they might have a future together. He'd been here because *she* had been gone.

Now she had returned, and Krnar had run to her.

Her heart splintered like a vrmefur, cracked open and lit on fire until every last drop of happiness had been burned away.

CHAPTER 36

The flaming half circle suspended on the horizon cast an orange glow that lit the edges of the leaves overhead and the tips of the grass before him. Krnar raced along the familiar path to Jahira's tent, and when he saw her, the ends of her hair glowed like a thousand tiny stars, drawing him to her.

He trilled, Jahira turned, her beautiful green eyes widened and her full lips split into a joyful grin. She dropped whatever had been in her hands and raced to meet him.

With arms open wide to receive her touch, he wrapped her in an embrace and held her to him. The first touch was like oil on a fire, like silver in a wound, burning and healing, comforting and torturing as sensation engulfed his body.

"I missed you," Jahira breathed the words against his neck, sending chills down his spine.

"I missed you, too," Krnar replied.

Pulling back enough that she could jump into his arms and wrap her legs around his torso, she leaned in and pressed her lips to his. Krnar drank in the taste of her, the salt and smoke flavor with a hint of fruit.

"When did you get back?" he asked, when they parted for air.

"Yesterday. It was late and I was exhausted. We unloaded and unpacked and had to talk to The General. Then, I looked for you this morning, but Ulletta said you'd gone hunting, so I went back to the boat to help Magnar clean it out after our trip. I'm so glad you came to find me."

"Plldoll told me that she and Tllomell saw you, and the boat."

"Oh, right! Plldoll seems really nice." Jahira worked her lower lip between her teeth. "Did Tllomell seem…okay? Anything…unusual about her?"

"No, she seemed fine," Krnar said, and then his eyes narrowed. "What happened to your nose? And your jaw?"

The tip of his finger traced the light scar along the edge of her jaw.

"It's a long story." After unwrapping her legs and placing her feet back on the ground, she pulled Krnar over to the fire. She looked at him as they sat beside each other. Her eyes widened and she gasped. "What happened to your shoulder?"

Reaching out slowly, she traced the lines of bare skin where the mllkallo teeth had torn through his flesh. "It's a long story."

"I guess we have a lot of catching up to do. You first."

"I was attacked by a mllkallo."

"What? Attacked! How? Where? What happened?"

"It would be easier to show you." Krnar tipped his head, asking permission to connect with her mind, and Jahira nodded.

Not that she could block him out yet, but he always made a point to ask her permission before projecting to her.

Dark lids hid the light of her green eyes and made Krnar smile. It was a habit he found endearing, her need to close her eyes to see his images. He started with his memories a few moments before the attack, when he'd realized the forest sounds had stopped.

Her emotions spiked as she watched the scene unfold. He felt her fear, her adrenaline, and finally her relief when the animal laid still and Krnar rose to his feet. Then he felt her curiosity, confusion...jealousy? When he retrieved his spear and made the throw to finish the second mllkallo, which had sunk its teeth into Tllomell's thigh.

Green eyes pierced his, sparking with emotion, and he retreated from her mind. "There were two mllkallo," she said. "And two Leroni. Who was that with you?"

"Tllomell was there. We both fought a mllkallo, and were both injured, but survived."

That explains the scars on her leg, Jahira said to herself. "Were you hunting with her?"

"No," Krnar replied. "Not intentionally. We were both searching for Grollon."

"Oh," Jahira's hand went to her nose for a moment and then dropped. He wondered at the gesture, but then she continued. "He followed us."

"Followed you? And Magnar?"

"Yes."

"On foot?"

"No, he flew."

Krnar trilled in surprise. "I didn't know he still could," he said.

"Neither did I," Jahira replied. "We were lucky he can, though. He saved us."

"Saved you? From what?"

Jahira then told him her story of their trip, starting from the beginning. She described the new wildlife, the people, and finally, their capture by the other humans and unexpected rescue by Grollon.

Blood boiled in Krnar's veins at the thought of Jahira being tied up and beaten. He wished now that he'd gone with her. "I do not want you to go there again," he said.

"I don't intend to," Jahira replied.

Her eyes locked with his and slowly, she reached up and traced a circle on his forehead.

Letting his mind open, he felt all traces of jealousy flee in the wake of her desire.

"Are you hungry?" she asked.

"No," he replied, his voice suddenly thick.

"Good." Jahira smiled and took his hand, and then led him into her tent.

Sometime later the nighttime insects buzzed, hummed, and peeped at random intervals beyond the thin walls of the tent. Krnar listened, wondering if he'd ever get used to the constant noise in this land. Growing up on the third continent had been so different. The silence there was so intense he'd sometimes thought he could hear the fish swimming in the sea at the bottom of the cliff while he lay awake in the community cavern.

Then there was Nall'Urrok, the Season of Ice. There in the bowels of the world in a darkness so complete one could begin to believe there was no such thing as sunlight, he had endured stretches of stillness that would last for days in an effort to con-serve energy and reduce the need for food and water.

Here, noise and heat and food and *life* filled every day and every night.

Muting out his light, Jahira's dark arm draped across his chest and her left leg trapped both of his beneath its weight. He felt blissfully happy.

His eyes were just drifting closed when a loud ripping sound caused them to spring open. Adrenaline coursed through him. Next to him, Jahira jerked awake and pulled her limbs off of him, allowing him to rise to a crouch.

A long tear appeared in the side of the tent.

Krnar barely had time to wonder how it had gotten there when glowing blue-white fingers thrust through the opening and ripped the wall apart.

Krnar gaped, frozen in disbelief.

Beyond the opening, Tllomell hissed, eyes wide and wild and in her right hand she gripped her knife like her life depended on it.

"Tllomell? What are you doing?"

"You're here with *her*! You've mated with *her*!"

Instinct forced him forward, putting himself between Tllomell and Jahira and getting to better defensive ground.

With his hands out to the sides, demonstrating his lack of weapons, he stepped through the gaping hole.

"What's going on, Tllomell? Why are you here?" He kept his voice calm and steady. His eyes were locked on hers, but he could see her knife in his peripheral vision.

Behind him he heard the rustle of Jahira pulling on clothes. He could sense when she stopped behind him.

"It should have been *me*. You were meant for *me*. They have a plant that can harm us! Do you see?" she held out her foot and, in the glow of her fur, he could see that the bottom of her foot was raw and blistered. No fur covered the sole.

Tllomell's chest rose and fell in rapid succession. Her eyes found Jahira and she bared her teeth and hissed.

Krnar sidestepped, blocking Tllomell's view of Jahira and took a step closer. "Tllomell, you need to leave. I won't let you hurt Jahira."

Tllomell's eyes snapped to his. Krnar could see the turmoil before her lids narrowed. "I didn't come for her," she said.

Before Krnar could react, she plunged her knife into his gut.

Shock numbed him. He didn't feel anything at first, almost as if his soul had left his body.

A scream ripped through the night. He didn't know who it came from.

His legs, no longer able to support his weight, gave out. Knees slammed against the ground, forcing a grunt of pain past his lips. His fingers wrapped around the bone handle, still warm from Tllomell's hand.

He pulled, and that's when the pain hit like an avalanche. It seared through him like a thousand mllkallo claws. With the heels of both hands, he pressed the wound, trying to hold in the blood, his blood. Dark red liquid seeped below and through his fingers and began to drip down his leg.

"Krnar! Krnar look at me!" He blinked hard, trying to focus on Jahira's face. "Krnar, listen to me."

Now he could see her eyes, so green, so much a part of this world of light and heat and color.

"I'm going to get help. I'll be right back. DO NOT die on me, do you understand?"

He tried to nod but her hands were holding his face. "Will you be my mate?" he asked.

Did I say that in my language or hers? he wondered. *Did she understand?* A sound somewhere between and laugh and cry preceded a series of sniffles. *Is she crying? Jahira never cries.*

"Just stay alive. We'll talk about that later." She'd heard him.

Something wrapped around him and sent a bolt of pain through his gut when it tightened on his wound. Then he felt his body being eased to the ground.

"I'll be right back. Stay alive!"

He thought he nodded. He tried to nod. Did she see him? He tried to say her name but his lips felt numb. Ice crept from his fingertips up to his elbows. *Don't take too long*, he projected.

Could anyone hear him?

CHAPTER 37

Tllomell's feet splashed into the cold creek. The weight of the water pulled against her ankles and she tipped forward, crashing to her knees. Rocks sliced into her palms.

Hard spasms gripped her insides and the contents of her stomach spewed into the water. Once her gut felt as hollow as her heart, she lifted a hand to sip but stopped before it reached her lips.

Dark splotches clung to her fur. Blood.

His blood.

She hissed and plunged her hands back into the water, scrubbing vigorously. She gripped handfuls of sand and scoured her arms, her chest, her legs.

Her stomach clenched again but there was nothing left.

Eventually she stood, forced her feet forward. She had to get away from him, from what she'd done. Stumbling through the grove, her mind reeled.

What have I done? She hadn't followed Krnar with the intent to harm anyone.

Aruvel help me, she thought, *I stabbed him. Did I kill him? He could be dead by my hand.*

She had followed, when he'd left her and Plldoll standing there. She'd followed as if pulled by an invisible line looped through their belts. At first, she'd stayed close, and then her hand and foot had begun to itch and burn, forcing her to stop and tend to them.

Bile had filled her throat when she'd looked at the sole of her foot and saw a patch of raw, blistered flesh where the fur had fallen away. *The leaf*, she remembered.

The leaf on the boat that Jahira had called *bad*. She'd stepped on it and then held it between the two fingers that now peeled and itched.

She had known what the plant would do. How had she known? Why did she have it?

She should find Ellall. She should find Frmar.

But instead, she'd followed Krnar.

She saw their embrace. She watched the human female pull Krnar into her tent. She couldn't see what went on inside, but she knew, and something inside her snapped.

He'd betrayed her. He'd betrayed them all. He tore them from their home to this place they did not belong and then fell in love with one of *them*. Did he know they had plants that could harm the Leroni?

She had to confront him. She had to know why he'd done this to her, to all of them.

I should go back, she thought. *I should make sure he is alright.*

Are you kidding? He'll kill you, or that human female will kill you. Have you seen her knife? You can't go back there. You can't ever go back there.

How will I face him? How will I face any of them?

You won't.

Her breathing evened and her steps grew steady.

Under the light of Leron's moons, Tllomell stole across the field until she'd reached Frmar's hearth.

Frmar, she pushed against his sleeping mind as she shifted her weight from foot to foot outside his ring of rocks.

He didn't stir.

Frmar! she pushed harder. Frmar opened his eyes, blinked several times, and then turned his head from side to side, searching for what had woken him. *Frmar, I'm here.* She stepped over the threshold without invitation.

He finally registered her presence and frowned. "Tllomell?" he said aloud.

Tllomell hissed softly. *Quiet. We must leave.*

Leave? Where are we going?

North.

After locating Frmar's pack, Tllomell began to stuff his belongings inside.

You said one moon, Tllomell continued. *It's time to go.*

You're coming? Frmar's body caught up with his brain and he sprang into action. With a *give it here* motion he reclaimed his pack. He emptied and repacked the items Tllomell had haphazardly shoved inside.

I'd better pack, she said.

We need to wake the others, Frmar said. *Some of them may not be ready; they may need more time.*

Whoever does not come now can catch up later.

Why the rush? What changed your mind?

When she didn't respond immediately, Frmar paused and glanced at her face.

Emotions warred inside her. Should she tell Frmar? Would he make her stay and answer to Ellall, and to Krnar? She would leave, anyway. She would go without him, but she didn't want to go alone. Without answering, Tllomell turned, ready to run if she must.

Tllomell.

She paused and listened, heart racing.

I'm coming with you. You can tell me when you're ready.

384

A long exhalation helped to calm her nerves. She nodded. *I'll go pack. You can wake the others. I will wait at the northern edge of the grove. Meet me there.*

Frmar trilled softly in acknowledgment.

By the time she'd made it to her own hearth, several glowing bodies had risen and were rolling up sleeping hides, sliding on already full packs, or placing their personal items into hides to be wrapped and tied.

After every item within her hearth circle had been wrapped, rolled, tied, and secured, she hustled for the cover of the trees. Her eyes remained fixed on the silver trunks. It took all of her willpower not to glance at the faces of those she would be leaving behind, friends she might never see again.

The skin on her back tingled and crawled. At any moment Krnar would charge into the field, shouting accusations, or Ellall would stop her and ask her where she was going, or Plldoll. What if Plldoll saw her? What would she say?

The tension in her gut eased somewhat once she reached the shelter of the grove. Visions began crowding into her brain: Krnar's eyes going wide when the knife parted his flesh, Krnar's blood spilling down his legs, splashing on her hands.

*One, two, three, four...*she counted leaves, counted rocks, counted her heartbeats, anything to keep her mind from those images.

She passed through the grove, crossed another field, and didn't stop until she'd reached the edge of the forest. She would give Frmar a little time to catch up, but she could not wait long. She had to be gone before Allorkan rose again.

A lifetime of pacing had her nerves frazzled. She couldn't wait any longer.

Tllomell.

Her head turned toward the grove as several glowing forms emerged from the shadows between the silver trunks.

A sigh of relief collapsed her chest.

Frmar and the others who'd been prepared to leave immediately gathered around her. Tllomell nodded.

"The rest will meet us within the forest at this location." He projected an image of one of their many clandestine meeting places.

Tllomell nodded again.

Without another word, they began to walk. The faint rustling of the ever-moving leaves above them made the hairs on the back of her neck tingle. She hoped the mllkallo were strictly daytime hunters.

Unbidden, a memory of Grollon's words popped into her head,

Some choices are so big, there's no turning back.

Nicole L. Bates

CHAPTER 38

With fists clenched so hard that her short nails dug into her palms, Jahira pounded on the wall of Tala's house.

She kept pounding until Tala's head popped out of a crack in the doorway. "Who the—Jahira!"

"Tala, I need you to go get Medic, send him to my tent, as fast as you can, please." Her chest heaved, her nostrils flared, and her eyes were wide with panic. She must have looked insane.

"Are you okay?"

"I'm fine. It's Krnar. He's been stabbed."

Tala's face went slack with shock. She didn't waste any more time with questions. She hopped out her doorway, alternating feet as she pulled on some shoes. "Meet you there."

Jahira nodded and raced back to her tent.

Krnar lay on the ground where she'd left him. The makeshift bandage she'd tied around the wound was soaked with blood.

Is his glow fading? she wondered. He didn't seem to be glowing quite as bright as before. Was that possible? *I think I'm losing it.*

Dropping to her knees by his side, she slowly but firmly pressed down on the site of his wound in an effort to slow the bleeding.

A low moan pushed past his lips.

"I'm so sorry," Jahira whispered. "Medic will be here soon, just hang on a little longer."

"Oranlo."

The word was so faint Jahira could barely make it out. "What did you say?" Her scalp tingled and she saw a brief flash of a silver pool in her mind. "Oh, oranlo. I didn't think of that, but it's too far, and I can't carry you. Medic is coming. Medic will know what to do. You're going to be okay."

Medic, please hurry.

The wait felt like an eternity.

Sitting there in the cold grass, she began to shiver. She tried to keep her hands still. She didn't want to cause Krnar any additional pain. The wait gave her plenty of time to replay what had happened.

Tllomell stabbed him.

A Leroni, someone she'd thought was his friend.

Krnar had stayed between them, between her and Tllomell. He'd believed Tllomell might try to hurt her. He had been trying to protect her. He'd never imagined she would harm him.

What will Ellall do? Was there any kind of trial or legal system in their culture?

He asked me to be his mate. Shaking her head in disbelief, she left that train of thought for another time. He'd been severely injured. People in pain said crazy things. *Usually the things they've been meaning to say for a long time.*

"Jahira!"

"Oh, thank goodness," Jahira breathed.

She shifted to the opposite side to give Medic room.

"What happened?" Medic asked as he pulled items out of a case.

"He was stabbed by a Leroni with that knife." Jahira pointed to the offending weapon that lay on the ground at Krnar's side.

Medic cut away the bandage and sprinkled a packet of white powder over the wound.

That stuff hurts like hell.

Jahira gripped Krnar's hand, waiting for him to groan or convulse. He barely reacted, which made Jahira break into a cold sweat.

Medic used a long filament with a tiny fork at the end that appeared to work like miniature fingers. The ends attached to flesh and held it together, allowing Medic to use a laser to seal everything that needed to be closed up on the inside. Finally, he sealed the outer wound and rocked back on his heels.

"He lost a lot of blood. I'd like to give him a transfusion, but I don't have any stock of Leroni blood and I have no idea how to test for their blood type."

"We should ask Ellall, or Grollon, see if there's anything else we can do," Jahira said. "He wanted to go to the silver pools. Can we take him there?"

"He's not going to be able to walk. We might be able to take him on a stretcher but I really don't think he should be moved. I'll hook up an IV and get some fluids into him. Once we see if he...revives," Medics eyes cut to Jahira and she knew that was not what he'd started to say. "Then we can think about moving him."

"Okay, whatever we need to do, just tell me."

"Let's get a blanket under him, and over him. I know they're adapted for the cold, but we need to keep all his energy working toward healing, not heating."

Jahira acted immediately.

She and Tala pulled out her sleeping bag and Krnar's sleeping hide. They followed Medic's instructions to get Krnar onto the sleeping bag without jostling him too much, and then covered him with the hide.

Medic hooked up a self-pump IV and scanned his vitals. "Now we wait," Medic said.

"Thank you, both of you, for your help," Jahira said.

Medic placed a hand on her shoulder. "I have to go back but I'll come and check on him in the morning. Send Tala if there's an emergency."

"Okay. I will. Thank you."

The clips on Medic's case snapped shut. He rose and walked away.

Tala sat down beside Jahira.

"You don't have to stay. Go get some sleep," Jahira said.

"Yeah, right. Someone scared the hell out of me by pounding on my house in the middle of the night and then sent me running off into the cold, dark night. I'm so full of adrenaline I won't sleep for a week."

A grin tugged at the corners of Jahira's mouth. "Sorry," she said.

"You should be," Tala replied. "Now I need details. Which Leroni stabbed him, and why?"

Jahira filled her in, as much as she could.

"She loved him," Tala said.

"You think so?"

"Definitely. She loved him. He loves you. Apparently the Leroni are not immune to jealousy."

"There's more than that, though, she was talking about him bringing them here, and she had blisters on her foot where she stepped on the leaf. I don't know. I think there's more to it."

The cold night air began to penetrate her temperature-regulating clothes. Jahira blew on her hands and tucked them under her armpits for warmth. She longed to curl up under the hide next to Krnar, but she didn't want to wake him.

"So now what?"

"What do you mean?"

"Well, do you avenge him? Does she go to alien prison? Now what?"

"I don't know. As soon as she stabbed him, she ran. I don't know how they deal with these things."

"Jahira?" Both women gasped and leaned forward.

"Krnar, can you hear me? I'm right here. Are you okay?"

"I hear you. I hurt."

Relief drowned her like a tsunami hitting a drought-hardened shore. "Do you need anything? Are you thirsty? Are you cold?"

"Meat."

"Meat? You want meat?"

A soft trill confirmed the statement.

"His body's probably craving the blood, or iron, or whatever it is their bodies need," Tala said.

"Tala?" Krnar whispered.

"Yep, I'm here too, big guy. Hang in there."

"Uh, do you have any raw meat?" Jahira asked Tala.

"Ewww, why does it have to be raw?"

"The blood, he needs the blood." Jahira stood, took a few steps, and then stepped through the gaping hole in the tent wall. She returned with her pack. "I guess I'm going to need a new house."

"I guess so."

After rifling through the contents of her pack, Jahira pulled out a strip of dried meat.

"Krnar, all I have is dried srlen. Can you take a bite?"

"NNhnn," he replied.

Slipping one hand behind his head for support, Jahira placed the dried meat against his lips and tried to lift his head slightly to make it easier to swallow. Krnar worked a small piece loose with his teeth. Slowly, he chewed and finally swallowed. "More," he said.

"Are you sure this is okay? Don't sick people need broth or something?"

"I'm not sick, I'm wounded," Krnar said.

"I guess if that's what his body is craving, that must be what he needs. At least he feels like eating," Tala said.

"That's true," Jahira agreed. "That must be a good sign."

"I think I'll start a fire and make that broth anyway. I'm freezing my butt off out here."

"Me, too. Thanks, Tala."

After a few more bites, Krnar held up his hand and closed his eyes.

With careful, gentle movements, Jahira laid his head back on the sleeping bag and went to join Tala by the fire. "I think we'll be alright, Tala. You should really get some sleep."

"I told you, I can't. I think I will run home and get my sleeping bag and let Leiko know where I am, though. I'll be right back."

"Okay."

Tala took off at a jog. Jahira crossed her legs and rested her elbows on her inner thighs, then rested her head in her hands. The adrenaline was wearing off. Fatigue began to pull at her, making her whole body feel heavy, like someone had turned up the gravity.

"Jahira?"

Her head jerked up and she returned to Krnar's side. "Yeah, I'm here. What do you need?"

"Just you," he said.

Her dark fingers slipped into his glowing palm and they stayed there together, beneath the winking stars of Empyrean.

CHAPTER 39

Chills shook Krnar's body despite the warmth of the sun soaking into the hide that covered his body. He wanted to ask for another hide, or to pull Jahira close and add her body heat to his own, but he didn't want to wake her.

Jahira's body curved around their clasped hands, forming a half moon in the grass. She'd stayed up with him all night and she needed to rest.

Medic had come and gone, changed the needle in his arm, and waved some object over his body. Everything must have been okay because Jahira had smiled, Tala had left, and the moment everyone departed, she'd collapsed into the grass and passed out.

In an effort to redirect his focus from his quaking body and sticky mouth, he watched the clouds float overhead, forming and reforming in a thousand different shapes.

A dark shadow blocked the sun from his face.

Krnar's heart began to race, thinking perhaps Tllomell had returned to finish what she'd started. His head turned and relief washed through him. *Ulletta*, he projected.

Krnar! There you are! What a relief!

Ulletta sat by his side, opposite where Jahira lay.

We've been looking all over for you! She glanced at his arm and over the Jahira, still asleep and clutching his hand. *What is going on?*

Tllomell stabbed me.

"*What?*" Ulletta yelled.

Krnar blanched and Ulletta shot an apologetic glance at Jahira, who stirred and scratched her nose. Her eyes stayed closed.

She came here, during the night. She cut a hole in Jahira's tent. I thought she was going to harm Jahira, but she stabbed me instead.

Are you okay?

I think so. Their healer has been here. He lifted the arm with its trailing tube to demonstrate his point. *I am chilled and thirsty, but I am alive.*

Ulletta nodded. She helped Krnar take a drink from a water bag attached to her belt and then, once he was settled, her eyes fixed on the horizon. There seemed an unusual tension about her, and then it dawned on Krnar that she hadn't known what happened but had still been looking for him.

Why were you searching for me? Krnar asked.

Her gaze wandered back to his and she sighed. *Tllomell is gone.*

Gone? Gone where?

To the north. We woke this morning to find several hearths empty and more of The People packing to leave.

Several hearths? Why? What is going on?

There are some who are not happy with life here. They fear the humans, and The Marked. They have decided to make their own way.

"What?" It was Krnar's turn to yell as he tried to push himself up. His head immediately protested and spun until he thought he would vomit.

Lie down. There is nothing you can do. They are gone. We just...we worried, when we couldn't find you, we thought you might have left with them.

You thought I would leave?

Not really, but you'd been spending a lot of time with Tllomell lately, and she was one of those missing, we didn't know what to think...

We?

Arkan and I, we went searching in different directions. Ellall is meeting with the elders to discuss what should be done.

Who else left? How many?

We don't know for sure. Some people are missing, but their belongings remain. They are probably out hunting or fishing. We're still trying to get an accurate count.

I must go. I must go after them.

You're not going anywhere right now. Rest, heal, I will tell Ellall that you are still with us.

Did Ellall know this would happen?

Ulletta tipped her head, thinking before she answered. *She did not seem surprised...only sad.*

Where will they go? How will they survive?

I guess that is up to them now.

Closing his eyes, his mind reeled with the new information.

Sudden heat from inside his body pushed sweat through his pores. Alternate kicks with his feet removed the hide from his body and cool air chilled the moisture that coated his fur. He lay panting from the small effort.

Do you need more water?

Krnar nodded, breathing too hard to speak.

Mine is by the pack, near the tent wall.

Ulletta rose, retrieved Jahira's canteen, and returned to Krnar's side.

After carefully removing his fingers from Jahira's grasp, he rose up on one elbow and tilted his torso to one side so that he

402

could drink without choking. Wincing with pain, he bit down on his lower lip to hold in the groan that fought to come out.

"Krnar," Jahira's voice behind him was filled with worry. "Oh, Ulletta, hi."

Ulletta smiled and helped Krnar sip from the mouth of the canteen.

The hide that he'd kicked off returned to cover his legs and torso.

"You need to stay warm," Jahira said.

"I am *too* warm," Krnar replied after swallowing a dribble of lukewarm water.

"Did he tell you what happened?" Jahira asked, addressing Ulletta.

Ulletta nodded, recapped the canteen, and looked up. "Tllomell is gone," she said.

"Ran away?" Jahira asked.

"Many left with her, they go north."

Deep furrows lined Jahira's brow.

"There were some who were not happy here. They have been planning to leave. Tllomell went with them," Krnar explained.

"Did you know?" Jahira asked.

"No," Krnar said.

"I'm sorry," Jahira said.

Krnar nodded. He knew that she meant she was sorry about his people leaving. She could certainly empathize. The humans had recently faced a similar parting of ways, though they seemed to have adapted easily and moved on with their lives.

For Krnar, this cut to the core of who his People were. They had, for generations, been driven by two goals: to survive until the next season of light, and to find the warm land.

They'd counted on each person's contribution to achieve the first, and honored the sacrifices necessary to hope for the second. Each birth, each season, each memory made had been made together. This felt like the ultimate betrayal.

Ulletta said those who left had feared the influence of the humans, and The Marked, but they would have faced the changes together, as a People. Now, they were a People divided.

"I will go tell Ellall and find Arkan. They will want to know what has happened. Arkan will wish to come and see you. Do you need anything?"

"Meat," Krnar said. "I must regain my strength."

"I will be back soon."

Krnar tried to tip his head in a small bow. Since he was lying down it only bunched the skin under his chin.

"Can I get you anything?" Jahira asked once Ulletta had departed.

"I've got water now," Krnar said, patting the canteen leaning against his side. "You should rest."

"I'll make some broth."

"You do not need to do that."

Jahira's face softened and she smiled at him in a way that made his heart quicken. "I want to. We take care of the people we love."

Krnar grinned.

She had never answered his question about being his mate and she hadn't brought it up since. Her words gave him hope.

By the time the broth was ready, Krnar felt strong enough to sit up and sip from the bowl.

The second bag of fluid, which Medic had changed that morning, was now empty. Jahira removed the needle from his arm and placed a small, spongy circle over the bead of blood inside his elbow.

The ache in his gut made him wince if he moved too fast, but his head didn't spin.

Both of their heads lifted when a trill bounced off the silver trees and echoed across the field. Ulletta had returned, with Arkan, Mrkon, and much to Krnar's surprise, Ellall.

With Jahira's help, Krnar managed to rise to his feet and bow his head.

Ellall waved him back down.

The Akaruvel sat cross-legged in the grass. Krnar shot a questioning look at Arkan, but his brother gave nothing away.

Once everyone had seated themselves in a small circle, all eyes trained on Krnar. His skin crawled under the scrutiny. He felt much like he had as a child, on display, everyone watching him with their minds blocked so he couldn't know what they were thinking. He hated that feeling.

"How are you?" Ellall asked.

Krnar blinked. Such a mild question took him aback for a moment. "I will be fine," he replied.

"Ulletta told us what happened. Tllomell did this to you," she said, gesturing toward the wound in his torso.

Krnar nodded.

"The human healer took care of you?"

"Yes, he did a fine job. I am feeling stronger every minute."

"Good." Ellall paused and took a deep breath before continuing. "Ulletta told you about Tllomell, and many others, leaving the grove."

"Yes."

Piercing blue eyes met his and froze him in place. "We have a problem, Krnar."

"Yes, the division of The People is a serious problem—"

Ellall held up a hand to stop him.

Krnar's brows drew together.

"That is a concern, yes, but we have a bigger issue."

"Bigger?" Krnar repeated in confusion. "What could be bigger than a third of our number leaving us?"

"Frmar has gone with them."

Shock exploded in Krnar's brain. *"Frmar?* He left? He has abandoned his duty?" Krnar knew the man had been angry and confrontational lately, but leaving The People? Leaving the Akaruvel? What if something happened to Ellall? He took their past and future with him.

"I don't think he feels he's abandoned his duties," Ellall explained. "I think he believes he's fulfilling them."

Realization dawned. "He has become Akaruvel...to them."

Ellall tipped her head in acknowledgement.

"Is he ready?"

Ellall smiled. "One is never truly ready for that kind of re-sponsibility. I thought I had chosen wisely, that he would be the kind of person to face fear and grow stronger through challenges.

I was wrong. He fed his fears, and the fears of those around him, until they could see no other way than to run from change."

As Krnar considered her words, a stirring began in his gut. "What do you plan to do?" he asked.

Pulling her shoulders back, Ellall locked her gaze with his. "Krnar, I would like you to become my new apprentice."

Even though he'd half expected it, surprise rolled over him like an icy wave, leaving him numb.

"You don't have to answer right away," Ellall assured him. "Take some time to think about it."

"Have you asked Allnall?" Krnar asked.

"She volunteered to go after those who left. Most of the information we have has been gleaned from the stragglers. She plans to catch up to Tllomell and Frmar, find out where they plan to settle, and perhaps, convince some to come back. She may not be able to return until the snows recede, and we cannot wait that long."

Krnar absorbed this news. "I am not sure I'm the best person," he said.

He glanced at Jahira, whose brow furrowed in concentration as she tried to follow the conversation. With a fortifying breath, he reached out and took her hand. "I've asked Jahira to be my mate."

Arkan's eyes flew open. Ulletta grinned. Ellall simply nodded.

Honestly, he'd expected a stronger reaction.

"It's a new world, Krnar. We have to adapt. We have to learn to live with the humans, and they with us. We can learn from them, and we also need to feel confident enough to teach them what we know. You and Jahira will form the line that holds us all together."

"So you approve?"

"I do."

"You will allow me to be mated to a human and become your apprentice?"

"Change is never easy. It becomes impossible if those in authority are not willing to make the changes themselves. I think Jahira should learn with you, and teach us about her people in return."

"I will need to ask her."

"Of course."

"If she agrees," Krnar said, giving Jahira's hand a squeeze. "Then I accept."

CHAPTER 40

"Okay, translate please," Jahira said once their guests had left. Her language skills were improving, but there were some words that simply didn't come up in conversation between her and Krnar. She felt like she'd missed some important pieces.

"Frmar left, he went north with the Tllomell."

"Okay, I caught that. Frmar is the one who is learning from Ellall, right?"

Krnar nodded. "Now Ellall needs to teach a new Akaruvel."

The whites appeared around Jahira's bright green eyes. "She asked you, didn't she? You're going to be the next Akaruvel!"

His eyes danced, but his face remained serious. "It depends," he said.

"On what?"

"On you."

Jahira felt her eyebrows jump.

"I told Ellall that I want you to be my mate and, traditionally, the Akaruvel does not take a mate."

A twist of apprehension churned through her. "What did she say?" If Ellall forbade it, or even disapproved, would it change Krnar's mind about her? Or would his feelings for her prevent him from fulfilling his purpose? She didn't want to be responsible for something like that.

"She said it is a new world, we must adapt. She believes that you and I, together, will help to bring our two peoples together. She wants you to learn with me, and to teach us."

Excitement followed close on the heels of Jahira's relief. She thought of Gavin and Brenna's little girl; of Tala and Leiko, who hoped to become parents soon; of Krnar's nephew Mrkon; and she thought of Zarya. If her sister were here, what kind of world would Jahira want her to grow up in?

Beaming from ear to ear, she grasped Krnar's hands. "We could start a school!"

"School?" Krnar tipped his head.

"All the children, human and Leroni, we bring them together for a little while each day and teach them! We can teach them both languages, the stories, memories, of both of our people! You could teach them to hunt and teach the human kids how to focus their minds. I could teach them about solar power and engineering. We could take hikes and learn about the plants and animals!" In her excitement, she'd stood and begun to pace as she shouted out ideas.

She felt filled with purpose for the first time since saving Magnar. She could have a job to do that would mean something. When she paused to take a breath, Krnar beamed up at her.

"This could be really great," she said.

"I think it will be," Krnar agreed. "Does that mean your answer is yes?"

Jahira knew he wanted her response to both questions. Dropping to her knees, she took his hands in hers again. "Yes," she said. "Definitely, yes."

Krnar slipped his fingers from her grasp and pulled her forehead to his. They locked eyes and kept them locked as Jahira leaned in and pressed her lips against his.

"We should tell Ellall," Krnar said when they pulled apart.

"We'll have to tell everyone," Jahira said. "But they can wait until tomorrow. You still need to rest."

The sky to the west was streaked with orange and pale pink. The night birds were cautiously testing their voices, alerting the insects of their imminent demise.

"I am tired," Krnar said.

"It's been a long day. I'll set up the bed in the tent and seal the hole. It got a little too cold for me last night."

"I think it's time for a new shelter," Krnar said.

"Yeah, I guess so," Jahira agreed reluctantly. "What kind of place would you want? Something like Tala and Leiko? Or should we wait for the snow and build an ice cave."

"Wouldn't you be cold?"

"Most likely, yes. But you could keep me warm," Jahira said and tossed a grin over her shoulder as she repaired the tent wall.

"I do not like Tala's hearth. It reminds me of being underground during Nall'Urrok. I feel trapped inside."

"Fair enough. Maybe we'll just have to get creative and come up with our own design."

Standing and taking a step back, Jahira inspected her repair. "I think it will hold unless we have a major storm," she said. "Can you stand? I'll get the sleeping bag and set up the bed."

Rising slowly, Krnar tested his balance on weak knees.

Jahira hurried to put a shoulder beneath his arm and support his weight. "Are you okay?"

"I will be fine."

Jahira helped Krnar to a seat by the fire and then moved the bedding into the tent, after giving it a good shake.

They settled inside, and Jahira felt the weight of her exhaustion pulling on her limbs. With her head resting on Krnar's shoulder, she had a perfect view of the dark line stretching the full length of the wall where she'd repaired the tent. "Tllomell is a little crazy," she said.

"More than a little," Krnar replied. "I'm thankful she did not go after you."

"She's lucky she didn't come after me. I wouldn't have stood there and let her stab me." Jahira smiled into his chest, hoping that he understood she was teasing.

His chest trembled with laughter, and then he cringed and coughed.

"Sorry," she said.

"Medic said the wound will not reopen. Laughter is good."

"Alright then, did I ever tell you about the woman with one leg who walked into a bar?"

"How did she walk with one leg?" Krnar asked. "And what is a bar?"

Jahira snorted, ruffling his fur under her nose. "Never mind," she said, stifling a huge yawn. "Get some rest."

Before long his breathing evened. Jahira placed one palm over his heart. She watched it rise and fall, surrounded by slightly glowing fur. His heart drummed against her hand and her own heart filled with gratitude that he was here, breathing, next to her. She hadn't lost him.

Memories of her family filled her mind then, bittersweet recollections that made her smile and cry at the same time. She longed to talk to them about everything that had happened, about her ideas for the future. She wished they could know Krnar.

She would do her best to honor their memory.

The sun beat down on the tent from its location directly above them by the time Jahira woke the next day. After carefully extracting her limbs from Krnar's, she stepped over his torso and opened the door to the brisk afternoon air. Her breath clouded in front of her face.

Shivers shook her body as cold air pressed against her skin even while the sun warmed her hair. A few extra logs on the fire and a cup of hot tea drove the chills from her body, but not from the world around her. Her eyes sought the silver trees and, sure enough, they were beginning to change. The golden fruits had shrunk to near invisibility and the inner veins of the leaves were darker. She couldn't quite tell what color they would become. Soon the grove would change and the snow would come.

We need to name each of the fruits, she thought, wondering what the next one would be. Hoping there would be a next one.

Many things on this planet needed a name. A whole world of discoveries waited for them, and the kids could help! It would be exciting. It would be challenging. It would be a whole new adventure.

"You are happy this morning," Krnar growled as he poked his head through the tent door.

"I am," Jahira said. "The happiest that I've been since we arrived here."

Two weeks later, human and Leroni gathered together under a steel grey sky. There remained a natural separation. Tala, Leiko, Dan, Cholie, Magnar, Kato, Creed, Gavin, Brenna, their daughter Chava, and The General formed one half of the circle. Arkan, Ulletta, Mrkon, Plldoll, Krag, Erget, Kllealla, several of the elders, though not all, and Ellall formed the other half.

Jahira took her place in the center of the circle with Krnar.

Such a small group, she thought.

Her gaze took in Mrkon and Chava, the only two children present. *They will learn to accept and appreciate each other instead of fearing or revering that which is simply different*, she thought.

In front of her, Krnar held his hands up, palms forward. Jahira pressed her palms against his.

"Are you ready?" Ellall asked.

A sense of calm filled her, wrapping her insides with warmth, just as the mllkallo-fur coat Krnar had given her warmed her on the outside.

This is good, she thought. *This is right.* "I'm ready," she said.

"I am ready," Krnar said.

Ellall spoke for a long time. Jahira only half listened. Krnar had connected with her mind, filling her head and heart with his emotions. She tried to do the same and, for a moment, felt the flush of embarrassment heat her face.

She thought she was improving with her focus, and hoped only Krnar could feel what she was feeling, but what if all the Leroni present could sense the emotions between them?

Then she decided that she didn't care.

Ellall drew a circle in the air around one set of joined hands, and then the other.

With gentle pressure, she pushed their heads forward until their foreheads touched and drew a circle in the air around their heads.

A chant rose up from the Leroni. A few of the humans joined the second time through, and then silence descended on the crowd.

Jahira's breath mingled with Krnar's in the cold morning air.

Dots of cold kissed the back of her neck and Krnar's eyes danced.

Jahira lifted her head and looked up.

Huge, intricate stars of frozen water clung to her lashes and rested on the backs of her hands before melting into small spots of liquid and trailing down her skin.

A wide grin stretched her full lips, and then she began to laugh. "The first snow!" she whispered reverently.

Dancing green eyes found Krnar's ice-blue ones and he smiled back at her.

"Aruvel blesses us," he said.

"It's perfect," she whispered.

Trills erupted from the Leroni. Cheers rose up from the humans.

The sounds complement each other, Jahira thought, but so many voices were missing. *There will be more*, she vowed. *From now on, we'll make sure of it.*

For the first time since she'd lost her family, she felt excited for the future.

Nicole L. Bates

DICTIONARY OF LERONI WORDS

Akaruvel (ä kä' roo vel'): The One Who Remembers; the spiritual leader of the Leroni who in the past, was formed by the merging of two individuals as they passed through the Gateway to Aruvel and were endowed with the Knowledge of Eternity. Since their exile, the term is still used, but for only one individual whose job it is to retain the Memories and pass them to an apprentice.

Alara (ä lä' rä): The silver trees of the sacred grove surrounding the five sacred pools.

Allorkan (ä lōr' kan): The primary sun of the solar system; always visible from the first and second continents—never visible from the third continent.

Allorkan a tal (ä lōr' kan ä täl): A greeting that when translated means "May the sun shine on you."

Aruvel (ä roo vel'): The One Who Knows All; the single deity of the Leroni.

Darno a tal (där' nō ä täl): "My soul to you," *darno* is the word a male would use, *dallno* the word a female would use to refer to one's soul.

Eroki (e rō' kē); The ice worm that lives within the Great Ice.

Frtikdi (fr tēk' dē): A type of insect that inhabits the grove.

Glluna (gloo' nä): A slug-like creature that clings to the rocks in and along the river.

420

Grolloni (grō lä nē'): The Marked; named after Grollon—the first Marked.

Kllkoa (kl kō' ä): The dancing trees; those trees in the forest surrounding the sacred grove whose leaves never cease to move.

Krska (kr' skä): The cave lizards that live within the rocks of the third continent.

Laro (lä rō'): The living islands that move through the seas on the currents.

Leron (lā rōn'): The World; the native name for the planet.

Leroni (lā' rōn ē'): The People of Leron.

Marnar (mär' när): Brother.

Mllkallo (ml kä' lō): The primary cat-like predator of The Warm Land that lives in the dancing forest.

Mrkellan (mr ke' len): The secondary sun of the solar system; visible every six years at the third continent for a period of two years—these two-year intervals are the Season of Light and the Season of Sacrifice, when the Leroni lived on the surface of the third continent. The six-year intervals of dark are the Seasons of Ice when the Leroni lived in the underground caves.

Nall'Mrkellan (näl' mr ke' len): The Season of Light on the third continent. The season lasts for two years and occurs every six, though every other season of light is more commonly referred to as the Season of Sacrifice.

Nall'Olara (näl' ō lä rä'): The Season of Sacrifice on the third continent. This season lasts for two years and occurs every fourteen years. This is the warmest season and is the season when the Junction occurs—the equidistant alignment of the planet between its two suns, which opens the Gateway within the oranlodi.

Nall'Urok (näl' oo rōk'): The Season of Ice on the third continent. This season lasts for six years, during which time the Leroni live deep below the surface in caves. Nall'Urok occurs every other season with a two-year interval between when The People live on the surface of the glacier-covered third continent.

Oranlo (ō ran' lō): The name of a single pool of silver outside of the sacred grove.

Oranlodi (ō ran' lō dē'): The Five Sacred Pools within the grove; always referred to together.

Plinka (plin' kä): Primary type of fish in ice world.

Srlen (sr len') – plural **srlendi** (sr len' dē): The four-legged herd beasts of The Warm Land. The animals range across the southern half of the second continent and the northern half of the first continent.

Tllafarr (tla far'): Rain.

Ulok (oo läk'): Snow.

Urillan (oo ri län'): The sea.

Urok (oo rōk'): Ice.

Vllusta (vloo sta'): The poisonous plant that grows on the first continent.

Vrmefur (vr' me fur'): Flame of the sea; a barnacle-like creature with glowing orange tendrils that clings to the rocks beneath the surface of the sea. It is filled with an oily interior that burns slowly and this creature is used for The People's fires on the third continent.

Vrsat (vr sat): Knife.

ACKNOWLEDGEMENTS

First and foremost I want to thank all of the friends, family, and unknown readers who read and shared the news of *Empyrean* and *Empyrean's Fall*. I am so grateful for the support and enthusiasm that have surrounded me on this journey. You all were truly the motivation for continuing. Thank you so much!

Thank you to my amazing critique partners: Sarah Fox, James Knapp, Vaughn Roycroft, and D.D. Falvo. These four people are truly fantastic human beings, as well as great writers! Find them, read their work, and support them; they truly deserve it!

Huge thanks to the amazing Jeannine Thibodeau for her editing expertise. Any errors, or weird formatting issues, you might find in this book are completely my fault. If you need an editor, hire her!

The gorgeous cover art is the work of Natasja Hellenthal of BeyondBookCovers. Thank you so much, Natasja, for making my convuluted vision come to life in a simple, beautiful image!

And, finally, thank you to YOU! You read this book! You gave it a chance, and that means the world to me.

About The author

Nicole L. Bates is the author two science fiction adventures, *Empyrean* and *Empyrean's Fall*. She grew up in Northern Michigan, exploring forest trails and devouring books. After moving seven times, she has once again settled in her home state with her family. You can find out more about Nicole and her work at www.NicoleLBates.com, follow Nicole L. Bates on Facebook at https://www.facebook.com/WriterNicoleLBates/, or on twitter at https://twitter.com/NicoleLBates .